For some reason I had imagined that the Sturm vacuum programming would make me insensitive to all pain. Quite illogical, since you could permanently damage your body all too easily in that situation. I felt the agony of expansion through my intestines, as the air rushed out of all my body cavities. My mouth was performing an automatic yawning and gasping, emptying the Eustachian tube to protect my ear drums and delicate inner ear. My eyes were closed to protect the eyeballs from freezing, and open just often enough to guide my body movements.

Holding Wicklund between us, McAndrew and I pushed off into the open depths of space. Ten seconds later, we intersected the landing tower about twenty meters up. Sturm couldn't make a human comfortable in space, but he had provided a set of natural movements that corresponded to a zero gee environment. They were needed. If we missed the tower there was no other landing within light years.

CHARLES SHEFFIELD
THE
McANDREW
CHRONICLES

A
JIM BÆN
PRESENTATION

TOR

A TOM DOHERTY ASSOCIATES BOOK

The McAndrew Chronicles

Copyright © 1983 by Charles Sheffield

A TOR Book

Published by Tom Doherty Associates
8-10 West 36th Street
New York, New York 10018

First TOR printing, June 1983

ISBN: 48-566-2

Cover art by Vincent DiFate

Acknowledgments: Portions of this work have appeared previously in revised form, as follows:
Killing Vector, copyright UPD Publications, 1978
Moment of Inertia, copyright Davis Publications, 1980
All the Colors of the Vacuum, copyright Davis Publications, 1981
The Manna Hunt, copyright Davis Publications, 1982
Rogueworld, copyright Mercury Press Inc., 1983

Printed in the United States of America

Distributed by:
Pinnacle Books
1430 Broadway
New York, New York 10018

To Larry Niven, whose stories brought me back to science fiction; to Jim Baen, who bought my first story and encouraged me to keep writing; and to Jerry Pournelle, whose demand for "a good black hole story" gave birth to McAndrew and Jeanie Roker.

INTRODUCTION • THE McANDREW CHRONICLES

Writers, readers and critics of science fiction often seem unable to produce a workable definition of the field, but one of the things they all agree on is the existence of a particular branch that is usually termed "hard" science fiction. People who like this branch will tell you it is the only subdivision that justifies the word *science* in sf, and that everything else is simple fantasy; and they will use words like "authentic", "scientifically accurate", "extrapolative", and "inventive" to describe it. People who don't like it say it is dull and bland, and use words like "characterless", "mechanical", "gadgetry", or "rockets and rayguns" to describe it. Some people can't stand hard sf, others will read nothing else.

Hard science fiction can be defined in several different ways. My favorite definition is an operational one: if you can take the science and scientific speculation away from a story, and not do it serious injury, then it was not hard sf to begin with. Here is another popular definition that I like rather less well: in a hard sf story, the scientific techniques of observation, analysis, logical theory, and experimental test must be applied, no matter where or when the story takes place. My problem with this definition is that it would classify many mystery stories as hard science fiction.

Whatever the exact definition, there is usually little difficulty deciding whether a particular story is "hard" or "soft" science fiction. And although a writer never knows quite what he or she has written into a book, and readers often pull things out that were never consciously put in, I certainly think of the book you are holding as hard sf, and expect it will mostly be read as such. That being the case I feel a special responsibility to the reader, one that derives from my own early experiences with science fiction.

I discovered the field for myself as a teenager (as did almost everyone else I knew — in school we were tormented with Wordsworth and Bunyan, while Clarke and Heinlein had to be private after-school pleasures). Knowing a negligible amount of real science, I swallowed whole and then regurgitated to my friends everything presented as science in the sf magazines. That quickly built me a reputation as a person stuffed with facts and theories — many of them wrong and some of them decidedly weird. The writers didn't bother to distinguish the scientific theories that they borrowed, from the often peculiarly unscientific theories that they made up for the story. Neither did I.

I knew all about the canals on Mars, the dust pools on the Moon, and the swamps on Venus, about the Dean drive and dianetics and the Hieronymus machine. I believed that men and pigs were more closely related than men and monkeys; that atoms were miniature solar systems; that you could shoot men to the moon with a cannon (a belief that didn't survive my first course in dynamics); that the pineal gland was certainly a rudimentary third eye and probably the seat of parapsychological powers; that Rhine's experiments at Duke University had made telepathy an unquestioned part of modern science; that with a little ingenuity and a few electronic bits and pieces you could build in your backyard a spacecraft to take you to the Moon; and that, no matter what alien races might have developed on other worlds and be scattered around the Galaxy, humans would prove to be the smartest, most resourceful, and most wonderful species to be found anywhere.

That last point may even be true. As Pogo remarked long ago, true or false, either way it's a mighty sobering thought.

What I needed was a crib sheet. We had them in school for the works of Shakespeare. They were amazingly authoritative, little summaries that outlined the plot, told us just who did what and why, and even informed us exactly what was in Shakespeare's head when he was writing the play. If they didn't say what he had for lunch that day, it was only because that subject never appeared on examination papers.

I didn't know it at the time, but the crib sheets were what I was missing. Given the equivalent type of information about sf, I would not have assured my friends (as I did) that the brains of industrial robots made use of positrons, that the work of Dirac and Blackett would lead us to a faster-than-light drive, or that the notebooks of Leonardo da Vinci gave all the details needed to construct a moon rocket.

As Mark Twain remarked, it's not what we don't know that causes the trouble, it's the things we know that ain't so.* That's why this book comes complete with crib sheet. The Appendix sorts out the real science, based on and consistent with today's theories (but probably not tomorrow's), from the "science" that I made up for these stories. I have tried to provide a clear dividing line, at the threshold where fact stops and fiction takes over. But even the invented material is designed to be consistent with and derived from what is known today. It does not contradict current theories, although you will not find papers about it in the *Physical Review* or the *Astrophysical Journal*.

Not yet, that is. But a few years from now . . . who knows?

Charles Sheffield, November 1982.

* This is an example of the problem. I was sure this was said by Mark Twain, but when I looked it up I found it was first said by Josh Billings. Since then I have seen it attributed to Artemus Ward.

iv

FIRST CHRONICLE: KILLING VECTOR

Everyone on the Control Stage found a reason to be working aft when Yifter came on board. There was maximum security, of course, so no one could get really close without a good reason. Even so, we all took the best look that we could manage — you don't often have a chance to see a man who has killed a billion people.

Bryson from the Planetary Coordinators' Office was at Yifter's elbow. The two men weren't shackled or anything melodramatic like that. Past a certain level of notoriety, criminals are treated with some deference and even respect. Bryson and Yifter were talking together in a friendly way, although they were in the middle of a group of top-rank security men, all heavily armed and watchful.

They were taking safety to extremes. When I stepped forward to greet Bryson and his prisoner, two guards carefully frisked me before I could get within hand-kill range, and they stood close beside me when the introductions were made. I haven't lived on Earth for a long time, and they must have known that I have no close relatives there; but they were taking no chances. Yifter was a prime target for personal revenge. A billion people leave a lot of friends and relatives.

From a distance of one meter, Yifter's appearance did not match his reputation. He was of medium height, slightly built, with bushy, prematurely white hair and mild, sad eyes. He smiled at me in a tired, tolerant way as Bryson introduced us.

"I am sorry, Jeanie Roker," he said. "Your ship will be filled with strangers on this trip. I'll do my best to keep out of your way and let you do your job."

I hoped he could live up to his words. Since I took over the runs to Titan, I've carried most things in the connected set of cargo spheres that make up the Assembly. Apart from the kernels, and we carry a few of those on the outbound leg of every trip, we've had livestock, mega-crystals, the gravity simulator, and the circus. That's right, the circus. They must have had a terrible agent, that's all I can say. I took them both ways, to Titan and back to L-5. Even with all that, Yifter was still a novelty item. After he had been caught and the rest of the Lucies had gone underground, nobody had known quite what to do with him. He was Earth's hottest property, the natural target for a billion guns and knives. Until they decided how and when he would come to trial, they wanted him a long way from Earth. It was my job to deliver him to the Titan penal colony, and return him when they got themselves sorted out on Earth.

"I'll arrange for you and your guards to travel in a separate part of the Assembly," I said. "I assume that you will prefer privacy."

Yifter nodded agreeably, but Bryson wasn't having any.

"Captain Roker," he said. "Let me remind you that Mr. Yifter has not been found guilty on any charge. On this journey, and until his trial, he will be treated with proper courtesy. I expect you to house both of us here in the Control Stage, and I expect that you will invite us to take our meals here with you."

In principle, I could have told him to go and take a walk outside. As captain, I said who would travel in the Control Stage, and who would eat with me — and innocent people were not usually sent to the Titan penal colony, even before their trial. On the other hand, Bryson was from the Planetary Coordinators' office, and even off-Earth that carried weight.

I suppressed my first reaction and said quietly, "What about the guards?"

"They can travel in the Second Section, right behind the Control Stage," replied Bryson.

I shrugged. If he wanted to make nonsense of Earth's security efforts, that was his choice. Nothing had ever happened on any of my two-month runs from Earth to Titan, and Bryson was probably quite right; nothing would happen this time. On the other hand, it seemed like a damned silly charade, to ship twenty-five guards to keep an eye on Yifter, then house them in a separate part of the Assembly.

Yifter, with an uncanny empathy, had read through my shrug. "Don't worry about security, Jeanie Roker," he said. He smiled again, that tired, soothing smile that began deep in his sad, brown eyes. "You have my assurance, I will be a model prisoner."

He and Bryson walked on past me, into the main quarters. Was that really Yifter, the bogey-man, the notorious head of the Hallucinogenic Freedom League? It seemed hard to believe. Three months earlier, the Lucies — under Yifter's messianic direction — had planted hallucinogenic drugs in the water supply lines of most of Earth's major cities. An eighth of the world had died in the resulting chaos. Starvation, epidemic, exposure and mindless combat had re-visited the Earth and exacted their age-old tribute. The monster who had conceived, planned and directed that horror was difficult to match with Yifter, the seemingly mild and placid man.

My thoughts were quickly diverted to more immediate practical matters. We had the final masses of all the cargo, and it was time for the final balancing of the whole Assembly. One might assume that just means balancing the kernels correctly, since they out-mass everything else by a factor of a million. But each Section containing a kernel has an independent drive unit, powered by the kernel itself. We leave those on Titan, and travel back light, but on the trip out the dynamic balancing is quite tricky.

I reviewed the final configuration, then looked around for McAndrew. I wanted him to look over the balance calculations. It's my responsibility, but he was the kernel expert. I realized that he hadn't been present when Yifter came aboard. Presumably he was over on one of the other Sections, crooning over his beloved power sources.

I found him in Section Seven. The Assembly is made up of a variable number of Sections, and there would be twelve on this trip, plus the Control Stage. Until we accelerate away from the Libration Colony station, all the Sections are physically connected — with actual cables — to each other and to the Control Stage. In flight, the coupling is done electromagnetically, and the drives for the powered Sections are all controlled by a computer on the Control Stage. The Assembly looks like a small bunch of grapes, but the stalks are non-functional — there are no cables in the System that could take the strains, even at lowest acceleration. Moving among the spherical Sections when we're in flight isn't easy. It means we have to cut the drives, and turn off the coupling between the Sections. That's why I thought the idea of having Yifter's guards in a different Section was so dumb — from there, they couldn't even reach the Control Stage when the drives were on.

I wanted McAndrew to check the configuration that we would hold in flight, to see if he agreed that the stresses were decently balanced among the different Sections. We never run near the limit on any of them, but there's a certain pride of workmanship in getting them all approximately equal, and the stresses as low as possible.

He was standing on the ten-meter shield that surrounded the Section Seven kernel, peering through a long boresight in towards the center. He was aware of my presence but did not move or speak until the observation was complete. Finally he nodded in satisfaction, closed the boresight cap, and turned to me.

"Just checking the optical scalars," he said. "Spun up nicely, this one. So, what can I do for you, Jeanie?"

I led him outside the second shield before I handed him the trim calculations. I know a kernel shield has never failed, but I'm still not comfortable when I get too close to one. I once asked McAndrew how he felt about working within ten meters of Hell, where you could actually feel the gravity gradient and the inertial dragging. He looked at me with his little, introspective smile, and made a sort of throat-clearing noise — the only trace of his ancestry that I could ever find in him.

"Och," he said. "The shields are triply protected. They won't fail."

That would have reassured me, but then he had rubbed his high, balding forehead and added, "And if they do, it won't make any difference if you are ten meters away, or five hundred. That kernel would radiate at about two gigawatts, most of it high-energy gammas."

The trouble was, he always had the facts right. When I first met McAndrew, many years ago, we were taking the first shipment of kernels out to Titan. He had showed up with them, and I assumed that he was just another engineer — a good one, maybe, but I expected that. Five minutes of conversation with him told me that he had probably forgotten more about Kerr-Newman black holes — kernels — than I was ever likely to learn. I have degrees in Electrical Engineering and Gravitational Engineering, in my job I have to, but I'm really no gravity specialist. I felt like an idiot after our first talk. I made a few inquiries, and found that McAndrew was a full professor at the Penrose Institute, and probably the System's leading expert on space-time structure.

When we got to know each other better, I asked him why he would give up his job for four months of the year, to ride herd on a bunch of kernels being shipped around the Solar System. It was a milk-run, with lots of time and very little to do. Most people would be bored silly.

"I need it," he said simply. "It's very nice to work with colleagues, but in my line of business the real stuff is mostly worked out alone. And I can do experiments here that wouldn't be allowed back home."

After that, I accepted his way of working, and took vicarious pride in the stream of papers that appeared from McAndrew at the end of each Titan run. He was no trouble on the trips. He spent most of his time in the Sections carrying the kernels, only appearing in the Control Stage for his meals — and frequently missing them. He was a tinkerer as well as a theorist. Isaac

Newton was his idol. His work had paid off in higher shielding efficiencies, better energy extraction methods, and more sensitive manipulation of the charged kernels. Each trip, we had something new.

I left the trim calculations with him, and he promised to check them over and give me his comments in an hour or two. I had to move along and check the rest of the cargo.

"By the way," I said, elaborately casual as I turned to go. "We'll be having company for dinner on this trip. Bryson insists that Yifter should eat with us."

He stood quietly for a moment, head slightly bowed. Then he nodded and ran his hand over his sandy, receding hair-line.

"That sounds like Bryson," he said. "Well, I doubt if Yifter will eat any of us for breakfast. I'm not sure he'll be any worse than the rest of you. I'll be there, Jeanie."

I breathed a small sigh of relief, and left him. McAndrew, as I knew from experience, was the Compleat Pacifist. I had wanted to be sure that he could stand the idea of meals with Yifter.

Four hours later, all our checks were complete. I switched on the fields. The dull grey exterior of each Section turned to silver, shattering the sunlight and turning the Assembly to a cluster of brilliants. The cables linking the Sections were still in position, but now they were hanging loose. All stresses had been picked up by the balancing fields. In the Control Stage, I gradually turned on the propulsion units of each powered Section. Plasma was fed through the ergosphere of each kernel, picked up energy, and streamed aft. The relative positions of the Sections, Mössbauer-controlled to within fractions of a micrometer, held steady. We accelerated slowly away from L-5, and began the long spiral of a continuous-impulse orbit to Titan.

My work was just about finished until crossover time.
The computers monitored the drive feeds, the accelerations, and all the balance of the Sections. On this trip,
we had three units without operating drive units: Section Two, where Yifter's guards were housed, just
behind the Control Stage; Section Seven, where McAndrew had taken the kernel out of commission for his
usual endless and mysterious experiments; and of
course, the Control Stage itself. I had made the mistake
of asking McAndrew what experiments he was planning for this trip. He looked at me with his innocent
blue eyes and scribbled an answer full of twistor dia-
grams and spinor notation — knowing damn well that
I wouldn't be able to follow it. He didn't like to talk
about his work "half-cooked", as he put it.

I had been more worried than I wanted to admit
about dinner on that first ship-evening. I knew we
would all be itching to ask Yifter about the Lucies, but
there was no easy way to introduce the subject into
the conversation. How could we do it? "By the way,
I hear that you killed a billion people a few months ago.
I wonder if you would like to say a few words on the
subject? It would liven up the table-talk at dinner." I
could foresee that our conversation might be a little
strained.
     As it turned out, my worries were unnecessary. The
first impression that I'd had of Yifter, of a mild and
amiable man, strengthened on longer exposure. It was
Bryson, during dinner, who caused the first tricky
moment.
     "Most of Earth's problems are caused by the United
Space Federation's influence," he said as the robo-
server, always on best form at the beginning of the trip,
rolled in the courses. "If it weren't for the U.S.F., there
wouldn't be as much discontent and rioting on Earth.

It's all relative, living space and living standards, and the U.S.F. sets a bad example. We can't compete."

According to Bryson, three million people were causing all the problems for ten billion — eleven, before Yifter's handiwork. It was sheer nonsense, and as a U.S.F. citizen, I should have been the one to bridle; but it was McAndrew who made a growling noise of disapproval, down in his throat; and it was Yifter, of all people, who sensed the atmosphere quickest, and deftly steered the conversation to another subject.

"I think Earth's worst problems are caused by the power shortage," he said. "That affects everything else. Why doesn't Earth use the kernels for power, the way that the U.S.F. does?"

"Too afraid of an accident," replied McAndrew. His irritation evaporated immediately at the mention of his specialty. "If the shields ever failed, you would have a Kerr-Newman black hole sitting there, pumping out a thousand megawatts — mostly as high-energy radiation and fast particles. Worse than that, it would pull in free charge and become electrically neutral. As soon as that happened, there'd be no way to hold it electromagnetically. It would sink down and orbit inside the Earth. We couldn't afford to have that happen."

"But couldn't we use smaller kernels on Earth?" asked Yifter. "They would be less dangerous."

McAndrew shook his head. "It doesn't work that way. The smaller the black hole, the higher the effective temperature and the faster it radiates. You'd be better off with a much more massive black hole. But then you've got the problem of supporting it against Earth's gravity. Even with the best electromagnetic control, anything that massive would sink down into the Earth."

"I suppose it wouldn't help to use a non-rotating, uncharged hole, either," said Yifter. "That might be easier to work with."

"A Schwarzschild hole?" McAndrew looked at him in disgust. "Now, Mr. Yifter, you know better than that." He grew eloquent. "A Schwarzschild hole gives you no control at all. You can't get a hold of it electromagnetically. It just sits there, spewing out energy all over the spectrum, and there's nothing you can do to change it — unless you want to charge it and spin it up, and make it into a kernel. With the kernels, now, you have control."

I tried to interrupt, but McAndrew was just getting warmed up. "A Schwarzschild hole is like a naked flame," he went on. "A caveman's device. A kernel is *refined*, it's controllable. You can spin it up and store energy, or you can use the ergosphere to pull energy out and spin it down. You can use the charge on it to move it about as you want. It's a real working instrument — not a bit of crudity from the Dark Ages."

I shook my head, and sighed in simulated despair. "McAndrew, you have an unconsummated love affair with those blasted kernels." I turned to Yifter and Bryson, who had watched McAndrew's outburst with some surprise. "He spends all his waking hours spinning those things up and down. All the last trip, he was working the kernels in gravitational focusing experiments. You know, using the fact that a gravity field bends light rays. He insists that one day we won't use lenses for optics — we'll focus light using arrays of kernels."

I made the old joke. "We hardly saw him on that trip. We were convinced that one day he'd get careless with the shields, fall into one of the kernels, and really make a spectacle of himself."

They didn't get it. Yifter and Bryson looked at me blankly, while McAndrew, who'd heard it all ten times before, chuckled. I knew his simple sense of humor —

a bad joke is always funny, even if it's the hundredth time you've heard it told.

It's a strange thing, but after the first half-hour I had stopped thinking of Yifter as our prisoner. I could understand now why Bryson had objected to the idea of surrounding Yifter with armed guards. I'd have objected myself. He seemed the most civilized man in the group, with a warm personality and a very dry and subtle sense of humor.

When Bryson left the table, pleading a long day and a lack of familiarity with a space environment, Yifter, McAndrew and I stayed on, chatting about the previous trips I had made to Titan. I mentioned the time I had taken the circus.

"Do you know, I'd never seen most of those animals before," I said. "They were all on the list of endangered species. I don't think you could find them on Earth any more, except in a circus or a zoo."

There was a moment of silence, then Yifter spoke. His eyes were mild and smiling, and his voice sounded dreamy and distant.

"Endangered species," he said. "That's the heart of it. Earth has no room for failures. The weaker species, like weaker specimens of a species, must be eliminated. Only the strong — the mentally strong — may survive. The weak must be culled, for our own sake; whether that means one tenth, one half, or nine tenths of the total."

There was a chilling pause. I looked at Yifter, whose expression had not changed, then at McAndrew, whose face reflected the horror that I was feeling. Yet behind all that, I could feel the unique power of the man. My mind was rejecting him, but I still had a sense of well-being, of warmth in the pit of my stomach, as he was speaking.

"We have made a beginning," went on Yifter quietly.

"Just a beginning. Last time we were less successful than I had hoped. We had a breakdown in the distribution system for the drugs. I managed to eliminate the responsible individuals, but it was too late to correct the problem. Next time, God willing, it will be different."

He rose to his feet, white hair shining like silver, face beatific. "Good night, Captain. Good night, Professor McAndrew. Sleep well."

After he had left, McAndrew and I sat and looked at each other for a long time. Finally, he broke the spell.

"Now we know, Jeanie. We should have guessed it from the beginning. Mad as a hatter. The man's a raving lunatic. Completely psychotic."

That said most of it. McAndrew had used up all the good phrases. I nodded.

"But did you feel the strength in him?" went on McAndrew. "Like a big magnet."

I was glad that the penal colony was so far from Earth, and the avenues of communication so well-guarded. "Next time . . . it will be different." Our two-month trip suddenly seemed to have doubled in length.

After that single, chilling moment, there were no more shocks for some time. Our regular meal-time conversations continued, and on several occasions McAndrew voiced views on pacifism and the protection of human life. Each time, I waited for Yifter's reply, expecting the worst. He never actually agreed with Mac — but he did not come out with any statement that resembled his comments of the first ship-evening.

We soon settled into the ship-board routine. McAndrew spent less and less time in the Control Stage, and more in Section Seven. On this trip, he had brought a new set of equipment for his experiments, and I was very curious to know what he was up to. He wouldn't tell. I had only one clue. Section Seven was drawing enormous energy from the other kernels, in the rest of the Assembly. That energy could only be going to one place — into the kernel in Section Seven. I suspected that McAndrew must be spinning it up — making it closer to an "extreme" kernel, a Kerr-Newman black hole where the rotation energy matches the mass energy. I knew that couldn't be the whole story. McAndrew had spun up the kernels before, and he had told me that there was no direct way of getting a really extreme kernel — that would take an infinite amount of energy. This time, he was doing something different. He insisted that Section Seven had to be off-limits to everybody.

I couldn't get him to talk about it. There would be a couple of seconds of silence from him, then he would stand there, cracking his finger joints as though he were snapping out a coded message to me. He could be a real sphinx when he chose.

Two weeks from Earth, we were drawing clear of the main Asteroid Belt. I had just about concluded that my worries for the trip were over, when the radar reported another ship, closing slowly with us from astern. Its spectral signature identified it as the Lesotho, a cruise liner that usually ran trajectories in the Inner System. It was broadcasting a Mayday, and flying free under zero drive power.

I thought about it for a moment, then posted Emergency Stations throughout the Assembly. The computed trajectory showed that we would match velocities at a separation of three kilometers. That was incredibly close, far too close to be accidental. After closest approach, we would pull away again — we were still under power, accelerating outward, and would leave the Lesotho behind.

I was still watching the displays, trying to decide

whether or not to take the next step — shutting off the drives — when Bryson appeared, with Yifter just behind him.

"Captain Roker," he said, in his usual imperious manner. "That's an Earth ship there, giving you a distress signal. Why aren't you doing anything about it?"

"If we wait just a few minutes," I said, "we'll be within spitting distance of her. I see no point in rushing in, until we've had a good look at her. I can't think what an Inner System ship would be doing, free-falling out here beyond the Belt."

That didn't cool him. "Can't you recognize an emergency when you see one?" he said. "If you won't do something productive with your people, I'll do something with mine."

I wondered what he wanted me to do, but he walked away from me without saying anything more, down the stairs that led to the rear communication area of the Control Stage. I turned back to the displays. The *Lesotho* was closing on us steadily, and now I could see that her locks were open. I cut our propulsion to zero and switched off all the drives. The other ship was tumbling slowly, drive lifeless and aft nacelles crumpled. Even from this distance, I could see that she would need extensive repairs before she could function again.

I was beginning to think that I had been over-cautious when two things happened. Yifter's guards, who had been housed behind the Control Stage in Section Two, began to float into view on the viewing screen that pointed towards the *Lesotho*. They were all in space armor and heavily weaponed. At the same time two suited figures appeared in the open forward lock of the other vessel. I cut in the suit frequencies on our main board.

"—shield failure," said the receiver. "Twenty-seven survivors, and bad injuries. We must have pain-killers, medical help, water, food, oxygen and power-packs."

With that, one group of our guards outside began to move towards the two suited figures in the *Lesotho's* lock, while the remainder stayed close to the Assembly, looking across at the other ship. Subconsciously, I noted the number of our guards in each party, then gave them my full attention and did a rapid re-count. Twenty-five. All our guards. I swore and cut in the transmitter.

"Sergeant, get half of those men back inside the Assembly shields. This is Captain Roker. I'm over-riding any other orders you may have received. Get the nearer party—"

I was interrupted. The display screen flashed bluewhite, then over-loaded. The whole Control Stage rang like a great bell, as something slapped hard on the outer shield. I knew what it was: a huge pulse of hard radiation and highly energetic particles, smashing into us in a fraction of a microsecond.

Yifter had been floating within a couple of meters of me, watching the screens. He put his hand to the wall to orient himself as the Control Stage vibrated violently. "What was that?"

"Thermonuclear explosion," I said shortly. "Hundred megaton plus. On the *Lesotho*."

All the screens on that side were dead. I activated the standby system. The *Lesotho* had vanished. The guards had vanished with it, vaporized instantly. All the cables linking the parts of the Assembly, all the scanners and sensors that were not protected behind the shields, were gone. The Sections themselves were intact, but their coupling fields would have to be completely re-calibrated. We wouldn't be arriving at Titan on schedule.

I looked again at Yifter. His face was now calm and thoughtful. He seemed to be waiting, listening expectantly. For what? If the Lesotho had been a suicide mission, manned by volunteers who sought revenge on Yifter, they hadn't had a chance. They couldn't destroy the Assembly, or get at Yifter. If revenge were not the purpose, what *was* the purpose?

I ran through in my mind the events of the past hour. With the drives switched off in the Assembly, we had an unprotected blind spot, dead astern. We had been putting all our attention on the Lesotho. Now, with the guards all dead, the Control Stage was undefended.

It was quicker to go aft and take a look, than to call Bryson or McAndrew and ask them what they could see from the rear viewing screens of the Control Stage. Leaving Yifter, I dived head-first down the stairway — a risky maneuver if there were any chance that the drive might come back on, but I was sure it couldn't.

It took me about thirty seconds to travel the length of the Control Stage. By the time that I was half-way, I knew I had been thinking much too slowly. I heard the clang of a lock, a shout, and the sputtering crackle of a hand laser against solid metal. When I got to the rear compartment it was all finished. Bryson, pale and open-mouthed, was floating against one wall. He seemed unhurt. McAndrew had fared less well. He was ten meters further along, curled into a fetal ball. Floating near him I saw a family of four stubby pink worms with red-brown heads, still unclenching with muscle spasm. I could also see the deep burn on his side and chest, and his right hand, from which a laser had neatly clipped the fingers and cauterized the wound instantly as it did so. At the far end of the room, braced against the wall, were five suited figures, all well-armed.

Heroics would serve no purpose. I spread my arms wide to show that I was not carrying a weapon, and one of the newcomers pushed off from the wall and floated past me, heading towards the front of the

Control Stage. I moved over to McAndrew and inspected his wounds. They looked bad, but not fatal. Fortunately, laser wounds are usually very clean. I could see that we would have problems with his lung unless we treated him quickly. A lobe had been penetrated, and his breathing was slowly breaking the seal of crisped tissue that the laser had made. Blood was beginning to well through and stain his clothing.

McAndrew's forehead was beaded with sweat. As the shock of his wound wore off, the pain was beginning. I pointed to the medical belt of one of the invaders, who nodded and tossed an ampoule across to me. I injected McAndrew intravenously at the big vein inside his right elbow.

The figure who had pushed past me was returning, followed by Yifter. The face plate of the suit was now open, revealing a dark-haired woman in her early thirties. She looked casually at the scene, nodded at last, and turned back to Yifter.

"Everything's under control here," she said. "But we'll have to take a Section from the Assembly. The ship we were following in caught some of the blast from the *Lesotho*, and it's no good for powered flight now."

Yifter shook his head reprovingly. "Impatient as usual, Akhtar. I'll bet you were just too eager to get here. You must learn patience if you are to be of maximum value to us, my dear. Where did you leave the main group?"

"A few hours' drive inward from here. We have waited for your rescue, before making any plans for the next phase."

Yifter, calm as ever, nodded approvingly. "The right decision. We can take a Section without difficulty. Most of them contain their own drives, but some are less effective than others."

He turned to me, smiling gently. "Jeanie Roker, which

Section is the best equipped to carry us away from the Assembly? As you see, it is time for us to leave you and rejoin our colleagues."

His calm was worse than any number of threats. I floated next to McAndrew, trying to think of some way that we could delay or impede the Lucies' escape. It might take days for a rescue party to reach us. In that time, Yifter and his followers could be anywhere.

I hesitated. Yifter waited. "Come now," he said at last. "I'm sure you are as eager as I am to avoid any further annoyance" — he moved his hand, just a little, to indicate McAndrew and Bryson — "for your friends."

I shrugged. All the Sections contained emergency life-support systems, more than enough for a trip of a few hours. Section Two, where the guards had been housed, lacked a full, independent drive unit, but it was still capable of propulsion. I thought it might slow their escape enough for us somehow to track it.

"Section Two should be adequate," I said. "It housed your guards in comfort. Those poor devils certainly have no need for it now."

I paused. Beside me, McAndrew was painfully straightening from his contorted position. The drugs were beginning to work. He coughed, and red globules floated away across the room. That lung needed attention.

"No," he said faintly. "Not Two, Yifter. Seven. Section Seven."

He paused and coughed again, while I looked at him in surprise.

"Seven," he said at last. He looked at me. "No Killing, Jeanie. No — Killing vector."

The woman was listening closely. She regarded both of us suspiciously. "What was all that about?"

My mouth was gaping open as wide as Bryson's. I

had caught an idea of what McAndrew was trying to tell me, but I didn't want to say it. Fortunately, I was helped out by Yifter himself.

"No killing," he said. "My dear, you have to understand that Professor McAndrew is a devoted pacifist — and carrying his principles through admirably. He doesn't want to see any further killing. I think I can agree with that — for the present."

He looked at me and shook his head. "I won't inquire what dangers and drawbacks Section Two might contain, Captain — though I do seem to recall that it lacks a decent drive unit. I think we'll follow the Professor's advice and take Section Seven. Akhtar is a very competent engineer, and I'm sure she'll have no trouble coupling the drive to the kernel."

He looked at us with a strange expression. If it didn't sound so peculiar, I'd describe it as wistful. "I shall miss our conversations," he said. "But I must say goodbye now. I hope that Professor McAndrew will recover. He is one of the strong — unless he allows himself to be killed by his unfortunate pacifist fancies. We may not meet again, but I am sure that you will be hearing about us in the next few months."

They left. McAndrew, Bryson and I watched the screens in silence, as the Lucies made their way over to Section Seven and entered it. Once they were inside, I went over to McAndrew and took him by the left arm.

"Come on," I said. "We have to get a patch on that lung."

He shook his head weakly. "Not yet. It can wait for a few minutes. After that, it might not be necessary."

His forehead was beading with sweat again — and this time it was not from pain. I felt my own tension mounting steadily. We stayed by the display screen, and as the seconds ticked away my own forehead began to film with perspiration. We did not speak. I had one question, but I was terribly afraid of the answer I might get. I think that Bryson spoke to both of us several times. I have no idea what he said.

Finally, a pale nimbus grew at the rear of the Section Seven drive unit.

"Now," said McAndrew. "He's going to tap the kernel."

I stopped breathing. There was a pause of a few seconds, stretching to infinity, then the image on the screen rippled slightly. Suddenly, we could see stars shining through that area. Section Seven was gone, vanished, with no sign that it had ever existed.

McAndrew took in a long, pained breath, wincing as his injured lung expanded. Somehow, he managed a little smile.

"Well now," he said. "That answers a theoretical question that I've had on my mind for some time."

I could breathe again, too. "I didn't know what was going to happen there," I said. "I was afraid all the energy might come out of that kernel in one go."

McAndrew nodded. "To be honest, that thought was in my head, too. At this range, the shields would have been useless. We'd have gone like last year's lovers."

Bryson had been watching the whole thing in confusion. We had been ignoring him completely. At last, pale and irritable, he spoke to us again.

"What are you two talking about? And what's happened to the Section with Yifter in it? I was watching on the screen, then it just seemed to disappear."

"McAndrew tried to tell us earlier," I said. "But he didn't want the Lucies to know what he was getting at. He'd been fiddling with the kernel in that Section. You heard what he said — no Killing vector. I don't know what he did, but he fixed it so that the kernel in Section Seven had no Killing vector."

"I'm sure he did," said Bryson tartly. "Now perhaps

you'll tell me what a Killing vector is."

"Well, Mac could tell you a lot better than I can. But a Killing vector is a standard sort of thing in relativity — I guess you never had any training in that. You get a Killing vector when a region of space-time has some sort of symmetry — say, about an axis of spin. And every sort of black hole, every sort of kernel we've ever encountered before, has at least one symmetry of that type. So if McAndrew had changed the kernel and made it into something with no Killing vector, it's like no kernel we've ever seen. Right, Mac?"

He looked dreamy. The drugs had taken hold. "I took it past the extreme Kerr-Newman form," he said. "Put it into a different form, metastable equilibrium. Event horizon had disappeared, all the Killing vectors had disappeared."

"Christ!" I hadn't expected that. "No event horizon? Doesn't that mean that you get—?"

McAndrew was still nodding, eye pupils dilated. "—a naked singularity. That's right, Jeanie. I had a naked singularity, sitting there in equilibrium in Section Seven. You don't get there by spinning-up — need different method." His speech was slurring, as though his tongue was swollen. "Didn't know what would happen if somebody tried to tap it, to use for a drive. Either the signature of space-time there would change, from three space dimensions and one time, to two space and two time. Or we might see the System's biggest explosion. All the mass coming out as radiation, in one flash."

It was slowly dawning on Bryson what we were saying. "But just where is Yifter now?" he asked.

"Gone a long way," I said. "Right out of this universe."

"And he can't be brought back?" asked Bryson.

"I hope not." I'd seen more than enough of Yifter.

"But I'm supposed to deliver him safely to Titan," said Bryson. "I'm responsible for his safe passage. What am I going to tell the Planetary Coordinators?"

I didn't have much sympathy. I was too busy looking at McAndrew's wounds. The fingers could be re-generated using the bio-feedback equipment on Titan, but the lung would need watching. It was still bleeding a little.

"Tell them you had a very singular experience," I said. McAndrew grunted as I probed the deep cut in his side. "Sorry, Mac. Have to do it. You know, you've ruined your reputation forever as far as I'm concerned. I thought you were a pacifist? All that preaching at us, then you send Yifter and his lot all the way to Hell — and good riddance to them."

McAndrew was drifting far away on his big dose of pain-killers. He half-winked at me and made his curious throat-clearing noise.

"Och, I'm a pacifist all right. We pacifists have to look after each other. How could we ever hope for peace with people like Yifter around to stir up trouble? There's a bunch more of them, a few hours' travel behind us. Fix me up quick. I should be tinkering with the other kernels a bit. Just in case the other Lucies decide to pay us a visit later..."

SECOND CHRONICLE: MOMENT OF INERTIA

"Now," said the interviewer, "tell us just what led you to tho ideas for the inertia-less drive."

She was young and vulnerable-looking, and I think that was what savod her from a hot reply. As it was, McAndrew just shook his head and said quietly — but still with feeling — "Not the *inertia-less* drive. There's no such thing. It's a *balanced* drive."

She looked confused. "But it lets you accelerate at more than fifty gees, doesn't it? By making you so you don't feel any acceleration at all. Doesn't that mean you must have no inertia?"

McAndrew was shaking his head again. He looked pained and resigned. I suppose that he had to go through this explanation twice a day, every day of his life, with somebody.

I leaned forward and lowered the sound on the video unit. I had heard the story too often, and my sympathies

were all with him. We had direct evidence that the
McAndrew Drive was anything but inertia-less. I doubt
if he'll ever get that message across to the average person, even though he's most people's idea of the "great
scientist", the ultimate professor.

I was there at the beginning of the whole thing. In
fact, according to McAndrew I *was* the beginning. We
had been winding our way back from the Titan Colony,
travelling light as we usually did on the in-bound leg.
We had only four Sections in the Assembly, and only
two of them carried power kernels and drive units, so
I guess we massed about three billion tons for ship and
cargo.

Halfway in, just after turn-over point, we got an
incoming request for medical help from the mining colony on Horus. I passed the word on to Luna Station,
but we couldn't do much to help. Horus is in the Egyp-
tian Cluster of asteroids, way out of the ecliptic, and
it would take any aid mission a couple of weeks to get
to them. By that time, I suspected their problem would
be over — one way or another. So I was in a pretty
gloomy mood when McAndrew and I sat down to
dinner.

"I didn't know what to tell them, Mac. They know
the score as well as I do, but they couldn't resist asking if we had a fast-passage ship that could help them.
I had to tell them the truth, there's nothing that can
get out there at better than two and a half gees, not
with people on board. And they need doctors, not just
drugs. Luna will have something on the way in a couple of days, but I don't think that will do it."

McAndrew nodded sympathetically. He knew that
I needed to talk it out to somebody, and we've spent
a lot of time together on those Titan runs. He's working
on his own experiments most of the time, but I know
when he needs company, too. It must be nice to be a

famous scientist, but it can be lonely travelling all the time inside your own head.

"I wonder if we're meant for space, Mac," I went on — only half-joking. "We've got drives that will let us send unmanned probes out at better than a hundred gees of continuous acceleration, but we're the weak link. I could take the Assembly here up to five gee — we'd be home in a couple of days instead of another month — but you and I couldn't take it. Can't you and some of your staff at the Institute come up with a system so that we don't get crushed flat by high accelerations? A thing like that, an inertia-less drive, it would change space exploration completely."

I was wandering on, just to keep my mind off the problems they had out on Horus, but what I was saying was sound enough. We had the power on the ships, only the humans were the obstacle. McAndrew was listening to me seriously, but he was shaking his head.

"So far as I know, Jeanie, an inertia-less drive is a theoretical impossibility. Unless somebody a lot brighter than I am can come up with an entirely new theory of physics, we'll not see your inertia-less drive."

That was a pretty definitive answer. There were no people brighter than McAndrew, at least in the area of physics. If Mac didn't think it could be done, you'd not find many people arguing with him. Some people were fooled by the fact that he took time off to make trips with me out to Titan, but that was all part of his way of working.

If you deduce from this that I'm not up at that rarefied level of thought, you're quite right. I can follow McAndrew's explanations — sometimes. But when he really gets going he loses me in the first two sentences.

This time, his words seemed clear enough for anyone to follow them. I poured myself another glass of ouzo and wondered how many centuries it would be before the man or woman with the completely new theory came along. Sitting across from me, Mac had begun to rub at his sandy, receding hairline. His expression had become vacant. I've learned not to interrupt when he's got that look on his face. It means he's thinking in a way that I can't follow. One of the other professors at the Penrose Institute says that Mac has a mind that can see round corners, and I have a little inkling what he means by that.

"Why inertia-less, Jeanie?" said McAndrew after a few minutes.

Maybe he hadn't been listening to me after all. "So we can use high accelerations. So we can get people to go at the same speeds as the unmanned probes. They'd be flattened at fifty gee, you know that. We need an inertia-less drive so that we can stand that acceleration without being squashed to a mush."

"But that's not the same thing at all. I told you that a drive with no inertia isn't possible — and it isn't. What you're asking for, now, it seems to me that we should be able..."

His voice drifted off to nothing, he stood up, and without another word he left the cabin. I wondered what I'd started.

If that was the beginning of the McAndrew Drive — as I think it was — then, yes, I was there at the very beginning.

So far as I could tell, it wasn't only the beginning. It was also the end. Mac didn't talk about the subject again on our way in to Luna rendezvous, even though I tried to nudge him a couple of times. He was always the same, he didn't like to talk about his ideas when they were "half-cooked", as he called it.

When we got to Luna, McAndrew went off back to the Institute, and I took a cargo out to Cybele. End of story, and it gradually faded from my thoughts, until the time came, seven months later, for the next run to Titan.

For the first time in five years, McAndrew didn't make the trip. He didn't call me, but I got a brief message that he was busy with an off-Earth project, and wouldn't be free for several months. I wondered, not too seriously, if Mac's absence could be connected with inertia-less spaceships, and then went on with the cargo to Titan.

That was the trip where some lunatic in the United Space Federation's upper bureaucracy decided that Titan was overdue for some favorable publicity, as a thriving colony where culture would be welcomed. Fine. They decided to combine culture and nostalgia, and hold on Titan a full-scale, old-fashioned Miss & Mister Universe competition. It apparently never occurred to the organizers — who must have had minds that could not see in straight lines, let alone around corners — that the participants were bound to take the thing seriously once it was started. Beauty is not something that good-looking people are willing to take lightly. I had the whole Assembly filled with gorgeous, jealous contestants, screaming managers, horny and ever-hopeful newshounds from every media outlet in the System, and any number of vengeful and vigilant wives, lovers and mistresses of both sexes. On one of my earlier runs I took a circus and zoo out to Titan, but that was nothing compared with this trip. Thank Heaven that the ship is computer-controlled. All my time was spent in keeping some of the passengers together and the rest apart.

It also hadn't occurred to the organizers, back on Earth, that a good part of the Titan colony is the prison. When I saw the first interaction of the prisoners and the contestants I realized that the trip out to Titan had been a picnic compared with what was about to follow.

I chickened out and went back to the ship until it was all over.

I couldn't really escape, though. When it *was* all over, when the winners had finally been chosen, when the protests and the counter-protests had all been lodged, when the battered remnants of the more persistent prisoners had been carried back to custody, when mayhem was stilled, and when the colonists of Titan must have felt that they had enjoyed as much of Inner System culture as they could stand for another twenty or thirty years, after all that it was my job to get the group back on board again, and home to Earth without further violence. The contestants hated their managers, the managers hated the judges, the judges hated the news media, and everyone hated the winners. It seemed to me that McAndrew may have had advance information about the trip, and drawn a correct conclusion.

I would like to have skipped it myself. Since I was stuck with it, I separated the Sections of the Assembly as much as I could, put everything onto automatic, and devoted myself to consoling one of the losers, a smooth-skinned armful from one of the larger asteroids.

We finally got there. On that day of rejoicing, the whole ghastly gaggle connected with the contest left the Assembly. I said a lingering farewell to my friend from Vesta — a most inappropriate origin for that particular contestant — and settled back for a needed rest.

It lasted for about eight hours. As soon as I called into the Com Center for news and messages, I got a terse summons on the com display: GO TO PENROSE INSTITUTE, L-4 STATION. MACAVITY.

Not an alarming message, on the face of it, but it worried me. It was from McAndrew, and it was addressed to me alone — no one else in the System called him Macavity, and I doubt if three people knew that I had given him that nickname when I found he was a specialist on theories of gravity ("Old Possum's Book Of Practical Cats" didn't seem to be widely read among Mac's colleagues).

Why hadn't he called me directly, instead of sending a com-link message? The fact that we were back from Titan would have been widely reported. I sat down at the terminal and placed a link to the Institute, person-to-person to McAndrew.

I didn't feel any better when the call went through. Instead of Mac's familiar face, I was looking at the coal-black complexion of Professor Limperis, the head of the whole Institute. He nodded at me seriously.

"Captain Roker, your timing is impressive. If we had received no response to Professor McAndrew's coded message in the next eight hours, we would have proceeded without you. Can you help?"

He hesitated, seeing my confused expression. "Did your message tell you the background of the problem?"

"Dr. Limperis, all I've had so far is half a dozen words — to go to the L-4 branch of the Institute. I can do that easily enough, but I have no idea what the problem is, or what use I could possibly be on it. Where's Mac?"

"I wish to God I could answer that." He sat silent for a moment, chewing on his lower lip, then shrugged. "Professor McAndrew insisted that we send for you — left a message specifically for you. He told us that you were the stimulus for beginning the whole thing."

"What whole thing?"

He looked at me in even greater surprise. "Why, the high acceleration drive — the balanced drive that McAndrew has been developing for the past year. McAndrew has disappeared testing the prototype. Can you come at once to the Institute?"

The trip out to the Institute, creeping along in the Space Tug from Luna Station, was one of the low points of my life. There was no particular logic to it — after all, I'd done nothing wrong. But I couldn't get rid of the feeling that I'd wasted a critical eight hours after the passengers had left the Assembly. If I hadn't been obsessed with sex on the trip back, maybe I would have gone straight to the com-link instead of taking a sleep break. And maybe then I would have been on my way that much earlier, and that would have been the difference between saving Mac and failing to save him . . .

You can see how my mind was running. Without any real facts, you can make bears out of bushes just as well in space as you can on Earth. All I had been told by Limperis was that McAndrew had left a week earlier on a test of the prototype of a new ship. If he was not back within a hundred and fifty hours, he had left that terse coded message for me, and instructions — orders might be a better word — to take me along on any attempted search for him.

Dr. Limperis had been very apologetic about it. "I'm only quoting Professor McAndrew, you understand. He said that he didn't want any rescue party setting out in the *Dotterel* if you weren't part of it. He said" — Limperis coughed uncomfortably — "we had a real need for your common sense and natural cowardice. We'll be waiting for you here as soon as you can arrange passage. The least we can do for Professor McAndrew in the circumstances is to honor his wishes on this."

I couldn't decide if I was being complimented or not. As L-4 Station crept into view on the forward screen, I peered at it on highest magnification, trying to see what the rescue ship looked like. I could see the bulk of the Institute structure, but no sign of anything that ought to be a ship. I had visions of a sort of super-

Assembly, a huge cluster of electromagnetically linked spheres. All I could see were living quarters and docking facilities, and, as we came in to dock, a peculiar construction like a flat, shiny plate with a long thin spike protruding from the center. It looked nothing like any USF ship, passenger or cargo.

Limperis may have spent his whole life in pure research, but he knew how to organize for emergency action. There were just five people in our meeting inside the Institute. I had never met them in person, but they were all familiar to me through McAndrew's descriptions, and from media coverage. Limperis himself had made a life study of high-density matter. He knew every kernel below lunar mass out to a couple of hundred astronomical units — many of them he had visited, and a few of the small ones he had shunted back with him to the Inner System, to use as power supplies.

Siclaro was the specialist in kernel energy extraction. The Kerr-Newman black holes were well-understood theoretically, but efficient use of them was still a matter for experts. When the USF wanted to know the best way to draw off power, for drives or for general use, Siclaro was usually called in. His name on a recommendation was like a stamp of approval that few would think to question.

With Gowers there as an expert in multiple kernel arrays, Macedo as the System authority in electromagnetic coupling, and Wenig the master of compressed matter stability, the combined intellect in that one room in the Institute was overpowering. I looked at the three men and two women who had just been introduced to me, and felt like a gorilla in a ballet. I might make the right movements, but I wouldn't know what was going on.

"Look, Dr. Limperis, I know what Professor McAndrew wants, but I'm not sure he's right." Might as well hit them with my worries at the beginning, and not ·waste everybody's time. "I can run a ship, sure — it's not hard. But I've no idea how to run something with a McAndrew Drive on it. Any one of you could probably do a better job."

Limperis was looking apologetic again. "Yes and no, Captain Roker. We could all handle the ship, any one of us. The concepts behind it are simple — a hundred and fifty years old. And the engineering has been kept simple, too, since we are dealing with a prototype."

"Then what do you want *me* for?" I won't say I was angry, but I was uneasy and unhappy, and there's a fine line between irritation and discomfort.

"Dr. Wenig will drive the *Dotterel,* he has handled it before in an earlier test. Actually, he handled the *Merganser,* the ship that Dr. McAndrew has disappeared in, but the *Dotterel* has identical design and equipment. Controlling the ship is easy — if everything behaves as we expect. If something goes wrong — and something must have gone wrong, or McAndrew would be back before this — then neither Dr. Wenig, nor any of the rest of us, has the experience that will be needed. We want you to tell Dr. Wenig what *not* to do. You've been through dangerous times before." He looked pleading. "Will you observe our actions, and use your experience to advise us?"

Uninvited, I flopped down into a seat and stared at the five of them. "You want me to be a bloody canary!"

"A canary?" Wenig was small and slight, with a luxuriant black mustache. He had a strong accent, and I think he was suspecting himself of a translation error.

"Right. Back when people used to go down deep in the earth to mine coal, they used to take a canary along with them. It was more sensitive to poisonous gases than they were. When it fell off the perch, they knew it was time to leave. The rest of you will fly the ship, and watch for me to fall off my seat."

They looked at each other, and finally Limperis nodded. "We need a canary, Captain Roker. None of us here knows how to sing at the right time. Will you do it?"

I had no choice. Not after Mac's personal cry for help. I could see one problem — I'd be telling them everything they did was dangerous. When you have a new piece of technology, it is risky, *whatever* you do with it.

"You mean you'll let me overrule all the rest of you, if I don't feel comfortable?"

"We would." Limperis was quite firm about it. "But the question will not arise. The *Merganser* and the *Dotterel* are both two-person ships. We saw no point in making them larger. Dr. Wenig will fly the *Dotterel,* and you will be the only other person. It just takes one person to handle the controls. You will be there to advise of hidden problems."

I stood up. "Let's go. I don't think I can see danger any better than you can, but I may be wrong. If Mac's on his own out there, wherever he is, we'd better get moving. I'm ready when you are, Dr. Wenig."

Nobody moved. Maybe McAndrew and Limperis were right about my antennae, because at that moment I had a premonition of new problems. I looked around at the uncomfortable faces.

"Professor McAndrew isn't actually *alone* on the *Merganser.*" It was Emma Gowers who spoke first. "He has a passenger on the ship."

"Someone from the Institute?"

She shook her head. "Nina Velez is with him."

"Nina Velez? You don't mean President Velez' daughter — the one with AG News?"

She nodded. "The same."

I sat down again in my chair. Maybe the Body-beautiful run to Titan had been an easier trip than I had realized.

Wenig may have come to piloting second-hand, but he certainly knew his ship. He wanted me to know it, too. Before we left the Institute, we'd done the lot — schematics, models, components, power, life support, mechanicals, electricals, electronics, controls, and back-ups.

When the ship was explained to me, I decided that McAndrew didn't really see round corners when he thought. It was just that things were obvious to him *before* they were explained, and obvious to other people afterwards. I had been saying "inertia-less" to Mac, and he had been just as often saying "impossible". But we hadn't been communicating very well. All I wanted was a drive that would let us accelerate at multiple gees without flattening the passengers. To McAndrew, that was a simple requirement, one that he could easily satisfy — but there was no question of doing away with inertia, of passengers or ship.

"Take it back to basics," said Wenig, when he was showing me how the *Dotterel* worked. "Remember the equivalence principle? That's at the heart of it. There is no way of distinguishing an accelerated motion from a gravitational field force, right?"

I had no trouble with that. It was freshman physics. "Sure. You'd be flattened just as well in a really high gravity field as you would in a ship accelerating at fifty gee. But where does it get you?"

"Imagine that you were standing on something with a hefty gravity field — Jupiter, say. You'd experience a downward force of about two and a half gee. Now suppose that somebody could accelerate Jupiter *away* from you, downwards, at two and a half gee. You'd fall towards it, but you'd never reach it — it would be accelerating at the same rate as you are. And you'd feel as though you were in free fall, but so far as the rest of the Universe is concerned you'd be accelerating at two and a half gee, same as Jupiter. That's what the equivalence principle is telling us, that acceleration and gravity can cancel out, if they're set up to be equal and opposite."

As soon as you got used to Wenig's accent, he was easy to follow — I doubt if anybody could get into the Institute unless he was more than bright enough to explain concepts in easy terms. I nodded.

"I can understand that easily enough. But you've just replaced one problem with a worse one. You can't find any drive in the Universe that could accelerate Jupiter at two and a half gee."

"We cannot — not yet, at any rate. Luckily, we don't need to use Jupiter. We can do it with something a lot smaller, and a lot closer. Let's look at the *Dotterel* and the *Merganser*. At McAndrew's request I designed the mass element for both of them."

He went across to the window that looked out from the inside of the Institute to raw space. The *Dotterel* was floating about ten kilometers away, close enough to see the main components.

"See the plate on the bottom? It's a hundred meter diameter disk of compressed matter, electromagnetically stabilized and one meter thick. Density's about eleven hundred and seventy tons per cubic centimeter — pretty high, but nothing near as high as we've worked with here at the Institute. Less than you get in anything but the top couple of centimeters of a neutron star, and nowhere near approaching kernel densities. Now, if you were sitting right at the center of that disk, you'd experience a *gravitational* acceleration of fifty gee pulling you down to the disk. Tidal forces on you would be one gee per meter — not enough to trouble you. If you stayed on the axis of the disk, and moved away from it, you'd feel an attractive force of one gee when you were two hundred and forty-six meters from the center of the disk. See the column growing out from the disk? It's four meters across and two hundred and fifty meters long."

I looked at it through the scope. The long central spike seemed to be completely featureless, a slim column of grey metal.

"What's inside it?"

"Mostly nothing." Wenig picked up a model of the *Dotterel* and cracked it open lengthwise, so that I could see the interior structure. "When the drives are off, the living-capsule is out here at the far end, two hundred and fifty meters from the dense disk. Gravity feels like one gee, towards the center of the disk. See the drives here, on the disk itself? They accelerate the whole thing *away* from the center column, so the disk stays flat and perpendicular to the motion. The bigger the acceleration that the drives produce, the closer to the disk we move the living-capsule, up the central column here. We keep it so the total force in the capsule, gravity less acceleration, is always one gee, *towards* the disk."

He slid the capsule along an electro-mechanical ladder closer to the disk. "It's easy to compute the right distance for any acceleration — the computer has it built-in, but you could do it by hand in a few minutes. When the drives are accelerating the whole thing at fourteen gee, the capsule is held a little less than fifty meters from the disk. I've been on a test run in the *Merganser* where we got up to almost twenty gee. Professor McAndrew intended to take it up to higher accelerations on this test. To accelerate at thirty-two gee, the capsule must be about twenty meters from the disk to keep effective gravity inside it to one gee. The

plan was to take the system all the way up to design
maximum — fifty gee thrust acceleration, so that the
passengers in the capsule would be right up against
the disk, and feel as though they were in free fall. Gravity and thrust accelerations will exactly balance."

I was getting goose bumps along the back of my neck.
I knew the performance of the unmanned med ships.
They would zip you from inside the orbit of Mercury
out to Pluto in a couple of days, standing start to standing finish. Once in a while you'd get a passenger on
them — accident or suicide. The flattened thing that
they unpacked at the other end showed what the
human body thought of a hundred gee.

"What would happen if the drives went off suddenly?" I said.

"You mean when the capsule is up against the disk—
at maximum thrust?" Wenig shook his head. "We designed a safeguard system to prevent that, even on the
prototypes. If there were a sign of the drive cutting off,
the capsule would be moved back up the column, away
from the disk. The system for that is built-in."

"Yeah. But McAndrew hasn't come back." I had the
urge to get on our way. "I've seen built-in-safe systems
before. The more foolproof you think something is, the
worse the failure when it happens. Can't we get
moving?"

"Come on." Wenig stood up. "Any teacher will tell
you, you can't get much into an impatient learner. I'll
give you the rest of the story as we go. We'll go out
along the same path as McAndrew did — that's plotted
out in the records back here."

"You think McAndrew went along with the nominal
flight plan?"

"We know he didn't." Wenig looked a lot less sure
of himself. "You see, when the drives are on maximum
the plasma round the life capsule column interferes

with radio signals. Fifty hours after they left the Institute, the *Merganser* was tracked from Triton Station. McAndrew came back into the Solar System, decelerating at fifty gee. He didn't cut the drive at all — just went right through the System and accelerated out again in a slightly different direction. We got the log, but we've no idea what he was doing — there was no way to get a signal to him or from him with the drive on."

"So they got all the way up to the maximum drive! And they came back here. God, why didn't Limperis tell me that when we were in the first meeting?" I went to the locker and pulled out a suit. "He took it up all the way, fifty gee or better. Let's get after him. If he kept that up, he'll be half-way to Alpha Centauri by now."

The living capsule was about three meters across and simply furnished. I was surprised at the amount of room there was, until Wenig pointed out to me how equipment and supplies that could take higher accelerations were situated on the outside of the capsule, on the side away from the gravity disk.

We had started with McAndrew's flight plan for only a few minutes when I took Limperis at his word that I'd be boss and changed the procedure. If we were to reach McAndrew, the less time we spent shooting off in the opposite direction to the one that he had gone, the better. He had come right through the System, and we ought to head in the direction that he was last seen to be heading.

"I'll take us up to fifty gee," said Wenig. "That way, we'll experience the same perturbing forces as the *Merganser* did. All right?"

"Christ, no." My stomach turned over. "Not all right. Look, we don't know what happened to Mac, but chances are it was some problem with the ship. If we do just what he did, we may finish up with the same trouble."

Wenig took his hands off the controls and turned to me, palms spread. "But then what can we do? We don't know where they were going, all we can do is try and follow the same track."

"I'm not sure. All I know is what we're *not* going to do — and we're not trying for top acceleration. Didn't you say you'd flown *Merganser* at twenty gee?"

"Several times."

"Then take us out along Mac's trajectory at twenty gee until we're outside the System. Then cut the drive. I want to use our sensors, and we won't be able to do that from the middle of a ball of plasma."

Wenig looked at me. I know he was mentally accusing me of cowardice. "Captain Roker," he said quietly. "I thought we were in a hurry. We may be weeks following *Merganser* the way you are proposing."

"Yeah. But we'll get there. Can Mac's support system last that long?"

"Easily."

"Then don't let's kick it around any more. Let's do it. Twenty gee, as soon as you can give it to us."

The *Dotterel* worked like a dream. At twenty gee acceleration relative to the Solar System, we didn't feel anything unusual at all. The disk pulled us towards it at twenty-one gee, the acceleration of the ship pulled us away from it at twenty gee, and we sat there in the middle at a snug and comfortable standard gravity. I couldn't even feel the tidal forces, though I knew they were there. We had poor communications with the Penrose Institute, but we'd known of that and expected to make up for it when we cut the drive.

Oddly enough, the first phase of the trip wasn't scary — it was boring. I wanted to get up to a good cruise speed before we coasted free. It gave me the chance to probe another mystery — one that seemed at least as strange as the disappearance of the *Merganser*.

"What were you doing at the Institute, allowing Nina Velez aboard the ship?"

"She heard that we were developing a new drive — don't ask me how. Maybe she saw the Institute's budget." Wenig sniffed. "I don't trust the security at the USF Headquarters."

"And you let her talk her way in, and you forced McAndrew to take her with him on a *test flight?*"

If I sounded mad, I felt madder. Mac's life meant more than the dignity of some smooth-assed bureaucrat in the Institute's front office.

Dr. Wenig looked at me coldly. "I think you misunderstand the situation. Nina Velez was not forced onto Professor McAndrew by the 'front office' — for one thing, we have no such thing. The Institute is run by its members. You want to know why Miss Velez is on board the *Merganser?* I'll tell you. McAndrew insisted that she go with him."

"Bullshit!" There were some things I couldn't believe. "Why the hell would Mac let himself go along with that? I know him, even if you don't. Over his dead body."

Wenig sighed. He was leaning on a couch across from me, sipping a glass of white wine — no hardship tours for him.

"Four weeks ago I'd have echoed your comments exactly," he said. "Professor McAndrew would never agree to such a thing, right? But he did. Putting this simply, Captain Roker, it is a case of infatuation. A bad one. I think that—"

He stopped, outraged. I had started to laugh, in spite of the seriousness of our situation.

"What's so funny, Captain?"

"Well." I shrugged. "The whole thing's funny. Not funny, it's preposterous. McAndrew is a great physicist, and Nina Velez may be the President's daughter, but she's just a young newswoman. Anyway, he and I — he wouldn't—"

Now I stopped. I wondered if Wenig was going to get up and hit me, he looked so mad.

"Captain Roker, I don't like your insinuation," he said. "McAndrew is a physicist — so am I. You may not be smart enough to realize it, but physics is a field of study, not a surgical operation. Castration isn't part of the Ph.D. exams, you know." His tone dripped sarcasm. I wouldn't have liked a two-month trip to Titan with young Dr. Wenig.

"Anyway," he went on. "You have managed to jump to a wrong conclusion. It was not Professor McAndrew that suffered the initial infatuation. It was Nina Velez. She thinks he is wonderful. She came to do an interview, and before any of us knew what was going on she was in his office all day. All night, too, after the first week."

I was wrong. I know that now, and I think I knew it then, but I was too peeved to make an immediate apology to Wenig. Instead, I said, "But if she was the one that wanted him, couldn't he just throw her out?"

"Nina Velez?" Wenig gave a bark of laughter. "You've never met her, I assume? She's a President's daughter, and whatever Nina wants, Nina gets. She started it, but inside a couple of days she had Professor McAndrew behaving like a true fool. It was disgusting, the way he went on."

(You're jealous, Wenig, I said, jealous of Mac's good luck — but I said it to myself.)

"And she persuaded McAndrew to let her go out on the *Merganser*? What were the rest of you doing?"

He reddened. "Professor McAndrew was not the only one behaving like a fool. Why do you think Limperis, Siclaro and I feel like murderers? The two women on the team, Gowers and Macedo, insisted that Nina Velez should not go near the ships. We overruled them. Now, Captain Roker, maybe you see why each of us wanted to come after McAndrew. We drew lots, and I was the winner."

"And maybe you should think of one other thing," he went on. "While you are looking at our motives, and laughing at them, maybe you ought to look at your own. You look angry. I think you are jealous — jealous of Nina Velez."

It's a good thing that we had to follow our flight plan at that point, and prepare to cut the drive, or I don't know what I would have done to Dr. Wenig. I'm a shade taller than he is, and I outweigh him by maybe ten pounds, but he looked fit and wiry. It wouldn't have been a foregone conclusion, not at all.

Our descent into savagery was saved by the insistent buzzer of the computer, telling us to be ready for the drive reduction. We sat there, furious and not looking at each other, as the acceleration was slowly throttled back and the capsule moved away from the disk to resume its free-flight position two hundred and fifty meters behind it. The move took ten minutes. By the time it was over we had cooled off. I managed a graceless apology for my implied insults, and Wenig just as uncomfortably accepted it and said that he was sorry for what he had been saying and thinking.

I didn't ask him what he *had* been thinking — there was a hint that it was much worse than anything that he had said.

We had cut the drive at a little more than one hundred astronomical units from the Sun and were coasting along at a quarter of the speed of light. The computer gave us automatic Doppler compensation, so that we could hold an accurate communication link back to the Institute, through Triton Station. Conversation wasn't easy, because the round-trip delay for signals was almost twenty-eight hours — all we expected to be able to do was send "doing fine" messages to Limperis and the others.

Our forward motion was completely imperceptible, though I fancied that I could see a reddening of stars astern and a bluer burn to stars ahead of us. We were out well beyond the edge of the planetary part of the System, out where only the comets and the kernels lived. I put all our sensors onto maximum gain and Wenig and I settled in to a quiet spell of close watching. He had asked me what we were looking for. I had told him the truth: I had no idea, of what or when.

We crept on, farther out. I don't know if you can creep, at a quarter of light speed, but that's the way it felt; blackness, the unchanging stars, and a dwarfed Solar System far behind us.

Our eyes were all wide open; radio receivers, infrared scanners, telescopes, flux meters, radar and mass detectors. For two days we found nothing, no signal above the hiss and shimmer of the perennial interstellar background. Wenig was growing more impatient, and his tone was barely civil. He wanted us to get the drive back on high, and dash off after McAndrew — wherever that might be.

He was fidgeting on his bunk and ignoring the scopes when I saw the first trace.

"Dr. Wenig. What am I seeing? Can you tune that IR receiver?"

He came alert and was over to the console in a single movement. After a few seconds of adjustment he shook his head and swore. "It's natural, not man-made. Look at that trace. We're seeing a hot collapsed body. About seven hundred degrees, that's why there's peak power in the five micrometer band. We can call back to Limperis if you like, but he's sure to have it in his catalog already. There must be lots of these within a few days' flight of us."

He left the display and slumped back on his bunk. I went over and stared at it for a couple of minutes. "Would McAndrew know that this is here?"

That made him think instead of just brooding. "There's a good chance that he would. Collapsed and high-density matter is Doctor Limperis' special study, but McAndrew probably would put a library of them into *Merganser's* computer before he left. He wouldn't want to run into something unexpected out here."

"We have McAndrew's probable trajectory stored there too?"

"We know how he left the System, where he was heading. If he cut the drive, or turned after he was outside tracking range, we don't have any information on it."

"Never mind that. Give me the library access codes, and let me get at the input console. I want to see if Mac's path shows intersection with any of the high-density objects out here."

Wenig looked skeptical. "The chances of such a close encounter are very small. One in millions or billions."

I was already calling up the access sequence. "By accident? I'd agree with you. But McAndrew must have had some reason to fly back through the System, and make the slight course change that you recorded. I think he was telling us where he was going. And the only place he could have been going between here and Sirius would be one of the collapsed bodies out in the Halo."

"But *why*?" Wenig was standing at my shoulder, fingers twitching.

"Don't know that." I stood up. "Here, you do it, you must have had plenty of experience with *Dotterel's* computer. Set it for anything that would put *Merganser* within five million kilometers of a high-density body. That's as close as I think we can rely on trajectory intersection."

Wenig's fingers were flying over the keys — he should have been a concert pianist. I've never seen anybody handle a programming sequence at that rate. While he was doing it the com-link whistled for attention. I turned to it, leaving Wenig calling out displays and index files.

"It's Limperis," I said. "Problems. President Velez is starting to breathe down his neck. Wants to know what has happened to Nina. When will she be back? Why did Limperis and the rest of you let her go on a test trip? How can the Institute be so irresponsible?"

"We expected that." Wenig didn't look up. "Velez is just blowing off steam. There's no way that any other ship could get out here to us in less than three months. Does he have anything useful to suggest?"

"No. He's threatening Limperis with punitive measures against the Institute. Says he'll want a review of the whole organization."

"Limperis is asking for our reply?"

"Yes."

Wenig keyed in a final sequence of commands and sat back in his seat. "Tell him Velez should go fuck himself. We've got enough to do without interference."

I was still reading the incoming signals from Triton Station. "I think Dr. Limperis has already sent that message to the President's office — not in those words, maybe. We'd better get Nina back safely."

"I know that." Wenig hit a couple of keys and an output stream began to fill the scope. "Here it comes. Closest approach distances for every body within five hundred a.u., assuming McAndrew held the same course and acceleration all the way out. I've set it to stop if we get anything better than a million kilometers, and display everything that's five million or closer."

Before I could learn how to read the display, Wenig banged both hands down on the desk and leaned forward.

"Look at that!" His voice showed his surprise and excitement. "See it? That's HC-183. It's 322 a.u. from the Sun, and almost dead ahead of us. The computer shows a fly-by distance for *Merganser* too small to compute — that's an underflow where we ought to see a distance."

"Suppose that McAndrew decelerated as he got nearer to it?"

"Wouldn't make much difference, he'd still be close to rendezvous — speeds in orbit are small that far out. But why would he want to rendezvous with HC-183?"

I couldn't answer that, but maybe we were at least going to find *Merganser*. Even if it was only a vaporized trace on the surface of HC-183, where the ship hit it.

"Let's get back with our drive," I said. "What's the mass of HC-183?"

"Pretty high." Wenig frowned at the display. "We show a five thousand kilometer diameter and a mass that's half of Jupiter's. Must be a good lump of collapsed matter at the center of it. How close do you want to take us? And what acceleration for the drive?"

"Give us a trajectory that lets us take a close look from bound orbit. A million kilometers ought to be enough. And keep us down to twenty gee or better. I'll send a message back to the Institute. If they have any more information on HC-183, we want it."

Wenig had been impatient before, when we weren't going anywhere in particular. Now that we had a target he couldn't sit still. He was all over our three-meter living capsule, fiddling with the scopes, the computer, and the control console. He kept looking wistfully at the drive setting, then at me.

I wasn't having any. I felt as impatient as he did, but when we had come this far I didn't want to find we'd duplicated *all* McAndrew's actions, including the one that might have been fatal. We smoothly turned after twenty-two hours, so our drive began to decelerate us, and waited out the interminable delay as we crept closer to the dark mass of HC-183. We couldn't see a sign of it on any of the sensors, but we knew it had to be there, hidden behind the plasma ball of the drive.

When the drive went off and we were in orbit around the black mass of the hidden proto-planet, Wenig was at the display console for visible wavelengths.

"I can see it!" he shouted.

My first feeling of relief and excitement lasted only a split second. There was no way we would be able to spot the *Merganser* from a million kilometers out.

"What are you seeing? Infra-red emission from HC-183?"

"No, you noodle. I can see the ship — McAndrew's ship."

"You can't be. We'd have to be right next to it to be able to pick it up with our magnifications." I spun my seat around and looked at the screen.

Wenig was laughing, hysterical with relief. "Don't you understand? I'm seeing the *drive*, not *Merganser* itself. Look at it, isn't it beautiful?"

He was right. I felt as though I was losing my reason. McAndrew might have gone into orbit about the body, or if he were unlucky he might have run into it — but it made no sense that he'd be sitting here with the drive on. And from the look of the long tail of glowing plasma that stretched across twenty degrees of the screen, that drive was on a high setting.

"Give me a Doppler read-out," I said. "Let's find out what sort of orbit he's in. Damn it, what's he doing there, sight-seeing?"

Now that it looked as though we had found them, I was irrationally angry with McAndrew. He had brought us haring out beyond the limits of the System, and he was sitting there waiting when we arrived. Waiting, and that was all.

Wenig had called up a display and was sitting there staring at it in perplexity. "No motion relative to HC-183," he said. "He's not in an orbit around it, he's got the ship just *hanging* there, with the drive balancing the gravitational attraction. Want me to take us alongside, so we can use a radar signal? That's the only way he'll hear us through the drive interference."

"I guess we'll have to. Take us up close to them." I stared at the screen, random thoughts spinning around my head. "No, wait a minute. Damn it, once we set up the computer to take us in there, it will do automatic drive control. Before we go in, let's find out what we're in for. Can you estimate the strength of HC-183's gravitational attraction at the distance that *Merganser* is at? Got enough data for it?"

"Give me a second." Wenig's fingers flew over the console again. If he ever decided that he didn't want to work at the Penrose Institute, he'd make the best space-racer in the System.

He looked at the output for a second, frowned, and said, "I think I must have made an error."

"Why?"

"I'm coming up with a distance from the surface of about nine thousand kilometers. That means the *Merganser* would be feeling a pull of fifty gee — their drive would be full on, as high as it's designed to go. It wouldn't make sense for them to hang there like that, on full drive. Want to go on down to them?"

"No. Hold it where we are." I leaned back and closed my eyes. "There has to be a pattern to what Mac's been doing. He went right through the System back there with the drive full on, now he's hanging close in to a high-density object with the drive still full on. What the hell's he up to?"

"You won't find out unless we can get in touch with him." Wenig was sounding impatient again. "I say we should go on down there. Now we know where he is it's easiest just to go and ask him."

It was hard to argue with him, but I couldn't get an uneasy feeling out of the back of my head. Mac was holding a constant position, fifty gees of thrust balancing the fifty gee pull of HC-183. We couldn't get alongside him unless we were willing to increase *Dotterel's* drive to fifty gee.

"Give me five more minutes. Remember why I'm here. It's to keep you from doing anything too brave. Look, if we were to hang on our drive with a twenty gee thrust, how close could we get to the *Merganser?*"

"We'd have to make sure we didn't fry them with our drive," said Wenig. He was busy for a couple of minutes at the computer, while I tried again to make sense of the pieces.

"We can get so we're about sixty thousand kilometers from them," said Wenig at last. "If we want to talk to them through the microwave radar link, the best geometry would be one where we're seeing them side-on. We'd have decent clearance from both drives there. Ready to do it?"

"One minute more." I was getting a feeling, a sense that everything that McAndrew had done had been guided by a single logic. "Look, I asked you what would happen if the drive failed when the life capsule was up close to the mass disk, and you said the system would move the capsule back out again. But look at it the other way round now. Suppose the drive works fine — and suppose it was the system that's supposed to move the life capsule up and down the column that wouldn't work? What would that do?"

Wenig stroked at his luxuriant mustache. "I don't think it could happen, the design looked good. If it did happen, everything would depend where the capsule stuck."

"Suppose it stuck up near the disk, when the ship was on a high-thrust drive."

"Well, that would mean there was a big gravitational acceleration. You'd have to cancel it out with the drive, or the passengers would be flattened." He paused. "It would be a bugger. You wouldn't dare to turn the drive *off* — you'd need it on all the time, so that your acceleration compensated for the gravity of the disk."

"Damn right. If you couldn't get yourself farther from the disk, you'd be forced to keep on accelerating. That's what happened to the *Merganser*, I'll bet my ass and hat on it. Get the designs of the capsule movement-train up on the screen and let's see if we can spot anything wrong with it."

"You're an optimist, Captain Roker." He shrugged. "We can do it, but those designs have been looked at twenty times. Look, I see what you're saying, but I find it hard to swallow. What was McAndrew doing when he came back through the System and then out again?"

"The only thing he *could* do. He couldn't switch the drive off, even though he could turn the ship around. He could fly off to God knows where in a straight line — that way we'd never have found him. Or he could fly in bloody great circles, and we'd have been able to see him but never get near to him for more than a couple of minutes at a time — there's no other manned ship that could match that fifty gee thrust. Or he could do what he did do. He flew back through the System to tell us the direction he was heading, out to HC-183. And he balanced here on his drive tail, and sat and waited for us to get smart enough to figure out what he was doing."

I paused for breath, highly pleased with myself. Out of a sphere of trillions of cubic miles, we had tracked the *Merganser* to its destination. Wenig was shaking his head and looking very unhappy.

"What's wrong," I said cockily. "Find the logic hard to follow?"

"Not at all. A rather trivial exercise." He looked down his nose at me. "But you don't seem able to follow your own ideas to a conclusion. McAndrew knows all about *this* ship. He knows it can accelerate at the same rate as *Merganser*. So your idea that he couldn't fly around in big circles and wait for us to match his position can't be right — the *Dotterel* could do that."

He was right.

"So why didn't Mac do that? Why did he come out all this way?"

"I can only think of one answer. He's had the chance to look at the reason the life capsule can't be moved back along the axis, so the drive mustn't be switched off. And he thinks that this ship has the same problem."

I nodded. "See now why I wouldn't let you take the *Dotterel* all the way up to fifty gee?"

"I do. You were right, and I would have taken us into trouble if you hadn't been along. Now then" — Wenig looked gloomier than ever at some new thought — "let's take the logic a step further. McAndrew is hanging down there near HC-183 in a fifty gee gravity field. We can't get there to help him unless we do the same — and we're agreed that we daren't do that, or we'll end up with the same difficulty that he has, and we won't be able to turn off the drive."

I looked out of the port, towards the dark bulk of

HC-183 and the *Merganser*, hovering on its plume of high-temperature plasma. Wenig was right. We daren't go down there.

"So how are we going to get them out?"

Wenig shrugged. "I wish I could tell you. Maybe McAndrew has an answer. If not, they're as inaccessible as if they were halfway to Alpha Centauri and still accelerating. We've got to get into communication with them."

When I was about eleven years old, just before puberty, I had a disturbing series of dreams. Night after night, for maybe three months, I seemed to wake on the steep face of a cliff. It was dark, and I could barely see handholds and toeholds in the rock.

I had to get to the top — something was hidden below, invisible behind the curve of the black cliff face. I didn't know what it was, but I knew it was awful.

Every night I would climb, as carefully as I could; and every night there would come a time when I missed a handhold, and began to slide downwards, down into the pit and the waiting monster.

I woke just as I reached the bottom, just as I was waiting for the first sight of my pit beast.

I never saw it. Puberty arrived, sex dreams replaced my fantasy. I forgot all about the cliff face, the terror, the feeling of force that could not be resisted. Forgot it totally — except that dream memories never disappear completely, they lie at some deep submerged level of the mind, until something pulls them out again.

And here I was again, back on the same cliff face, sliding steadily to my fate, powerless to prevent it. I woke up with my heart rate higher by thirty beats a minute, with cold perspiration on my forehead and neck. It took me a long time to return to the present, to banish the bygone fall into the pit.

I finally forced myself up to full consciousness and looked at the screen above me. The purple blaze of a plasma drive danced against the black backdrop of HC-183 and its surrounding star field. It hung there, falling forever but suspended on the feathery stalk of the drive exhaust. I lay there for about ten minutes, just watching, then looked across at Wenig. He was staring at me, his eyes unblinking.

"Awake at last." He made a sort of coughing noise, something that I think was intended to be a laugh. "You're a cool one, Captain Roker. I couldn't sleep with that hanging there" — he jerked his thumb at the screen — "even if you doped me up with everything in the robodoc."

"How long did I sleep?"

"About three hours. Ready to give up now?"

I was. It had been my idea, an insistence that we ought to try and get some sleep before we did the next phase of our maneuver around HC-183. Wenig had opposed it, had wanted to go on at once, but I thought we'd benefit from the rest. So I was wrong.

"I'm ready." My eyes felt as though they'd been filled with grit and my throat was dry and sore, but talking about that to Wenig wouldn't do much for McAndrew or Nina Velez. "Let's get into position and try the radar."

While Wenig juggled us over to the best position, sixty thousand kilometers from HC-183 and about the same distance from the *Merganser*, I wondered again about my companion. They had drawn lots to come with me, and he had won. The other four scientists back at the Institute seemed a little naive and unworldly, but not Wenig. He was tough and shrewd, and I had seen the speed of those hands, dancing over the keyboard. Had he done a bit of juggling when they drew lots, a touch of hand-faster-than-the-eye? I thought of his look when he spoke about Nina. If McAndrew was infatuated, perhaps Wenig shared the spell. Something strong was driving him along, some force that could keep him awake and alert for days on end. I wouldn't know if I was right or not unless we could find a way to haul *Merganser* back out of the field. The ship still hovered over its pendant of blue ionized gases, motionless as ever.

"How about this?" Wenig interrupted my thoughts. "I don't think I can get the geometry any better than it is now."

We were hanging there too, farther out from the proto-planet than *Merganser* but close enough to see the black disk occulting the star field. We could beam short bursts of microwaves at our sister ship and hope there was enough signal strength to bore through the sheaths of plasma emitted by the drives. It would be touch and go — I had never tried to send a signal to an unmanned ship on high-drive, but our signal-to-noise ratio stood right on the borderline of system acceptance. As it was, we'd have to settle for voice-links only.

I nodded, and Wenig sent out our first pulses, the simple ship I.D. codes. We sent it for a couple of minutes, then waited with our attention fixed on the screen.

After a while Wenig shook his head. "We're not getting through. It wouldn't take that long to respond to our signal."

"Send it with reduced information rate and more redundancy. We have to give McAndrew enough to filter out the noise."

He was still in send mode when the display screen began to crawl with green patterns of light. Something was coming in. The computer was performing a frequency analysis to pick out the signal content from the background, smoothing it, and speeding it up to standard communication rate. We were looking at the Fourier analysis that preceded signal presentation.

"Voice mode," said Wenig quietly.

"*Merganser.*" The computer reconstruction of McAndrew's voice was slow and hollow. "This is McAndrew from the *Merganser.* We're certainly glad to hear from you, *Dotterel.* Well, Jeanie, what kept you?"

"Roker speaking." I leaned forward and spoke into the vocal input system — too fast, but the computer would take care of that at the other end. "Mac, we're hanging about sixty kay out from you. Is everything all right in *Merganser?*"

"Yes."

"No," broke in another voice. "Get us out of here. We've been stuck in this damned metal box for sixteen days now."

"Nina," said Wenig. "We'd love to get you out — but we don't know how. Didn't Dr. McAndrew tell you the problem?"

"He said we couldn't leave here until the other ship you're on came for us."

Wenig grimaced at me and turned away from the input link. "I ought to have realized that. McAndrew hasn't told her the problem with the drives — not all of it."

"Maybe he knows an answer." I faced back to the microphone. "Mac, as we see it we shouldn't put the *Dotterel* up as high as fifty gee thrust. Correct?"

"Of course." McAndrew sounded faintly surprised at my question. "Why do you think I went to such lengths to get to this holding position out here? When you go to maximum setting for the drive, the electromechanical coupling for moving the life capsule gets distorted, too."

"How did we miss it on the design?" Wenig sounded unconvinced.

"Remember the last-minute increase in stabilizing fields for the mass plate?"

"It was my recommendation — I'm not likely to forget it."

"We re-calculated the effects on the drive and on the exhaust region, but not the magnetostrictive effects on the life-support column. We thought they were second-order changes."

"And they're not? I ought to be drawn and quartered — that was my job!" Wenig was sitting there, fists clenched and face red.

"Was it now? Och, your job, eh? And I've been sitting here thinking all this time it was my job." For someone in a hopeless position thirty billion miles from home, McAndrew sounded amazingly cool. "Come on now, we can sort out whose doing it was when we're all back at the Institute."

Wenig looked startled, then turned to me again. "Go along with him on this — I'm sure he's doing it for Nina's sake. He doesn't want her worried."

I nodded — but this time I was unconvinced. Mac must have something hidden away inside his head, or not even Nina Velez would justify his optimistic tone.

"What should we do, Mac?" I said. "We'd get the same effects if we were to accelerate too hard. We can't get down to you, and you can't get up to us without accelerating out past us. How are we going to get you out of there?"

"Right." The laugh that came over the com link sounded forced and hollow, but that may have been just the tone that the computer filters gave it. "You might guess that's been on my mind too. The problem's in the mechanical coupling that moves the life capsule along the column. It's easy enough to see, once you imagine that you've had a two millimeter decrease in column diameter — that's the effects of the added field on the mass plate."

Wenig was already calling the schematics out onto a second display. "I'll check that. Keep talking."

"You'll see that when the drive's up to maximum, the capsule catches on the side of the column. It's a simple ratchet effect. I've tried varying the drive thrust up and down a couple of gee, but that won't free it."

"I see where you mean." Wenig had a light-pen out and was circling parts of the column for larger scale displays. "I don't see how we can do anything about it. It would take a lateral impact to free it — you'll not do it by varying your drive."

"Agreed. We need some lateral force on us. That's what I'm hoping you'll provide."

"What is all this?" It was Nina's voice again, and she sounded angry. "Why do you just keep on talking like that? Anybody who know what he was doing would have us out by now — would never have got us into it in tho first place if he had any sense."

I raised an eyebrow at Wenig. "The voice of infatuation? I think the bloom's off the rose down there."

He looked startled, then pleased, then excited — and then tried to look nonchalant. "I don't know what McAndrew is getting at. How could we provide any help from here?" He turned to the input system. "Dr. McAndrew, how's that possible? We can't provide a lateral force on *Merganser* from here, and we can't come down safely."

"Of course you can." McAndrew's voice sounded pleased, and I was sure he was enjoying making the rest of us try and work out his idea. "It's very easy for you to come down here."

"How, Mac?"

"In a free-fall trajectory. We're in a fifty gee gravity field because we're in a stationary position relative to HC-183. But if you were to let yourself fall in a free orbit, you'd be able to swing in right past us, and away again, and never feel anything but free fall. Agreed?"

"Right. We'd feel tidal effects, but they'd be small." Wenig was calling out displays as he talked, fingers a blur over the computer console. "We can fly right past you, but we'd be there and away in a split second. What could we do in so short a time?"

"Why, what we need." McAndrew sounded surprised by the question. "Give us a good bang on the side as you go by."

It sounded easy, as McAndrew so glibly and casually suggested it. When we went into details, there were three problem areas. If we went too close, we'd be fried in the *Merganser's* drive. Too far off, and we'd never get a strong enough interaction. If all that was worked out correctly, we still had one big obstacle. For the capsule to be freed as *Dotterel* applied sideways pressure, the drive on the other ship would have to cut off completely. Only for a split second, but during that time McAndrew and Nina would feel a full fifty gee on them.

That's not quite as bad as it sounds — people have survived instantaneous accelerations of more than a hundred gee in short pulses. But it's not a picnic, either. Mac continued to sound cheerful and casual, mainly for Nina Velez's benefit. But when he listed the preparations that he was taking inside *Merganser*, I knew he was dealing with a touch-and-go situation.

After all the calculations (performed independently on the two ships, cross-checked and double-checked) we had started our free-fall orbit. It was designed to take us skimming past the *Merganser*, with a closest separation of less than two hundred meters. We daren't go nearer without risking crippling effects from their drive. We would be flying right through its region of turbulence.

Four hours of discussion between McAndrew and Wenig — with interruptions from Nina and me — had fixed the sequence for the vital half-second when we would be passing the Merganser. The ships would exert gravitational forces on each other, but that was useless for providing the lateral thrust on the life capsule system that McAndrew thought was needed. We had to give a more direct and harder push some other way.

Timing was crucial, and very tricky. Whatever we threw at the other ship would have to pass through the drive exhaust region before it could impact the life capsule column. If the drive were on, nothing could get through — at those temperatures it would be vaporized on the way, even if it were there for only a fraction of a second. The sequence had to be: launch mass from Dotterel; just before it got there, kill drive on Merganser; hold drive off just long enough for Dotterel to clear the area and for the mass to impact the Merganser support column; and back on with their drive, at once, because when the drive was off Merganser's passengers would be feeling the full fifty gees of the mass plate's gravity.

McAndrew and Wenig cut the time of approach of the two ships into millisecond pieces. They decided exactly how long each phase should last. Then they let the two on-board computers of the ships talk to each other, to make sure that everything was synchronized between them — at the rate things would be happening, there was no way that humans could control them. Not even Wenig, with his super-fast reflexes. We'd all be spectators, while the two computers did the real work and I nursed the abort switch.

There was one argument. McAndrew wanted to use a storage tank as the missile that we would eject from our ship to impact theirs. It would provide high

momentum transfer for a very brief period. Wenig
argued that we should trade off time against intensity,
and use a liquid mass instead of a solid one. Endless
discussion and calculations, until Mac was convinced
too. We would use all our spare water supply, about
a ton and a half of it. That left enough for drinking
water on a twenty gee return to the Inner System, but
nothing spare for other uses. It would be a scratchy
and smelly trip home for *Dotterel's* passengers.

Drive off, we felt only the one-gee pull of our mass
plate as we dropped in to close approach. On *Merganser*, McAndrew and Nina Velez were lying in water
bunks, cushioned with everything soft on the ship. We
were on an impact course with them, one that would
change to a near-miss after we ejected the water
ballast. It looked like a suicide mission, running straight
into the blue furnace of their drive.

The sequence took place so fast it was anti-climactic.
I saw the drive cut off ahead of us, and felt the vibration along the support column as our mass driver threw
the ballast hard towards *Merganser*. The brief pulse
from our drive that took us clear of them was too quick
for me to feel.

We cleared the drive region. Then there seemed to
be a wait that lasted for hours. McAndrew and Nina
were now in a ship with drive off, dropping towards
HC-183. They were exposed to the full fifty gees of their
mass plate. Under that force, I knew what happened
to the human body. It had not been designed to operate
when it suddenly weighed more than four tons. Mem-
branes ruptured, valves burst, veins collapsed. The
heart had never evolved to pump blood that weighed
hundreds of pounds, up a gravity hill of fifty gee. The
only thing that Mac and Nina had going for them was
the natural inertia of matter. If the period of high gee
were short enough, the huge accelerations would not

have time to produce those shattering physical effects.

Wenig and I watched on our screens for a long, long moment, until the computer on *Merganser* counted off the last microsecond and switched on the drive again. If the life capsule was free to move along its column, the computer would now begin the slow climb out of HC-183's gravity well. No action was needed from the passengers. When we completed our own orbit we hoped we would see the other ship out at a safe distance, ready for the long trip home.

And on board the ship? I wasn't sure. If the encounter had lasted too long, we might find no more than two limp and broken sacks of blood, tissue and bone.

It was another long day, waiting until we had carried around in our orbit and could try and rendezvous the two ships. As soon as we were within radar range again, Nina Velez appeared on the com screen. The drive was cut back, so we could get good visual signals. My heart sank when I saw the expression on her face.

"Can you get over to this ship — quickly?" she said.

I could see why all the professors at the Institute had lost their senses. She was small and slight, with a childlike look of trust and sad blue eyes. All a sham, according to everything I'd been told, but there was no way of seeing the strong personality behind the soft looks. I took a deep breath.

"What's happening there?" I said.

"We're back under low gee drive, and that's fine. But I haven't been able to wake him. He's breathing, but there's blood on his lips. He needs a doctor."

"I'm the nearest thing to that in thirty billion miles." I was pulling a suit towards me, sick with a sudden fear. "I've had some medical training as part of the Master's License. And I think I know what's wrong with McAndrew. He lost part of a lung lobe a couple of years ago. If anything's likely to be hemorrhaging, that's it. Dr. Wenig, can you arrange a rendezvous with the mass plates at maximum separation and the drives off?"

"I'll need control of their computer." He was pulling his suit on, too. I didn't want him along, but I might need somebody to return to the *Dotterel* for medical supplies.

"What should I be doing?" Thank Heaven Nina showed no signs of panic. She sounded impatient, with the touch of President Velez in her voice. "I've sat around in this ship for weeks with nothing to do. Now we need action but I daren't take it."

"What field are you in now? What net field?"

"One gee. The drive's off now, and we've got the life capsule right out at the end of the column."

"Right. I want you to stay in that position, but set the drive at one gee acceleration. I want McAndrew in a zero-gee environment to slow the bleeding. Dr. Wenig, can you dictate instructions for that while we are rendezvousing?"

"No problem." He was an irritating devil, but I'd choose him in a crisis. He was doing three things at once, putting on his suit, watching the computer action for the rendezvous, and giving exact and concise instructions to Nina.

Getting from one ship to the other wasn't as easy as it might sound. We had both ships under one gee acceleration drives, complicated by the combined attraction of the two mass plates. The total field acting on us was small, but we had to be careful not to forget it. If we lost contact with the ships, the nearest landing point was back on Triton Station, thirty billion miles away.

Nina in the flesh was even more impressive than she was over the video link, but I gave her little more than a cursory once-over. McAndrew's color was bad and even while I was cracking my suit open and hustling out of it I could hear a frightening bubbling sound in his breathing. Thank God I had learned how to work in zero gee — required part of any space medicine course. I leaned over him, vaguely aware of the two others intently watching. The robodoc beside me was clucking and flashing busily, muttering a faint complaint at McAndrew's condition and the zero gee working environment. Standard diagnosis conditions called for at least a partial gravity field.

I took the preliminary diagnosis and prepared to act on it even while the doc was still making up its mind. Five cc's of cerebral stimulant, five cc's of metabolic depressant, and a reduction in cabin pressure. It should bring Mac up to consciousness if his brain was still in working order. I worried about a cerebral hemorrhage, the quiet and deadly by-product of super-high gees. Ten minutes and I would know one way or the other.

I turned to Wenig and Nina who were still watching the robodoc's silent body trace. "I don't know how he is yet. We may need emergency treatment facilities ready for us as soon as we get back to the System. Can you go over to *Dotterel*, cut the drive and try to make contact with Triton Station? By the time you have the connection we should have the diagnosis here."

I watched them leave the ship, saw how carefully Wenig helped Nina in the transfer, and then I heard the first faint noise behind me. It was a sigh, with a little mutter of protest behind it. The most wonderful sound I ever heard in my life. I glanced over at the doc. Concussion — not too bad — and a little more bleeding than I wanted to see from the left lung. Hell, that was nothing. I could patch the lung myself, maybe even start the feedback regeneration for it. I felt a big grin of delight spreading like a heat wave over my face.

"Take it easy, Mac. You're doing all right, just don't

try and rush yourself. We've got lots of time." I secured his left arm so that he couldn't disturb the rib cage on that side. He groaned.

"Doing fine, am I?" He suddenly opened his eyes and stared up at me. "Holy water, Jeanie, that's just like a medic. I'm in agony, and you say it's a little discomfort. How's Nina doing?"

"Not a mark on her. She's not like you, Mac, an old bag of bones. You're getting too old for that sort of crap."

"Where is she?"

"Over on *Dotterel*, with Wenig. What's the matter, still infatuated?"

He managed a faint smile. "Ah, none of that now. We were locked up on *Merganser* for more than two weeks, in a three meter living sphere. Show me an infatuation, and I'll show you a cure for it."

The com link behind me was buzzing. I cut it in, so that we could see Wenig's worried face.

"All right here," I said, before he had time to worry any more. "We'll be able to take our time going back. How are you? Got enough water?"

He nodded. "I took some of your reserve supply to make up for what we threw at you. What should we do now?"

"Head on back. Tell Nina that Mac's all right, and say we'll see you both back at the Institute."

He nodded again, then leaned closer to the screen and spoke with a curious intensity. "We don't want to run the risk of having a stuck life capsule again. I'd better keep us down to less than ten gee acceleration."

And he cut off communication, without another word. I turned to McAndrew.

"How high an acceleration before you'd run into trouble with these ships?"

He was staring at the blank screen, a confused look

on his thin face. "At least forty gee. What the devil's got into Wenig? And what are you laughing at, you silly bitch?"

I came over to him and took his right hand in mine. "To each his own, Mac. I wondered why Wenig was so keen to get here. He wants his shot at Nina — out here, where nobody else can compete. What did you tell her — some sweet talk about her lovely eyes?"

He closed his eyes again and smiled a secret smile. "Ah, come on, Jeanie. Are you telling me you've been on your best behavior since I last saw you? Gi' me a bit of peace. I'm not soft on Nina now."

"I'll see." I went across to the drive and moved us up to forty gee. "Wait until the crew on Titan hears about all this. You'll lose your reputation."

He sighed. "All right. I'll play the game. What's the price of silence?"

"How long would it take a ship like this to get out to Alpha Centauri?"

"You'd not want this one. We'll have the next one up to a hundred gee. Forty-four ship days would get you there, standing start to standing finish."

I nodded, came back to his side and held his hand again. "All right, Mac, that's my price. I want one of the tickets."

He groaned again, just a bit. But I knew from the dose the doc had put into him that it wasn't a headache this time.

THIRD CHRONICLE:
ALL THE COLORS OF THE VACUUM

As soon as the ship got back from the mid-year run to Titan I went down to Earth and asked Woolford for a leave of absence. I had been working hard enough for six people, and he knew it. He nodded agreeably as soon as I made the formal request.

"I think you've earned it, Captain Roker, no doubt about that. But don't you have quite a bit of leave time saved up? Wouldn't that be enough?" He stopped staring out of the window at the orange-brown sky and called my records onto the screen in front of him.

"That won't do it," I said, while he was still looking.

Woolford frowned and became less formal. "It won't? Well, according to this, Jeanie, you've got at least..." He looked up. "Just how long *do* you want to take off?"

"I'm not exactly sure. Somewhere between nine and sixteen years, I think."

I would have liked to break the news more gently, but maybe there was no graceful way.

It had taken McAndrew a while to deliver on his promise. The design of the more advanced ship contained no new theory, but this time he intended that the initial tests would be conducted more systematically. I kept pushing him along, while he tried to wriggle out of the commitment. He had been full of drugs and painkillers at the time, he said — surely I didn't consider it fair, to hold him to what he'd been silly enough to promise then?

Fair or not, I wouldn't listen to him. I had called him as soon as we were on the final leg of the Titan run.

"Yes, she's ready enough to go." He had a strange expression on his face, somewhere between excitement and perplexity. "You've still got your mind set on going, then, Jeanie?"

I didn't even reply to that.

"How soon can I come out to the Institute?"

He cleared his throat, making that odd sound that spoke to me of his Scots ancestry. "Och, if you're set on it, come as soon as you please. I'll have things to tell you when you get here, but that can wait."

That was when I went down and made my request to Woolford for a long leave of absence. McAndrew had been strangely reluctant to discuss our destination, but I couldn't imagine that we'd be going out past Sirius. Alpha Centauri was my guess, and that would mean we would only be away about nine Earth years. Shipboard time would be three months, allowing a few days at the other end for exploration. If I knew McAndrew, he would have beaten the hundred gee acceleration that he projected for the interstellar prototype. He was never a man to talk big about what he was going to do.

The Penrose Institute had been moved out to Mars' orbit since the last time I was there, so it took me a couple of weeks of impatient ship-hopping to get to it. When we finally closed to visible range I could see the old test ships, *Merganser* and *Dotterel*, floating a few kilometers from the main body of the Institute. They were easy to recognize from the flat mass disk with its protruding central spike. And floating near them, quite a bit bigger, was a new ship of gleaming silver. That had to be the *Hoatzin*, McAndrew's newest plaything. The disk was twice the size, and the spike three times as long, but *Hoatzin* was clearly *Merganser's* big brother.

It was Professor Limperis, the head of the Institute, who greeted me when I entered. He had put on weight since I last saw him, but that pudgy black face still hid a razor-sharp mind and a bottomless memory.

"Good to see you again, Captain Roker. I haven't told McAndrew this, but I'm very glad you'll be going along to keep an eye on him." He gave what he once described as his "hand-clapping nigger laugh" — a sure sign he was nervous about something.

"Well, I don't know that I'll be much use. I'm expecting to be just a sort of passenger. Don't worry. If my instincts are anything to go by there won't be much danger in a simple stellar rendezvous and return."

"Er, yes." He wouldn't meet my eye. "That was my own reaction. I gather that Professor McAndrew has not mentioned to you his change of target?"

"Change of target? He didn't mention any target at all." Now my own worry bead was beginning to throb. "Are you suggesting that the trip will *not* be to a stellar rendezvous?"

He shrugged and waved his hands along the corridor. "Not if McAndrew gets his way. Come along, he's inside at the computer. I think it's best if he is present when we talk about this further."

Pure evasion. Whatever the bad news was, Limperis wanted me to hear it from McAndrew himself.

We found him staring vacantly at a completely blank display screen. Normally I would never interrupt him when he looks as imbecilic as that — it means that he is thinking with a breadth and depth that I'll never comprehend. I often wonder what it would be like to have a mind like that. Humans, with rare exceptions, must seem like trained apes, with muddied thoughts and no ability for abstract analysis.

Tough luck. It was time one of the trained apes had some of her worries put to rest. I walked up behind McAndrew and put my hands on his shoulders.

"Here I am. I'm ready to go — if you'll tell me where we're going."

He turned in his chair. After a moment his slack jaw firmed up and the eyes brought me into focus.

"Hello, Captain." No doubt about it, as soon as he recognized me he had that same shifty look I had noticed in Limperis. "I didn't expect you here so soon. We're still making up a flight profile."

"That's all right. I'll help you." I sat down opposite him, studying his face closely. As usual he looked tired, but that was normal. Geniuses work *harder* than anyone else, not less hard. His face was thinner, and he had lost a little more hair from that sandy, receding mop. My argument with him over that was long in the past.

"Why don't you grow it back? It's such a minor job, a couple of hours with the machines every few months and you'd have a full head of hair again."

He had sniffed. "Why don't you try and get me to grow a tail, or hair all over my body? Or maybe make my arms a bit longer, so they'll let me run along with them touching the ground? Jeanie, I'll not abuse a biofeedback machine to run evolution in the wrong direction. We're getting less hairy all the time. I know your fondness for monkeys" — a nasty crack about an engineering friend of mine on Ceres, who was a bit hairy for even my accommodating tastes — "but I'll be just as happy when I have no hair at all. It gets in the way, it grows all the time, and it serves no purpose whatsoever."

McAndrew resented the time it took him to clip his fingernails, and I'm sure that he regarded his fondness for food as a shameful weakness. Meanwhile, I wondered who in the Penrose Institute cut his hair. Maybe they had a staff assistant, whose job it was to shear the absent-minded once a month.

"What destination are you planning for the first trip out?" If he was thinking of chasing a comet, I wanted that out in the open.

McAndrew looked at Limperis. Limperis looked at McAndrew, handing it back to him. Mac cleared his throat.

"We've discussed it here and we're all agreed. The first trip of the *Hoatzin* won't be to a star system." He cleared his throat again. "It will be to pursue and rendezvous with the Ark of Massingham. It's a shorter trip than any of the star systems," he added hopefully. He could read my expression. "They are less than two light years out. With the *Hoatzin* we can be there and docked with the Ark in less than thirty-five ship days."

If he was trying to make me feel better, McAndrew was going about it in quite the wrong way.

Back in the twenties, the resources of the Solar System must have seemed inexhaustible. No one had been able to *catalog* the planetoids, still less analyze their composition and probable value. Now we know everything out to Neptune that's bigger than a hundred meters across, and the navigation groups want that down to fifty meters in the next twenty years. The idea of grabbing an asteroid a couple of kilometers across and using it how you choose sounds like major theft. But it hadn't merely been permitted — it had been encouraged.

The first space colonies had been conceived as utopias, planned by earth idealists who wouldn't learn from history. New frontiers may attract visionaries, but more than that, they attract oddities. Anyone who is more than three sigma away from the norm, in any direction, seems to finish out there on the frontier. No surprise in that. If a person can't fit, for whatever reason, he'll move away from the main group of humanity. They'll push him, and he'll want to go. How do I know? Look, you don't pilot to Titan without learning a lot about your own personality. Before we found the right way to use people like me, I would probably have been on one of the Arks.

The United Space Federation had assisted in the launch of seventeen of them, between ninety and forty years ago. Each of them was self-supporting, a converted asteroid that would hold between three and ten thousand people at departure time. The idea was that there would be enough raw materials and space to let the Ark grow as the population grew. A two-kilometer asteroid holds five to twenty billion tons of matter, and a total life-support system for one human needs less than ten tons of that.

The Arks had left long before the discovery of the McAndrew balanced drive, before the discovery of even the Mattin Drive. They were multi-generation ships, bumbling along into the interstellar void with speeds that were only a few percent of light speed.

And who was on board them when they left? Any fairly homogeneous group of strange people, who shared enough of a common philosophy or delusion to prefer the uncertainties of star travel to the known problems within the Solar System. It took courage to set out like that, to sever all your ties with home except occasional laser and radio communication. Courage, or an overpowering conviction that you were part of a unique and chosen group.

To put that another way, McAndrew was proposing to take us out to meet a community about which we knew little, except that by the usual standards they were descended from madmen.

"Mac, I don't remember which one was the Ark of Massingham. How long ago did it leave?"

Even mad people can have sane children. Four of the Arks, as I recalled, had turned around and were on their way back to the System.

"Seventy-five years ago. It's one of the earlier ones, with a final speed a bit less than three percent of light speed."

"Is it one of the Arks that has turned back?"

He shook his head. "No. They're still on their way. Target star is Tau Ceti. They won't get there for another three hundred years."

"Well, why pick them out? What's so special about the Ark of Massingham?" I had a sudden thought. "Are they having some problem that we could help with?"

We had saved two of the Arks in the past twenty years. For one of them we had been able to diagnose a recessive genetic element that was appearing in the children, and pass the test information and sperm filter technique over the communications link. The other had needed the use of an unmanned high-acceleration probe, to carry a couple of tons of cadmium out to them. They had been unlucky enough to choose a freak asteroid, one that apparently lacked the element even in the tiniest traces.

"They don't report any problem. We've never had a response to any messages we've sent to them, so far as the records on Triton Station are concerned. But we know that they are doing all right, because about every three or four years a message has come in from them. Never anything about the Ark itself, it has always been scientific information."

McAndrew had hesitated as he said that last phrase. That was the lure, no doubt about it.

"What kind of information?" I said. "Surely we know everything that they know. We have hundreds of thousands of scientists in the System, they can't have more than a few hundred of them."

"I'm sure you're right on the numbers." Professor Limperis spoke when McAndrew showed no inclination to do so. "I'm not sure it's relevant. How many scientists does it require to produce the work of one Einstein, or one McAndrew? You can't just sit down and count numbers, as though you were dealing with — with bars of soap, or with poker chips. You have to deal with individuals."

"There's a genius on the Ark of Massingham," said McAndrew suddenly. His eyes were gleaming. "A man or woman who has been cut off from most of physics for a whole lifetime, working alone. It's worse than Ramanujan."

"How do you know that?" I had seldom seen McAndrew so filled with feeling. "Maybe they've been getting messages from somebody in the System here."

McAndrew laughed, a humorless bark. "I'll tell you why, Jeanie Roker. You flew on Merganser. Tell me how the drive worked."

"Well, the mass plate at the front balanced the acceleration, so we didn't get any sensation of fifty gee." I shrugged. "I didn't work out the maths for myself, but I'm sure I could have if I felt like it."

I could have, too. I was a bit rusty, but you never lose the basics once you have them planted deep enough in your head.

"I don't mean the balancing mechanism, that was just common sense." He shook his head. "I mean the drive. Didn't it occur to you that we were accelerating a mass of trillions of tons at fifty gee? If you work out the mass conversion rate that you will need with an ideal photon drive, you'll consume the whole mass in a few days. The *Merganser* got its drive by accelerating charged particles up to within millimeters a second of light speed, that was the reaction mass. But how did it get the energy to do it?"

I felt like telling him that when I had been on *Merganser* there had been other details — such as survival — on my mind. I thought for a few moments, then shook my head.

"You can't get more energy out of matter than the rest mass energy, I know that. But you're telling me that the drives on *Merganser* and *Hoatzin* do it. That Einstein was wrong."

"No, I'm not." McAndrew looked horrified at the thought that he might have been criticizing one of his senior idols. "All I've done is build on what Einstein did. Look, you've done a fair amount of quantum mechanics. You know that when you calculate the energy for the vacuum state of a system you don't get zero. You get a positive value."

I had a hazy recollection of a formula swimming back across the years. What was it? $\frac{1}{2}hw$, said a distant voice.

"But you can set that to zero!" I was proud at remembering so much. "The zero point of energy is arbitrary."

"In quantum theory it is. But not in general relativity." McAndrew was beating back my mental

defenses. As usual when I spoke with him on theoretical
subjects, I began to feel I would know less at the end
of the conversation than I did at the beginning.

"In general relativity," he went on, "energy implies
space-time curvature. If the zero point energy is not
zero, the vacuum self-energy is real. It can be tapped,
if you know what you are doing. That's where *Hoatzin*
draws its energy. The reaction mass it needs is very
small. You can get that by scooping up matter as you
go along, or if you prefer it you can use a fraction —
a very small fraction — of the mass plate."

"All right." I knew McAndrew. If I let him get going
he would talk all day about physical principles. "But
I don't see how that has anything to do with the Ark
of Massingham. It has an old-fashioned drive, surely.
You said it was launched seventy-five years ago."

"It was." This was Limperis again, gently insistent.
"But you see, Captain Roker, nobody outside the Penrose Institute knows how Professor McAndrew has
been able to tap the vacuum self-energy. We have been
very careful not to broadcast that information until we
were ready. The potential for destructive use is enormous. It destroys the old idea that you cannot create
more energy at a point than the rest mass of the matter
residing there. There was nothing known in the rest
of the System about this use until two weeks ago."

"And then you released the information?" I was
beginning to feel dizzy.

"No. The basic equations for accessing the vacuum
self-energy were received by laser communication.
They were sent, with no other message, *from the Ark
of Massingham.*"

Suddenly it made sense. It wasn't just McAndrew
who was itching to get in and find out what there was
on the Ark — it was everyone at the Penrose Institute.
I could sense the excitement in Limperis, and he was

the most guarded and politically astute of all the members. If some physicist, working out there alone two light-years from Sol, had managed to parallel McAndrew's development, that was a momentous event. It implied a level of genius that was difficult to imagine.

I knew *Hoatzin* would be on the way in a few days, whether I wanted to go or stay. But there was one more key question.

"I can't believe that the Ark of Massingham was started by a bunch of physicists. What was the original composition of the group that colonized it?"

"Not physicists." Limperis had suddenly sobered. "By no means physicists. That is why I am glad you will be accompanying Professor McAndrew. The leader of the original group was Jules Massingham. In the past few days I have taken the time to obtain all the System records on him. He was a man of great personal drive and convictions. His ambition was to apply the old principles of eugenics to a whole society. Two themes run through all his writings: the creation of the superior human, and the idea of that superior being as an integrated part of a whole society. He was ruthless in his pursuit of those ends."

He looked at me, black face impassive. "From the evidence available, Captain, one might suggest that he succeeded in his aims."

Hoatzin was a step up from *Merganser* and *Dotterel*. Maximum acceleration was a hundred and ten gee, and the living capsule was a four-meter sphere. I had cursed the staff of the Institute, publicly and privately, but I had got nowhere. They were obsessed with the idea of the lonely genius out there in the void, and no one would consider any other first trip for *Hoatzin*. So at least I would check out every aspect of the system before we went, while McAndrew was looking at the rendezvous problem and making a final flight plan. We sent a message to the Ark, telling them of our trip and estimated arrival time. It would take two years to get there, Earth-time, but we would take even longer. They would be able to prepare for our arrival however they chose, with garlands or gallows.

On the trip out, McAndrew tried again to explain to me his methods for tapping the vacuum self-energy. The available energies made up a quasi-continuous "spectrum", corresponding to a large number of very high frequencies of vibration and associated wavelengths. Tuned resonators in the *Hoatzin* drive units selected certain wavelengths which were excited by the corresponding components in the vacuum self energy. These "colors", as McAndrew thought of them, could feed vacuum energy to the drive system. The results that had come from the Ark of Massingham suggested that McAndrew's system for energy extraction could be generalized, so that all the "colors" of the vacuum self-energy should become available. If that were true, the potential acceleration produced by the drive could go up by a couple of orders of magnitude. He was still working out what the consequences of that would be. At speeds that approached within a nanometer per second of light speed, a single proton would mass enough to weigh its impact on a sensitive balance.

I let him babble on to his heart's content. My own attention was mostly on the history of the Ark of Massingham. It was an oddity among oddities. Six of the Arks had disappeared without trace. They didn't respond to signals from Earth, and they didn't send signals of their own. Most people assumed that they had wiped themselves out, with accidents, wars, strange sexual practices, or all three. Four of the Arks had swung back towards normalcy and were heading in again for the System. Six were still heading out, but two of them were in deep trouble if the messages that came back to Triton Station were any guide. One was full of messianic ranting, a crusade of human folly propagating itself out to the stars (let's hope they never met anyone out there whose good opinion we would later desire). The other was quietly and peacefully insane, sending messages that spoke only of new rules for the interpretation of dreams. They were convinced that they would find the world of the Norse legends when they finally arrived at Eta Cassiopeia, complete with Jotunheim, Niflheim, and all the assembly of gods and heroes. It would be six hundred years before they arrived there, time enough for moves to rationality or to extinction.

Among this set, the Ark of Massingham provided a bright mixture of sanity and strangeness. They had sent messages back since first they left, messages that assumed the Ark was the carrier of human hopes and a superior civilization. Nothing that we sent — questions, comments, information, or acknowledgments — ever stimulated a reply. And nothing that *they* sent ever discussed life aboard the Ark. We had no idea if they lived in poverty or plenty, if they were increasing or decreasing in numbers, if they were receiving our transmissions, if they had material problems of any kind. Everything that came back to the System was science, delivered in a smug and self-satisfied tone. From all that science, the recent transmission on physics was the only one to excite more than a mild curiosity from System scientists. Usually the Ark sent "discoveries" that had been made here long ago.

Once the drive of the *Hoatzin* was up to full thrust there was no way that we could see anything or communicate with anyone. The drive was fixed to the mass plate on the front of the ship, and the particles that streamed past us and out to the rear were visible only when they were in collision with the rare atoms of hydrogen drifting in free space. We had actually settled for less than a maximum drive and were using a slightly dispersed exhaust. A tightly focussed and collimated beam wouldn't harm us any, but we didn't want to generate a death ray behind us that would disintegrate anything in its path for a few light years.

Six days into the trip, our journey out shared the most common feature of all long distance travel. It was boring. When McAndrew wasn't busy inside his head, staring at the wall in front of him and performing the mental acrobatics that he called theoretical physics, we talked, played and exercised. I was astonished again that a man who knew so much about so much could know nothing about some things.

"You mean to tell me," he said once, as we lay in companionable darkness, with the side port showing the eldritch and unpredictable blue sparks of atomic collision. "You mean that *Lungfish* wasn't the first space station? All the books and records show it that way."

"No, they don't. If they do, they're wrong. It's a common mistake. Like the idea back at the beginning of flight itself, that Lindbergh was the first man to fly across the Atlantic Ocean. He was more like the hundredth." I felt McAndrew turn his head towards me. "Yes, you heard me. A couple of airships had been over before him, and a couple of other people in aircraft. He was just the first person to fly *alone*. *Lungfish* was the first *permanent* space station, that's all. And I'll tell you something else. Did you know that in the early flights, even ones that lasted for months, the crews were usually all men? Think of that for a while."

He was silent for a moment. "I don't see anything wrong with it. It would simplify some of the plumbing, maybe some other things, too."

"You don't understand, Mac. That was at a time when it was regarded as morally wrong for men to form relationships with men, or women with women."

There was what I might describe as a startled silence.

"Oh," said McAndrew at last. Then, after a few moments more, "My God. How much did they have to pay them? Or was coercion used?"

"It was considered an honor to be chosen."

He didn't say any more about it; but I don't think he believed me, either. Politeness is one of the first things you learn on long trips.

We cut off the drive briefly at crossover, but there was nothing to be seen and there was still no way we could receive messages. Our speed was crowding light speed so closely that anything from Triton Station would scarcely be catching up with us. The Institute's message was still on its way to the Ark of Massingham, and we would be there ourselves not long after it. The *Hoatzin* was behaving perfectly, with none of the problems that had almost done for us on the earlier test ships. The massive disk of dense matter at the front of the ship protected us from most of our collisions with stray dust and free hydrogen. If we didn't come back, the next ship out could follow our path exactly, tracking our swath of ionization.

During deceleration I began to search the sky beyond the *Hoatzin* every day, with an all-frequency sweep that ought to pick up signals as soon as our drive went to reduced thrust. We didn't pick up the Ark until the final day and it was no more than a point on the microwave screen for most of that. The image we finally built up on the monitor showed a lumpy, uneven ball, pierced by black shafts. Spiky antennas and angled gantries stood up like spines on its dull grey surface. I had seen the images of the Ark before it left the System, and all the surface structures were new. The colonists had been busy in the seventy-seven years since they accelerated away from Ganymede orbit.

We moved in to five thousand kilometers, cut all drive, and sent a calling sequence. I don't remember a longer five seconds, waiting for their response. When it came it was an anti-climax. A pleasant-looking middle-aged woman appeared on our screen.

"Hello," she said cheerfully. "We received a message that you were on your way here. My name is Kleeman. Link in your computer and we'll dock you. There will be a few formalities before you can come inside."

I put the central computer into distributed mode and linked a navigation module through the comnet. She sounded friendly and normal but I didn't want her to have override control of all the *Hoatzin's* movements. We moved to a position about fifty kilometers away from the Ark, then Kleeman appeared again on the screen.

"I didn't realize your ship had so much mass. We'll hold there, and you can come on in with a pod. All right?"

We called the unit a capsule these days, but I know what she meant. I made McAndrew put on a suit, to his disgust, and we entered the small transfer vessel. It was just big enough for four people, with no air lock and a simple electric drive. We drifted in to the Ark, with the capsule's computer slaved through the *Hoatzin*. As we got nearer I had a better feel for size. Two kilometers is small for an asteroid, but it's awfully big compared with a human. We nosed in to contact with a landing tower, like a fly landing on the side of a wasp's nest. I hoped that would prove to be a poor simile.

We left the capsule open and went hand-over-hand

down the landing tower rather than wait for an electric lift. It was impossible to believe that we were moving at almost nine thousand kilometers a second away from Earth. The stars were in the same familiar constellations, and it took a while to pick out the Sun. It was a bright star, but a good deal less bright than Sirius. I stood at the bottom of the tower for a few seconds, peering about me before entering the air lock that led to the interior of the Ark. It was like a strange, alien landscape, with the few surface lights throwing black angular shadows across the uneven rock. My trips to Titan suddenly felt like local hops around the comfortable backyard of the Solar System.

"Come on, Jeanie." That was McAndrew, all brisk efficiency and already standing in the air lock. He was much keener than I to penetrate that unfamiliar world of the interior.

I took a last look at the stars, and fixed in my mind the position of the transfer capsule — an old habit that pays off once in a thousand times. Then I followed McAndrew down into the lock.

"A few formalities before you can come inside." Kleeman had a gift for understatement. We found out what she meant when we stepped in through the inner lock, to an office-cum-schoolroom equipped with a couple of impressive consoles and displays. Kleeman met us there, as pleasant and rosy-faced in the flesh as she had seemed over the comlink.

She waved us to the terminals. "This is an improved version of the equipment that was on the original ship, before it left your System. Please sit down. Before anyone can enter our main Home, they must take tests. It has been that way since Massingham first showed us how our society could be built."

We sat at the terminals, back-to-back. McAndrew

was frowning at the delay. "What's the test, then?" he grumbled.

"Just watch the screen. I don't think that either of you will have any trouble." She smiled and left us to it. I wondered what the penalty was if you failed. We were a long way from home. It seemed clear that if they had been improving this equipment after they left Ganymede, they must apply it to their own people. We were certainly the first visitors they had seen for seventy-five years. How had they been able to accept our arrival so calmly?

Before I could pursue that thought the screen was alive. I read the instructions as they appeared there, and followed them as carefully as possible. After a few minutes I got the knack of it. We had tests rather like it when I first applied to go into space. To say that we were taking an intelligence test would be an oversimplification — many other aptitudes were tested, as well as knowledge and mechanical skills. That was the only consolation I had. McAndrew must be wiping the floor with me on all the parts that called for straight brain-power, but I knew that his coordination was terrible. He could unwrap a set of interlocking multiple-connected figures mentally and tell you how they came apart, but ask him to do the same thing with real objects and he wouldn't be able to start.

After three hours we were finished. Both screens suddenly went blank. We swung to face each other.

"What's next?" I said. He shrugged and began to look at the terminal itself. The design hadn't been used in the System for fifty years. I took a quick float around the walls — we had entered the Ark near a pole, where the effective gravity caused by its rotation was negligible. Even on the Ark's equator I estimated that we wouldn't feel more than a tenth of a gee, at the most.

No signs of what I was looking for, but that didn't

mean much. Microphones could be disguised in a hundred ways.

"Mac, who do you think she is?"

He looked up from the terminal. "Why, she's the woman assigned to..." He stopped. He had caught my point. When you are two light years from Sol and have your first visitors for seventy-five years, who leads the reception party? Not the man and woman who recycle the garbage. Kleeman ought to be somebody important on the Ark.

"I can assist your speculation," said a voice from the wall. So much for our privacy. As I expected, we had been observed throughout — no honor system on this test. "I am Kal Massingham Kleeman, the daughter of Jules Massingham, and I am senior member of Home outside the Council of Intellects. Wait there for one more moment. I will join you with good news."

She was beaming when she reappeared. Whatever they were going to do with us, it didn't seem likely they would be flinging us out into the void.

"You are both prime stock, genetically and individually," she said. "I thought that would be the case when first I saw you."

She looked down at a green card in her hand. "I notice that you both failed to answer one small part of the inquiry on your background. Captain Roker, your medical record indicates that you bore one child. But what is its sex, condition, and present status?"

I heard McAndrew suck in his breath past his teeth, while I suppressed my own shock as best I could. It was clear that the standards of privacy in the System and on the Ark had diverged widely in the past seventy-seven years.

"It is a female." I hope I kept my voice steady. "Healthy, and with no neuroses. She is in first level education on Luna."

"The father?"

"Unknown."

I shouldn't have been pleased to see that now Kleeman was shocked, but I was. She looked as distressed as I felt. After a few seconds she grabbed control of her emotions, swallowed, and nodded.

"We are not ignorant of the unplanned matings that your System permits. But hearing of such things and encountering them directly are different things." She looked again at her green card. "McAndrew, you show no children. Is that true?"

He had taken his lead from me and managed a calm and literal reply. "No recorded children."

"Incredible." Kleeman was shaking her head. "That a man of your talents should be permitted to go so long without suitable mating..."

She looked at him hungrily, the way that I have seen McAndrew eye an untapped set of experimental data from out in the Halo. I could imagine how he had performed on the intellectual sections of the test.

"Come along," she said at last, still eyeing McAndrew in a curiously intense and possessive way. "I would like to show you some of Home, and arrange for you to have living quarters for your use."

"Don't you want more details of why we are here?" burst out Mac. "We've come nearly two light years to get to the Ark."

"You have been receiving our messages of the advances that we have made?" Kleeman's manner had a vast self-confidence. "So why should we be surprised when superior men and women from your System wish to come here? We are only surprised that it took you so long to develop a suitably efficient ship. Your vessel is new?"

"Very new." I spoke before McAndrew could get a word in. Kleeman's assumption that we were on the

Ark to stay had ominous overtones. We needed to know more about the way the place functioned before we told her that we were planning only a brief visit.

"We have been developing the drive for our ship using results that parallel some of those found by your scientists," I went on. I gave Mac a look that kept him quiet for a little while longer. "When we have finished with the entry preliminaries, Professor McAndrew would very much like to meet your physicists."

She smiled serenely at him. "Of course. McAndrew, you should be part of our Council of Intellects. I do not know just how high your position was back in your System, but I feel sure you have nothing as exalted — and as respected — as our Council. Well" — she placed the two green cards she was holding in the pocket of her yellow smock — "there will be plenty of time to discuss induction to the Council when you have settled in here. The entry formalities are complete. Let me show you Home. There has never been anything like it in the whole of human history."

Over the next four hours we followed Kleeman obediently through the interior of the Ark. McAndrew was itching to locate his fellow-physicists, but he knew he was at the mercy of Kleeman's decisions. From our first meeting with others on the Ark, there was no doubt who was the boss there.

How can I describe the interior of the Ark? Imagine a free-space bee-hive, full of hard-working bees that had retained an element of independence of action. Everyone on the Ark of Massingham seemed industrious, cooperative, and intelligent. But they were missing a dimension, the touch of orneriness and unpredictability that you would find on Luna or on Titan. Nobody was cursing, nobody was irrational. Kleeman guided us through a clean, slightly dull Utopia.

The technology of the Ark was simpler to evaluate.

Despite the immense pride with which Kleeman showed off every item of achievement, they were half a century behind us. The sprawling, overcrowded chaos of Earth was hard to live with, but it provided a constant pressure towards innovation. New inventions come fast when ten billion people are there to push you to new ideas. In those terms, life on the Ark was spacious and leisurely. The colony had constructed its network of interlocking tunnels to a point where it would take months to explore all the passages and corridors, but they were nowhere near exhausting their available space and resources.

"How many people would the Ark hold?" I asked McAndrew as we trailed along behind Kleeman. It would have taken only a few seconds to work it out for myself, but you get lazy when you live for a while with a born calculator.

"If they don't use the interior material to extend the surface of the Ark?" he said. "Give them the same room as we'd allow on Earth, six meters by six meters by two meters. They could hold nearly sixty million. Halve that, maybe, to allow for recycling and maintenance equipment."

"But that is not our aim," said Kleeman. She had overheard my question. "We are stabilized at ten thousand. We are not like the fools back on Earth. *Quality* is our aim, not mindless numbers."

She had that tone in her voice again, the one that had made me instinctively avoid the question of how long we would be staying on the Ark. Heredity is a potent influence. I couldn't speak about Jules Massingham, the founder of this Ark, but his daughter was a fanatic. I have seen others like her over the years. Nothing would be allowed to interfere with the prime objective: build the Ark's population on sound eugenic principles. Kleeman was polite to me — I was "prime stock" — but she had her eye mainly on McAndrew. He would be a wonderful addition to her available gene pool.

Well, the lady had taste. I shared some of that attitude myself. "Father unknown" was literally true and Mac and I had not chosen to elaborate. My daughter had rights too, and Jan's parentage would not be officially known unless she chose after puberty to take the chromosome matching tests.

Over the next six days, McAndrew and I worked our way into the life pattern aboard the Ark. The place ran like a clock, everything according to a schedule and everything in the right position. I had a good deal of leisure time, which I used to explore the less-popular corridors, up near the Hub. McAndrew was still obsessed with his search for physicists.

"No sense here," he growled to me, after a meal in the central dining-area, out on the Ark's equator. As I had guessed, effective gravity there was about a tenth of a gee. "I've spoken to a couple of dozen of their scientists. There's not a one of them would last a week at the Institute. Muddled minds and bad experiments."

He was angry. Usually McAndrew was polite to all scientists, even ones who couldn't understand what he was doing, still less add to it.

"Have you seen them all? Maybe Kleeman is keeping some of them from us."

"I've had that thought. She's talked to me every day about the Council of Intellects, and I've seen some of the things they've produced. But I've yet to meet one of them, in person." He shrugged, and rubbed at his sandy, receding hairline. "After we've slept I'm going to try another tack. There's a schoolroom over on the other side of the Ark, where I gather Kleeman keeps people who don't seem quite to fit into her ideas. Want to take a look there with me, tomorrow?"

"Maybe. I'm wondering what Kleeman has in mind for me. I think I know her plans for you, she sees you as another of her senior brains." I saw the woman herself approaching us across the wide room, with its gently curving floor. "You'd like it, I suspect. It seems to be like the Institute, but members of the Council have a lot more prestige."

I had immediate proof that I was right. Kleeman seemed to have made up her mind. "We need a commitment from you now, McAndrew," she said. "There will soon be a vacancy on the Council. You are the best person to fill it."

McAndrew looked flattered but uncomfortable. The trouble was, it really *did* interest him, I could tell that. The idea of a top-level brains trust had appeal.

"All right," he said after a few moments. He looked at me, and I could tell what he was thinking. If we were going to be on our way back home soon, it would do no harm to help the Ark while he was here. They could use all the help available.

Kleeman clapped her hands together softly; plump white hands that pointed out her high position — most people on the Ark had manual duties to keep the place running, with strict duty rosters.

"Wonderful! I will plan for your induction tomorrow. Let me make the announcement tonight, and we can speed up the proceedings for the outgoing member."

"You always have a fixed number of members?" asked McAndrew.

She seemed slightly puzzled by his question. "Of course. Exactly twelve. The system was designed for that number."

She nodded at me and hurried away across the dining area, a determined little woman who always got her way. Since we first arrived, she had never ceased to tell McAndrew that he must become the father of many children; scores of children; hundreds of children. He looked more and more worried as she increased the suggested number of his future progeny.

The next morning I went on with my own exploration of the Ark, while McAndrew made a visit to the Ark's oddities, the people who didn't seem to fit Kleeman's expectations. We met to eat together, as usual, and I had a lot on my mind. I had come across an area in the center of the Ark where power supply lines and general purpose tubes increased enormously, but it did not seem to be a living area. Everything led to one central area, and that was accessible only with a suitable code. I puzzled over it while I waited for McAndrew to appear.

The whole Ark was bustling with excitement. Kleeman had made the announcement of McAndrew's incorporation to the Council of Intellects. People who had scarcely spoken to him before stopped us and shook his hand solemnly, wishing him well and thanking him for his devotion to the welfare of the Ark. While I drank an aperitif of glucose and dilute ascorbic acid, preparations for a big ceremony were going on around me. A new Council member was a big event.

When I saw McAndrew threading his way towards me past a network of new scaffolding, I knew his morning had been more successful than mine. His thin face was flushed with excitement and pleasure. He slid into the seat opposite me.

"You found your physicist?" I hardly needed to ask the question.

He nodded. "Up on the other side, in a maximum gravity segment directly — right across from here. He's — you have no idea — he's—" McAndrew was practically spluttering in his excitement.

"Start from the beginning." I leaned across and took his hands in mine.

"Yes. I went out on the other side of the Ark, where there's a sort of tower built out from the surface. We must have passed it on the way over from the *Hoatzin* but I didn't notice it then. Kleeman never took us there — never mentioned it to me."

He reached out with one hand across the table, grabbed my drink and took a great gulp of it. "Och, Jeanie, I needed that. I've not stopped since I first opened my eyes. Where was I? I went on up to that tower, and there was nobody to stop me or to say a word. And I went on inside, farther out, to the very end of it. The last segment has a window all the way round it, so when you're there you can see the stars and the nebulae wheeling round past your head."

McAndrew was unusually stirred and his last sentence proved it. The stars were normally considered fit subjects only for theory and computation.

"He was out in that last room," he went on. "After I'd given up hope of finding anybody in this whole place who could have derived those results we got back through Triton Station. Jeanie, he looks no more than a boy. So blond, and so young. I couldn't believe that he was the one who worked out that theory. But he is. We sat right down at the terminal there, and I started to run over the background for the way that I renormalize the vacuum self-energy. It's nothing like his way. He has a completely different approach, different invariants, different quantization conditions. I think his method is a good deal more easy to generalize. That's why he can get multiple vacuum colors out when we look for resonance conditions. Jeanie, you should have seen his face when I told him that we probably had fifty people at the Institute who would be able to follow his proofs. He's been completely alone here. There's not another one who can even get close to following him, he says. When he sent back those equations, he didn't tell people how important he thought they might be. He says they worry most about the control on what comes in from the System, rather than what goes out from here. I'm awful glad we came here. God, he's an accident, a sport that shows up only once in a couple of centuries — and he was born out here in the void! Did you know, he's taken all the old path integral methods, and he has a form of quantum theory that looks so simple, you'd never believe it if you didn't see it..."

He was off again. I had to break in, or he would have talked without stopping, right through our meal. McAndrew doesn't babble often, but when he does he's hard to stop.

"Mac, hold on. Something here doesn't make sense. What about the Council of Intellects?"

"What about it?" He looked as though he had no possible interest in the Council of Intellects — even though the bustle that was going on all around us, with new structures being erected, was all to mark McAndrew's elevation to the Council.

"Look, just yesterday we agreed that the work you're interested in here must have originated with the Council. You told me you hadn't met one person who knew anything worth discussing. Are you telling me now that this work on the vacuum energy *doesn't* come from the people on the Council?"

"I'm sure it doesn't. I doubted that even before I met Wicklund, up there in the tower." McAndrew was looking at me impatiently. "Captain, if that's the impression I gave, it's not what I meant. A thing like this is almost always the work of a single person. It's not initiated by a group, even though a group may help to apply it in practice. This work, the vacuum color work, that's *all* Wicklund — the Council knows nothing of it."

"So what *does* the Council do? I hope you haven't forgotten that you're going to join it later today. I don't think Kleeman would take it well if you said you wanted to change your mind.''

He waved an impatient arm at me. "Now, Jeanie, you know I've no time for that. The Council of Intellects is some sort of guiding and advising group, and I'm willing to serve on it and do what I can for the Ark. But not now. I have to get back over to Wicklund and sort out some of the real details. Did I mention that I've explained all about the drive to him? He mops up new material like a sponge. If we can get him back to the Institute he'll catch up on fifty years of System science development in a few months. You know, I'd better go and talk to Kleeman about this Council of hers. What's the use of calling it a Council of Intellects, when people like Wicklund are not on it? And I'll have to tell her we want to take him back with us. I've already mentioned it to him. He's interested, but he's a bit scared of the idea. This is home to him, the only place he knows. Here, is that Kleeman over there by the scaffolding? I'd better catch her now."

He was up and out of his seat before I could stop him. He hurried over to her, took her to one side and began to speak to her urgently. He was gesturing and cracking his finger joints, in the way that he always did when he was wound up on something. As I moved to join them I could see Kleeman's expression changing from a friendly interest to a solid determination.

"We can't change things now, McAndrew," she was saying. "The departing member has already been removed from the Council. It is now imperative that the replacement be installed as soon as possible. That ceremony must take place tonight."

"But I want to continue my meetings with—"

"The ceremony will take place tonight. Don't you understand? The Council cannot function unless there are all twelve members meeting. I cannot discuss this further. There is nothing to discuss."

She turned and walked away. Just as well. McAndrew was all set to tell her that he was not about to join her precious Council, and he was planning to leave the Ark without fathering hundreds, scores, or even ones of children. And he was taking one of her colonists — her subjects — with him. I took his arm firmly and dragged him back to our table.

"Calm down, Mac." I spoke as urgently as I could. "Don't fly off wild now. Let's get this stupid Council initiation rite out of the way today, and then let's wait a while and approach Kleeman on all this when she's in a more reasonable mood. All right?"

"That damned, obstinate, overbearing woman. Who the hell does she think she is?"

"She thinks she's the boss of the Ark of Massingham, and she *is* the boss of the Ark of Massingham. Face facts. Slow down now, and go back to Wicklund. See if he's interested in leaving when we leave, but don't push it too hard. Let's wait a few days, there's nothing to be lost from that."

How naive can you get? Kleeman had told us exactly what was going on, but we hadn't listened. People hear what they expect to hear.

I found out the truth the idiot's way. After McAndrew had gone off again, calm enough to talk to his new protege, I had about four hours to kill. The great ceremony in which McAndrew would become part of the Council of Intellects would not take place until after the next meal. I decided I would have another look at the closed room that I had seen on my earlier roaming.

The room was still locked, but this time there was a servicewoman working on the pipes that led into it. She recognized me as one of the two recent arrivals on the Ark — the less important one, according to Ark standards.

"Tonight's the big event," she said to me, her manner friendly. 'You've come to take a look at the place your friend will be, have you? You know, we really need him. The Council has been almost useless for the past two years, with one member almost gone. Kleeman knew that, but she didn't seem happy to provide a new member until she met McAndrew."

She obviously assumed I knew all about the Council and its workings. I stepped closer, keeping my voice casual and companionable. "I'll see all this for myself tonight. McAndrew will be in here, right? I wonder if I could take a peek now, I've never been inside before."

"Sure." She went to the door and keyed in a combination. "There's been talk for a while now of moving the Council to another part of Home, where there's less vibration from construction work. No sign of it happening yet, though. Here we go. You won't be able to go inside the inner room, of course, but you'll find you can see most things from the service area."

As the door slid open I stepped through into a long, brightly-lit room. It was empty.

My heart began to pound urgently and my mouth was as dry as Ceres. Strange, how the absence of something can produce such a powerful effect on the body.

"Where are they?" I said at last. "The Council. You said they are in this room."

She looked at me in comical disbelief. "Well, you didn't expect to find them out here, did you? Take a look through the hatch at the end there."

We walked forward together and peered through a transparent panel at the far end of the room. It led through to another, smaller chamber, this one dimly lit by a soft green glow.

My eyes took a few seconds to adapt. The big, translucent tank in the center of the room slowly came into definition. All around it, equally spaced, were twelve smaller sections, inter-connected through a massive set of branching cables and optic bundles.

"Well, there they are," said the servicewoman. "Doesn't look right, does it, with one of them missing like this? It doesn't work, either. The information linkages are all built for a set of exactly twelve units, with a twelve-by-twelve transfer matrix."

Now I could see that one of the small tanks was empty. In each of the eleven others, coupled to a set of thin plastic tubes and contact wires, was a complex shape, a dark-grey ovoid swimming in a bath of green fluid. The surfaces were folded and convoluted, glistening with the sticky sheen of animal tissues. At the lower end, each human brain thinned away past the brain stem to the spinal cord.

I remember asking her just one question.

"What would happen if the twelfth member of the Council of Intellects were not connected in today?"

"It would be bad." She looked shocked. "Very bad. I don't know the details, but I think all the potentials would run wild in a day or two, and destroy the other eleven. It has never happened. There have always been twelve members of the Council, since Massingham created it. He is the one over there, on the far right."

We must have spoken further, but already my mind was winging its way back to the dining area. I was to meet McAndrew one hour before the big ceremony. "Incorporation", that was what Kleeman had called it, incorporation into the Council. De-corporation would be a better name for the process. But the Council of Intellects was well-named. After someone has been pared down, flesh, bone and organs, to a brain and a spinal column, intellect is all that can remain. Perhaps the thing that had upset me more than anything in that inner room had been their decision to leave the eyes

intact. They were there, attached to each brain by the
protruding stalks of their optic nerves. They looked like
the horns of a snail, blue, grey or brown balls projecting
from the frontal lobes. Since there were no muscles left
to change the focal length of the eye lenses, they were
directed to display screens set at fixed distances from
the tanks.

The wait in the dining area was a terrible period.
I had been all right on the way back from the Council
Chamber, there had been movement to make the tension tolerable, but when McAndrew finally appeared
my nerves had become awfully ragged. He was all set
to burble on about his physics discussions. I cut him
off before he could get out one word.

"Mac, don't speak and don't make any quick move.
We have to leave the Ark. Now."

"Jeanie!" Then he saw my face. "What about Sven
Wicklund? We've talked again and he wants to go with
us — but he's not ready."

I shook my head and looked down at the table top.
It was the worst possible complication. We had to move
through the Ark and transfer across to the *Hoatzin*,
without being noticed. If Kleeman sensed our intentions,
Mac might still make it to the Council. My fate was less
certain but probably even worse — if a worse fate is
imaginable. It would be hard enough doing what we
had to do without the addition of a nervous and inex-
perienced young physicist. But I knew McAndrew.

"Go get him," I said at last. "Remember the lock we
came in by?"

He nodded. "I can get us there. When?"

"Half an hour. Don't let him bring anything with
him — we'll be working with a narrow margin."

He stood up and walked away without another word.
So he probably wouldn't have agreed to go without
Wicklund; but he hadn't asked me for any explanation,

hadn't insisted on a reason why we had to leave. That sort of trust isn't built up overnight. I was scared shitless as I stood up and left the dining area, but in an obscure way I was feeling that warm glow you only feel when two people touch deeply. McAndrew had sensed a life-or-death issue.

Back at our sleeping quarters I picked up the comlink that gave me coded access to the computer on the *Hoatzin*. We had to make sure the ship was still in the same position. I followed my own directive and took nothing else. Kal Massingham Kleeman was a lady whose anger was best experienced from a distance — I had in mind a light-year or two. I was only concerned now with the first couple of kilometers of that. We might find it necessary to move out of the Ark in a hurry.

The interior of the Ark was a great warren of connecting tunnels, so there were a hundred ways between any two points. That was just as well. I changed my path whenever I saw anyone else approaching, but I was still able to move steadily in the direction of our entry lock.

Twenty minutes since McAndrew had left. Now the speaker system crackled and came to life.

"Everyone will assemble in Main Hall Five."

The ceremony was ready to begin. Kleeman was going to produce Hamlet without the Prince. I stepped up my pace. The trip through the interior of the Ark was taking longer than I expected, and I was going to be late.

Thirty minutes, and I was still one corridor away. The monitors in the passage ceiling suddenly came to life, their red lenses glowing. All I could do was keep moving. There was no way of avoiding those monitors, they extended through the whole interior of the Ark.

"McAndrew and Roker." It was Kleeman's voice,

calm and superior. "We are waiting for you. There will be punishment unless you come here at once to Main Hall Five. Your presence in the outer section has been noted. A collection detail will arrive there any moment now. McAndrew, do not forget that the Council awaits you. You are abusing a great honor by your actions."

I was at last at the lock. McAndrew stood there listening to Kleeman's voice. The young man by his side — as Mac had said, so blond, so young — had to be Sven Wicklund. Behind those soft blue eyes lay a brain that even McAndrew found impressive. Wicklund was frowning now, his expression indecisive. All his ideas on life had been turned upside down in the past days, and now Kleeman's words must be giving him second thoughts about our escape.

Without speaking, McAndrew turned and pointed towards the wall of the lock. I looked, and felt a sudden sickness. The wall where the line of suits should be hanging was empty.

"No suits?" I said stupidly.

He nodded. "Kleeman has been thinking a move ahead of you."

"You know what joining the Council would imply?"

He nodded again. His face was grey. "Wicklund told me as we came over here. I couldn't believe it at first. I asked him, what about the children Kleeman wanted me to sire? They would drain me for the sperm bank before they..." He swallowed. There was a long and terrible pause. "I looked out," he said at last. "Through the viewport there. The capsule is still where we left it."

"You're willing to chance it?" I looked at Wicklund, who stood there not following our conversation at all.

"I am." Mac nodded. "But what about him? There's no Sturm Invocation for people here on the Ark."

As I had feared, Wicklund was a major complication.

I walked forward and stood in front of him. "Do you still want to go with us?"

He licked his lips, then nodded.

"Into the lock." We moved forward together and I closed the inner door.

"Do not be foolish." It was Kleeman's voice again, this time with a new expression of alarm. "There is nothing to be served by sacrificing yourselves to space. McAndrew, you are a rational man. Come back, and we will discuss this together. Do not waste your potential by a pointless death."

I took a quick look through the port of the outer lock. The capsule was there all right, it looked just the same as when we left it. Wicklund was staring out in horror. Until Kleeman had spoken, it did not seem to have occurred to him that we were facing death in the void.

"Mac!" I said urgently.

He nodded, and gently took Wicklund by the shoulders, swinging him around to face him. I stepped up behind him and dug hard into the nerve centers at the base of his neck. He was unconscious in two seconds.

"Ready, Mac?"

Another quick nod. I checked that Wicklund's eyelids were closed, and that his breathing was shallow. He would be unconscious for another couple of minutes, pulse rate low and oxygen need reduced.

McAndrew stood at the outer lock, ready to open it. I pulled the whistle from the lapel of my jacket and blew hard. The varying triple tone sounded through the lock. Penalty for improper use of any Sturm Invocation was severe, whether you used spoken, whistled, or electronic methods. I had never invoked it before, but anyone who goes into space, even if it is just a short trip from Earth to Moon, must receive Sturm vacuum survival programming. One person in a million uses it.

I stood in the lock, waiting to see what would happen to me.

The sensation was strange. I still had full command of my actions, but there was also a new set of involuntary activities. Without any conscious decision to do so, I found that I was breathing hard, hyper-ventilating in great gulps. My eye-blinking pattern had reversed. Instead of open eyes with rapid blinks to moisten and clean the eyeball, my lids were closed except for brief instants. I saw the lock and the outside as quick snapshots.

The Sturm Invocation had the same effect on McAndrew, as his own deep programming took over for vacuum exposure. When I nodded, he swung open the outer lock door. The air was gone in a puff of ice vapor. As my eyes flicked open I saw the capsule at the top of the landing tower. To reach it we had to traverse sixty meters of the interstellar vacuum. And we had to carry Sven Wicklund's unconscious body between us.

For some reason I had imagined that the Sturm vacuum programming would make me insensitive to all pain. Quite illogical, since you could permanently damage your body all too easily in that situation. I felt the agony of expansion through my intestines, as the air rushed out of all my body cavities. My mouth was performing an automatic yawning and gasping, emptying the Eustachian tube to protect my eardrums and delicate inner ear. My eyes were closed to protect the eyeballs from freezing, and open just often enough to guide my body movements.

Holding Wicklund between us, McAndrew and I pushed off into the open depths of space. Ten seconds later, we intersected the landing tower about twenty meters up. Sturm couldn't make a human comfortable in space, but he had provided a set of natural movements that corresponded to a zero gee environment.

They were needed. If we missed the tower there was no other landing point within light years.

The metal of the landing tower was at a temperature several hundred degrees below freezing. Our hands were unprotected, and I could feel the ripping of skin at each contact. That was perhaps the worst pain. The feeling that I was a ball, over-inflated and ready to burst, was not a pain. What was it? That calls for the same sort of skills as describing sight to a blind man. All I can say is that once in a lifetime is more than enough.

Thirty seconds in the vacuum, and we were still fifteen meters from the capsule. I was getting the first feeling of anoxia, the first moment of panic. As we dropped into the capsule and tagged shut the hatch I could feel the black clouds moving around me, dark nebulae that blanked out the bright star field.

The transfer capsule had no real air lock. When I hit the air supply, the whole interior began to fill with warm oxygen. As the concentration grew to a perceptible fraction of an atmosphere, I felt something turn off abruptly within me. My eye blinking went back to the usual pattern, my mouth closed instead of gaping and gasping, and the black patches started to dwindle and fragment.

I turned on the drive of the transfer vessel to take us on our fifty kilometer trip to the *Hoatzin* and glanced quickly at the other two. Wicklund was still unconscious, eyes closed but breathing normally. He had come through well. McAndrew was something else. There was blood flowing from the corner of his mouth and he was barely conscious. He must have been much closer to collapse than I when we dropped into the capsule, but he had not loosened his grip on Wicklund.

I felt a moment of irritation. Damn that man. He had assured me that he would replace that damaged lung lobe after our last trip but I was pretty sure he had done nothing about it. This time I would see he had the operation, if I had to take him there myself.

He began to cough weakly and his eyes opened. When he saw that we were in the capsule and Wicklund was between us, he smiled a little and let his eyes close again. I put the drive on maximum and noticed for the first time the blood that was running from my left hand. The palm and fingers were raw flesh, skin ripped off by the hellish cold of the landing tower. I reached behind me and pulled out the capsule's small medical kit. Major fix-ups would have to wait until we were on the *Hoatzin*. The surrogate flesh was bright yellow, like a thick mustard, but it took away the pain. I smeared it over my own hand, then reached across and did the same for McAndrew. His face was beginning to blaze with the bright red of broken capillaries, and I was sure that I looked just the same. That was nothing. It was the bright blood dribbling down his blue tunic that I didn't like.

Wicklund was awake. He winced and held his hands up to his ears. There might be a burst eardrum there, something else we would have to take care of when we got to the *Hoatzin*.

"How did I get here?" he said wonderingly.

"Across the vacuum. Sorry we had to put you out like that, but I didn't think you could have faced a vacuum passage when you were conscious."

His gaze turned slowly to McAndrew. "Is he all right?"

"I hope so. There may be some lung damage that we'll have to take care of. Want to do something to help?"

He nodded, then turned back to look at the ball of the Ark, dwindling behind us. "They can't catch us now, can they?"

"They might try, but I don't think so. Kleeman probably considers anybody who wants to leave the Ark is not worth having. Here, take the blue tube out of the kit behind you and smear it on your face and hands. Do the same for McAndrew. It will speed up the repair of the ruptured blood vessels in your skin."

Wicklund took the blue salve and began to apply it tenderly to McAndrew's face. After a couple of seconds Mac opened his eyes and smiled. "Thank you, lad," he said softly. "I'd talk more physics with you, but somehow I don't quite feel that I'm up to it."

"Just lie there quiet." There was hero worship in Wicklund's voice. I had a sudden premonition of what the return trip was going to be like. McAndrew and Sven Wicklund in a mutual admiration society, and all the talk of physics.

After we had the capsule back on board the *Hoatzin* I felt secure for the first time. We installed McAndrew comfortably on one of the bunks while I went to the drive unit and set a maximum-acceleration course back to the Solar System. Wicklund's attention was torn between his need to talk to McAndrew and his fascination with the drive and the ship. How would Einstein have felt in 1905, if someone could have shown him a working nuclear reactor just a few months after he had developed the mass-energy relation? It must have been like that for Wicklund.

"Want to take a last look?" I said, my hand on the drive keyboard.

He came across and gazed at the Ark, still set on its long journey to Tau Ceti. He looked sad, and I felt guilty.

"I'm sorry," I said. "We should have asked you if you wanted to come with us before we put you under. But I'm afraid there's no going back now."

"I know." He hesitated. "You found Home a bad

place, I could tell from what McAndrew said. But it's not so bad. To me, it was home for my whole life."

"We'll talk to the Ark again. There may be a chance to come here later, when we've had more time to study the life that you lived. I hope you'll find a new life in the System."

I meant it, but I was having a sudden vision of the Earth we were heading back to. Crowded, noisy, short of all resources. Wicklund might find it as hellish as we had found life on the Ark of Massingham. It was too late to do anything about it now. I suspected that this sort of problem meant less to Wicklund than it would to most people. Like McAndrew, his real life was lived inside his own head, and all else was secondary to that private vision.

I pressed the key sequence and the drive went on. Within seconds, the Ark had vanished from sight.

I turned back and was surprised to see that McAndrew was sitting up in his bunk. He looked terrible, but he must be feeling better. His hands were yellow paws of surrogate flesh, his face and neck a bright blue coating of the ointment that Wicklund had applied to them. The dribble of blood that had come from his mouth had spread its bright stain down his chin and over the front of his tunic, mixing in with the blue fabric to produce a horrible purple splash.

"How are you, Mac?" I said.

"Not bad. Not bad at all." He forced a smile.

"You know, it's not good enough. You promised me ages ago that you'd schedule a repair for that lung — and you didn't do it. If you think I'm prepared to keep dragging you around bleeding and bubbling, you're wrong. When we get back, you have that lung fixed properly — if I have to drag you to the medics myself."

"Och, Jeanie." He gave a feeble shrug. "We'll see. It takes so much time away from work. Let's get on home, though, and we'll see. I've learned a lot on this trip, more than I ever expected. It's all been well worth it."

He caught my skeptical look. "Honest, now, this is more important than you realize. We'll make the next trip out together, the way I promised you — maybe next time we'll get to the stars. I'm sorry that you got nothing out of this one."

I stared at him. He looked like a circus clown, all smears and streaks of different clashing colors. I shook my head.

"You're wrong. I got something out of it."

He looked puzzled. "How's that?"

"I listen to you and the other physicists all the time, and usually I don't understand a word of it. This time I know just what you mean. Lie still, and you can see for yourself. I'll be back in a second."

All the colors of the vacuum? That was McAndrew. If a picture is worth a thousand words, there are times when a mirror is worth more than that. I wanted to watch Mac's face when he saw his own reflection.

FOURTH CHRONICLE: THE *MANNA* HUNT

We had been working hard for two months, preparing for the first long trip. Neither McAndrew nor I would admit to feeling excited, but every day I could see the pleasure and anticipation just bubbling up in him. I doubt that I was any harder to read.

It meant sixteen-hour work spells, day after day, checking every detail of the ship and mission. On an exploration that would take us away for four months of shipboard time and almost nine years of Earth-time, all the thinking had to be finished before we left the Institute.

Finally the launch date was only four days away.

That made the news of cancellation — when they plucked up the courage to tell us about it — hard to take.

I had been over on the *Hoatzin*, checking the condition of the big massplate at the front of the ship. It took longer than I expected. By the time I flew my inspection pod on its ten thousand kilometer hop back to the Penrose Institute we were well into the sleep period. I hadn't expected anyone in the dining hall when I slipped in to dial a late meal — and certainly I didn't expect to find Professor Limperis in close conversation with McAndrew.

"Working late—" I said. Then I saw their faces. Even Limperis, black as he was, looked drawn and a shade paler.

I sat down opposite them. "What's happened?"

McAndrew shrugged without speaking and jerked his head towards Limperis.

"We've had a directive from U.S.F. Headquarters," said the older man. He seemed to be picking his words carefully. "Signed by Korata — right from the top. There was a meeting last week between the Food and Energy Council of Earth and the United Space Federation. They called me two hours ago. The Penrose Institute is instructed to support certain high priority Council activities. This requires that we—"

"They've cancelled us, Jeanie," cut in McAndrew harshly. "The bastards. Without one word of discussion with anybody here. Our Alpha Centauri mission is dead — *finito*."

I gawped at Limperis. He nodded in an embarrassed way.

"Postponed, at least. With no new date set."

"They can't do that." I was beginning to feel my own anger rising. "The Institute doesn't answer to the Food and Energy Council, how the hell can they claim to order you around? This is an independent organization. Tell them to go away and play with themselves. You have the authority to do that, don't you?"

"Well..." Limperis looked even more embarrassed. "In *principle*, Captain Roker, it is as you say. I have the authority. But you know that's an oversimplification of the real world. We need political support as much as any other group — we rely partly on public funding. I like to pretend that we're pure research, answering to no one. In practice, we have our own political constituency in the Councils. I tried to explain this just now"—McAndrew grunted and glowered down at the table—"to point out why I can't really fight it without losing an awful lot. Three of our big supporters, Councillors who've done us big favors in the past, called me ten minutes after we got the first word. They want to use their credit on this one. The Alpha Centauri mission is off. The Council needs the use of the *Hoatzin* for other purposes."

"No way." I leaned forward until our faces were only six inches apart. "That's our ship — we've slaved over it. If they think they can call in and take it away from me and Mac without even asking us, and leave us—"

"They want you, too, Jeanie." Limperis leaned back a bit. In my excitement I was spitting all over him. "Both of you. The orders are very clear. They want you and McAndrew *and* the ship."

"And what the hell for?"

"For a mission of their own." He looked baffled. "For a mission so secret they wouldn't tell me anything about it."

That was the first shock. The others dribbled in one by one as McAndrew and I made our way from the Penrose Institute to the headquarters of the Food and Energy Council.

The Institute had been parked out near Mars' orbit. With the *Hoatzin*, and its hundred gee drive, or even with one of the prototypes like *Merganser* at fifty gee, we could have been to Earth in half a day. But Professor Limperis still insisted that the McAndrew Drive

should never be employed in the Inner System, and
McAndrew himself backed that decision completely.
We were stuck with a slow boat and a ten day journey.

Surprise Number One came soon after we powered
away from the Institute. I had assumed that we would
be running a confidential mission for the Energy
Department of the full Food and Energy Council. We
had worked together on high-energy projects in the
past, and I knew McAndrew was a real expert on the
subject. But our travel documents instructed us to
report to the Food Department. What did food programs need with a theoretical physicist, a spacecraft
captain, and a high-acceleration ship?

Three days from Earth we were hit with another surprise. The information came in as a brief, impersonal
directive that could be neither amplified nor ques-
tioned. I would not be the captain of the new mission.
Despite the fact that I had more experience with the
McAndrew Drive than anyone else in the System, a
Food Department official would give me my orders. I
became even angrier when, two days from Earth, we
learned the rest of it. McAndrew and I would serve
as "special advisors" reporting to a crew from the Food
and Energy Council. We would have about as much
decision-making authority on the mission as the
robochef. I had descended from captain to cabinboy.

For me, maybe they could persuade themselves that
it was a reasonable decision — some people have more
deep space experience than I do (but not much more)
and you could say that my talent is nothing more than
tricks for staying alive and out of trouble. But McAndrew was another matter. To assign him a role as a
simple information source suggested an ignorance or
an arrogance beyond my belief.

(All right, so I'm a McAndrew fan; I won't deny it.
When I got to Earth I would have words with the
bureaucrats of the Food Department.)

I needed to talk it out with somebody, but Mac was no use. He wasn't interested in arguments on non-technical subjects. Instead, he retreated as usual into his private world of tensors and twistors, and despite my own respectable scientific background I couldn't follow him there. For most of the journey he sat slack-jawed on his bunk, perfectly content, gazing at the blank wall and performing the invisible mental gymnastics that had earned him his reputation.

That sort of thinking is beyond me. I spent my time brooding, and by the time we were led into the Council's offices I was loaded for bear.

The Food Department enjoys a bigger staff and budget than anything else in System Government, and the opulence of its fittings was quite a contrast to the spartan furnishings of the Institute. We were conducted through four luxurious outer offices, each with its own secretaries and screening procedure. Ample working space spoke of prestige and power. The room we finally came to held a conference table big enough for forty people.

A woman was seated alone at the massive desk. I looked at her elegant dress, beautifully made-up eyes and carefully coiffured hair, and I suddenly felt scruffy and out-of-place. Mac and I were dressed for space work, in one-piece beige coveralls and loafers. My hair had been cropped to a few centimeters long. His thin, straggly mop as usual dipped untidily over his high forehead. Neither of us was wearing a touch of make-up.

"Professor McAndrew?" She stood up and smiled at us. I glowered back at her. "And Captain Roker, I assume. I must apologize for treating you in such cavalier fashion. You have had a long trip here, and no adequate explanation."

Good disarming waffle, the sort you get from an experienced politician or the highest level of bureaucrat, but her smile was broad and friendly. She came forward and held out a pudgy hand. As I took it I made a closer inspection of her appearance: thirty-five years old, maybe, and a bit overweight. Perhaps this messy situation wasn't her fault. I restrained my scowl and muttered conventional words of greeting.

She gestured us to sit down.

"I am Anna Lisa Griss," she went on. "Head of Programs for the Food Department. Welcome to Headquarters. Other staff members will join us in a few minutes, but first I want to point out the need for secrecy. What you will learn here cannot be mentioned to anyone outside this room without my permission. I will come to the point at once. Look at this."

She exuded an air of complete control. As she was speaking the lights dimmed and an image became visible on the screen at the far end of the room. It showed a column of calendar years, and alongside it two other columns of figures.

"Total System food reserves, present and projected," said Griss. "Look at the trend — it's a log scale — then look particularly at the behavior thirty years from now."

I was still trying to assimilate the first few numbers when McAndrew grunted and put his hand up to his face.

"That's ridiculous," he said. "You're showing a factor of two drop in less than three decades. What's the basis for that projection?"

If she felt surprise at his speed of response, she didn't show it. "We included population patterns, available acreages, plant yields, and capacity to manufacture synthetics. Would you like to see the details on any one of them?"

McAndrew shook his head. "Never mind the details.

That's disaster and starvation flashing on your screen."

"It is. It's the reason that you are here." She brought the lights back up to what I regarded as a dim, conspiratorial level and dropped her voice to match. "You can imagine the effect when that projection becomes public knowledge, especially if no one can see any way out. Even though we're talking about many years in the future, we'd see stockpiling — probably food wars."

I was feeling a growing anger. There had been rumors of a major future food shortage flying around the System for a long time. The Administration had denied every one, dismissing all gloomy forecasts as alarmist.

"If you're correct in your projections, you can't keep this a secret," I said. "People have a right to know so they can work on solutions."

McAndrew frowned at me, while Anna Lisa Griss gave me a quick probing glance (no smile now) and raised her dark eyebrows. The man's easy, her look said, but this one needs persuading.

"The problem is clear enough," she agreed. "It has been known to my group for almost a decade. Fairly soon it may be obvious to everybody. But it's the possible solution I want to talk about now. And involving the general public wouldn't help a bit — there's no chance that they could provide new insights."

I didn't like her superior manner, but in spite of my irritation I was becoming interested. "It has to be a supply side answer," I said. "The population growth won't budge."

"Obviously." She smiled again, a bit too broadly, and sneaked a look at her watch. "But think about that supply side. We'd like to increase the planted acreage, of course. But how? We're using every spare inch, unless we can move the lunar agricultural experiments to massive production — and nobody feels optimistic

about that. Plant yields are as high as they will go —
we're seeing bad effects of plant overbreeding already.
No hope there. So what's left?"

Before we could chance an answer or she could provide one, the door behind us opened. A skinny man with
plastered-down grey hair entered and stood deferen-
tially at the threshold.

"Come in, Bayes." Anna Lisa Griss looked again at
her watch. "You're late."

"Sorry." He remained at the door, hesitating.

"I began without you. Come in and sit down." She
turned to face us without offering introductions. "There
was one area still to be examined: alternative supplies
of organic materials that might easily be converted to
food. Six years ago, everyone thought that was a
hopeless avenue. Now, with the Griss-Lanhoff
Theory"—I could hear the capital letters in her voice
as she proclaimed the name—"we have new hope."

I was watching Bayes' face as she spoke. His lips
tightened when Anna Lisa Griss pronounced the name
of the theory, but he remained silent.

McAndrew cleared his throat.

"I'm afraid that I'm not as well up on the literature
of food production as I ought to be," he said. "Lanhoff's
a familiar name. If it's the same person, I knew him
fairly well ten years ago, when he was working on por-
phyrin syntheses. What's he doing now?"

"We don't know. Maybe you can help us to find out."
She leaned forward and looked at us intently. "Lanhoff has disappeared — out in the Halo, testing our
theory. Two weeks ago I learned that you have available a high-acceleration ship with an inertia-less
drive." (I saw McAndrew wince and mutter "not
inertia-less" to himself). "We need the use of that, for
a mission of the highest priority. We have to find out
what happened to Lanhoff's project. Three days from

now we must be on our way to the Halo."

It said something for the lack of efficiency of the Food Department that they would drag McAndrew and me all the way to Earth for a meeting, then shuttle us back to the Penrose Institute and the *Hoatzin* on a Government-owned ship less than four hours after we arrived. Anna Lisa Griss would follow to the Institute in another and even fancier vessel, but Bayes went with us to continue the briefing on the way. Without his boss around he lost his intimidated look and became a much cheerier person.

"Let's start with Lanhoff's ideas," he said. "Though after listening to Anna back in her office it's apparently going to be called the Griss-Lanhoff Theory, at least while Lanhoff's not on the scene. I'll keep it short, but I'm not sure where to begin. In the Halo, I guess. Professor McAndrew, do you know anything about the Halo?" He cackled with laughter at his joke.

Griss had asked McAndrew that same question when she was giving us our first briefing. I had watched Bayes' eyes bulge with astonishment. I felt the same way myself. McAndrew probably knew more about the Halo and the outer parts of the extended Solar System than anyone, living or dead — he had developed the entire theory that predicted the existence of the kernel ring, the broad belt of Kerr-Newman black holes that girdles the ecliptic at four hundred a.u., ten times the distance of Pluto. And of course he had travelled out there himself, in the first test of the McAndrew balanced drive. I assumed that any scientist worth the name would know all about McAndrew and his work, but apparently Anna Lisa Griss proved me wrong.

McAndrew laughed. He and Will Bayes had needed only ten minutes alone together to discover a mutual fascination with bad jokes, and they were getting along famously. I thought ahead to a long trip with the two of them and shuddered at the prospect.

"Lanhoff wandered into our offices six or seven years back," went on Bayes after he had had a good giggle at his own wit. "He'd been analyzing the results of Halo remote chemistry probes. Didn't you do some of that yourself, a few years ago?"

McAndrew rubbed at his sandy, receding hairline. "Och, just a little bit. I wanted to find power kernels, not low-density fragments, but as part of the survey we sneaked in a look at some other stuff as well. Most of the Oort Cloud's so poorly surveyed, you know, it's a crime not to explore it whenever you have the chance. But I never looked out more than a few hundred a.u. — it was before we had the drive, and probes were too expensive. I'm sure Lanhoff had all my results to work with when he started."

"He certainly knew your work," said Bayes. "And he remembered you well. You made quite an impression on him. He's an organic chemist, and he had been looking at all the data on the Halo, and plotting body chemical composition as a function of distance from the Sun. He has a special algorithm that allows him to look at the fractional composition of each object — I think it came from Minga's team. You probably don't remember Minga, he never published much himself. I met him once or twice, way back...no, maybe I'm thinking of Rooney. You know, he was the one who did the high-energy work, I think it was for the Emerald Project, wasn't it? I think so..."

It's probably a kindness if I edit Will Bayes' briefing of McAndrew and me. He tried hard enough, but everything he said reminded him of something else, and that something-else had to be explained too, and all the people involved in it reminded him of other people, and what they had done. Regression, *ad infinitum.*

We didn't mind too much, with a two day journey before we were back at the Institute, but I must say I thought a bit more kindly of Anna Griss before the trip was over. Staff meetings with Bayes must be hell.

Boiling Will's verbiage down to a minimum, it was a simple story: Lanhoff had done a systematic chemical analysis of the cometary Halo, from its beginnings not far past the orbit of Pluto, all the way to the fading outer edge nearly half a lightyear away, where the Sun's gravitational hold is so weak that the frozen bodies drift around in orbits with periods of millions of years.

That's the Oort Cloud, a great ball of loosely-held matter centered on the Sun. There are several hundred billion comets out there, ranging from near-planet-sized monsters a few hundred kilometers across to snowballs no bigger than your fist. Chapman's Rule applies as well to the cometary Halo as it does to the asteroid belt: for every object of given diameter, there are ten objects with one-third of that diameter.

The Halo has been described and studied since the middle of the twentieth century, but Lanhoff's interests were different. He divided the solar vicinity into regions, of different distances and inclinations to the plane of the ecliptic, and he looked at the percentage of different organic materials within each orbital regime. Naturally, with a trillion objects to work with he could only look at a tiny sample of the total, but even so, the analysis took him eight years. And he found something new and surprising. In a part of the Halo about 3,200 a.u. from the Sun, running out to maybe 4,000 a.u., the complexity of chemical compounds increases enormously. Instead of simple organic molecules like cyanogen, formaldehyde, and methane, his program told him he was finding higher compounds and complex polymers — macromolecules like polysaccharide chains.

"Like what?" At that point in the discussion I had interrupted Will Bayes' ramblings. Organic chemistry is low on the list of educational priorities for controlling a spacecraft.

"Organic polymers," said McAndrew thoughtfully. He had been frowning hard as Bayes talked of the chemical composition. "Chains of glucose molecules, to make starches and cellulose." He turned back to Bayes. "Did Lanhoff find any evidence of porphyrins, or nitrogen compounds like purines and pyrimidines?"

Bayes blinked. "You seem to know all about this already. Did Anna already brief you? Lanhoff's work is all supposed to be a big secret."

I had some sympathy with him. Briefing McAndrew is an unrewarding experience. At the end of it he seems to know everything you know and be able to apply it better. Now he was shaking his head and looking puzzled.

"She didn't mention any of this to us. But I knew most of it years ago. Not the particular place in the Halo where we might find complex organic materials, but at least the fact that they might be there. It's not a new theory at all. Hoyle suggested it more than a hundred years ago. I just don't understand why there's anything secret about it. A finding like this one ought to be available to anyone."

"There's a reason. Wait until you know Anna Griss a bit better and you'll understand." Bayes was looking outside for his first glimpse of the *Hoatzin*, which was now only a couple of hundred kilometers away. "She's the hardest worker I know, but she's super-ambitious. She wants to run the whole Council someday — tomorrow, if she had her way. When Lanhoff came to her with his proposal, the first thing she did was hit it with a classified label."

"Didn't anyone argue with her?" I said.

"No. Try it. It's not something you'll want to do more than once. There were a few mutterings, that was all. Anna offered some positive incentives, too. She thinks this will make her famous, and push everybody in the Department ten rungs up the management ladder."

"Just because we've got a bit more information about the composition of the Halo? Not much chance of that." McAndrew snorted his disbelief.

"No." Bayes was still peering out of the port. "Lanhoff persuaded her that he had the only answer to the System food problem. All he needed was money and a ship, and U.S.F. permission to make some orbit changes to a few bodies out in the Halo. Good God!" He turned back from the scope. "There's the oddest-looking ship out there. Surely we're not proposing to chase after Lanhoff in that thing?"

Lanhoff's suggestion sounded reasonable until you sat down to think about it. Out in the Halo, off where the Sun was nothing more than an extra-bright star, mountains of matter drift through space, moving to the tug of a faint gravitational current. Most of them are frozen or rocky fragments, water ice and ammonia ice bonding metals and silicates. But swarms of them, in a toroidal region three hundred billion miles from Earth, are made of more complex organic molecules. If Lanhoff were correct, we would find an endless supply of useful compounds there — all the prebiotic materials from which foodstuffs are easily made. They needed only warmth and a supply of the right enzymes to serve as catalytic agents. Cellulose, polypeptides, carotenoids and porphyrins could be transformed to sugars, starches, proteins and edible fats. The food supply of the whole Syhstem would be assured for a million years.

Now sit down and think about it again. How do you seed a hundred million worlds and turn them to giant candymountains, when the nearest of them is so far away? How do you heat them; how do you get them back where they will be useable?

If you are Arne Lanhoff, none of those questions will deter you. The enzymes you need are available in small amounts in the Inner System; once a body has been seeded and heat is available from a fusion reactor, enzyme production can proceed at an explosive pace. It will suffice to begin with just a few hundred thousand tons of the right enzymes, and make the rest where the supply of raw materials is assured. The types of enzymes needed to split polymer chains are well known, but the only sort of ship that can carry this much load is a boost-and-coast vessel with a maximum short-duration acceleration of only two-tenths of a gee. So be it. Plan on a trip out to the Halo that will take a couple of years, and allow another year or two to trundle around from one cometary body to the next, seeding and performing necessary orbital adjustments. The continuous-thrust engines that will be attached to each body add another two million tons to the ship's initial payload. So be it. Fusion heaters to warm the frozen interiors will add a million more. Don't worry about it. For a project of this size and importance, the Food and Energy Council will find the money and equipment.

McAndrew had shaken his head when Will Bayes described the plan to place the seeded bodies into radial orbits, thrusting in toward the Sun. "Man, do you realize what it will take to stop one of them? We'll be trying to catch a billion tons travelling at two thousand kilometers a second."

"Arne Lanhoff knew that before he left. He was planning just enough drive to bring them to the Inner

System in twenty years. By that time they'll be warmed and transformed in content." Bayes smiled contentedly. "He felt sure that you'd find ways to catch them and slow them. It's the sort of thing your group finds challenging."

"Challenging! He's insane." But two minutes later McAndrew was miles away, working on his new puzzle. Arne Lanhoff knew his man rather well.

The ship that had left the Inner System four years ago did so with no fanfares or publicity. The *Star Harvester* was a massive set of linked cargo spheres with electromagnetic coupling. Each Section had an independent drive unit powered by its own kernel. It was quite similar to the Assembly that I pilot on the Earth-Titan run, and I was glad to know that I'd have no trouble handling it if the need arose.

That need might well arise. The Food Department had received regular communications from the *Star Harvester* crew during the long trip out — two years Earth-time, and the ship was too slow to make it noticeably shorter in shipboard time. Lanhoff had finally reached his first suitable target, a fifteen-kilometer chunk of ice and organics. He had officially named the body *Cornucopia*, planted the enzyme package, the fusion furnace, and the drive, and then started it on the long drop in towards the Sun. Without the drive it would fall for millennia. With a little continuous-thrust assistance *Cornucopia* would be crossing the orbit of Jupiter sixteen years from now. By that time it would be a fertile mass of the raw materials of nutrition, enough to feed the System for five years.

"No problems. Complete success in all phases," read Arne Lanhoff's message as they moved on to the next selected target, a mere five hundred million miles away.

The mission had operated perfectly for another five targets — each one named, processed, and directed toward the Inner System. *Ambrosia; Harvest Festival; Persephone; Food of the Gods;* and *Demeter.*

Then the pattern was broken. The seventh target had been reached ninety days ago. After an initial message announcing contact with the body *Manna*, a huge organic fragment sixty kilometers in length and incredibly rich in complex compounds, *Star Harvester* became inexplicably silent. A message of inquiry beamed to it from Triton Station fled off on its nineteen-day journey, and an automatic signal of message receipt finally returned. But no message originated in the ship's transmission equipment. Arne Lanhoff and his crew of four had vanished into the void, three hundred billion miles from home.

Our troubles didn't wait until we were out in the Halo. As soon as Anna Lisa Griss arrived on board the *Hoatzin*, only six hours before our scheduled departure time, we had a problem. She looked around the living quarters disbelievingly.

"You mean we're supposed to stay in this little space — all of us? It can't be more than three meters across."

"Nearer to four." I paused in my run-through of firing sequence checks. "We left information about that with you before we came here — didn't you look at it?"

"I looked at the size of the ship, and the column for the living quarters was hundreds of meters long. Why can't we use all of it?"

I sighed. She had the authority to commandeer the *Hoatzin*, but had never bothered to learn the first thing about how it operated.

"The living-capsule moves up and down that column," I said. "Nearer or closer to the mass disk, depending on the ship's acceleration. We can put the supplies outside the capsule area, but if we want to live in a one-gee environment we're stuck with this part — it's not bad, plenty of space for four people."

"But what about my staff?" She gestured at the five people who had followed her into the *Hoatzin*. I realized for the first time that they might be more than merely carriers of luggage.

"Sorry." I tried to sound it. "This ship is rated for a four-person crew, maximum."

"Change it." She gave me the full force of her imperial manner. I suddenly understood why Will Bayes chose not to argue with her.

I stared back at her without blinking.

"I can't. I didn't make that rule — check with the U.S.F. back at Lunar Base if you like, but they'll confirm what I'm telling you."

She took her lower lip between her teeth, turned her head to survey the cabin, and finally nodded. "I believe you. Damnation. But if there is a four-man limit we still have a problem. I need Bayes and I want my own pilot. And I need McAndrew. You'll have to stay behind."

She didn't look at me this time. I took a deep breath. I didn't want to do it, but if we were going to bang heads we might as well get it over with — now was as good a time as any.

"I suggest that you discuss this with McAndrew," I said. "Better talk to your pilot, too, while you're at it. I think you'll find that Mac will refuse to go along without me — just as I wouldn't go without him. This is not a conventional vessel. Ask your own pilot how many hours of experience he has with the McAndrew Drive. Mac and I have essential experience and skills for the successful performance of this mission. Take your pick. Both, or neither."

My voice sounded trembly. Instead of replying she turned to head for the steps to the lower level of the living capsule.

"Prepare us for departure," she said over her shoulder as she went. Her voice was so calm that I was shocked by my own tension. "I will talk to Bayes. He must assume additional duties on this project." She turned again when just her head and shoulders were visible. "Did you ever consider taking a job down on Earth? You have abilities that are wasted out here in the middle of nowhere."

I swivelled my chair to face the console screen and wondered what sort of victory I had won — if any. Anna Lisa Griss was wise in the ways of political infighting, while I was a raw novice. But I was damned if I'd give up my place on this trip without a struggle. The ship was easy to handle, but I'd never admit that to Anna Griss.

Will Bayes came in to stand beside me while I was still having trouble getting my attention back to the status reports.

"Now you've done it," he said. "What did you say to her? I've never seen her in such a weird mood. I can't read her at all. She just told Mauchly and the rest of her staff to get back to Headquarters — no explanation. And I've been given double duty for the duration."

I ran the trajectory parameters out onto the screen, jabbing viciously at the buttons. Then I gave him a quick sideways glance. "I had to make a choice. Which would you rather have: Anna Lisa Griss in a peculiar mood, or a ship run by people who don't know the McAndrew Drive from a laser-sail?"

He grunted and stared gloomily at the screen. "It's not an easy decision. You've never seen Anna when she's really annoyed. I have. Let me tell you, it's not something I want to go through again." He leaned forward. "Hey, Jeanie. Surely that's not the plot of our flight out you've got on the display there."

"It certainly is." I rotated axes so that all coordinates were in ecliptic spherical polars and stored the result. "Don't you like it?"

"But it looks so *simple*." He moved his finger along the screen. "I mean, it's just a straight line. Not a real trajectory at all. What about the Sun's gravitational field? And you're not making any allowance for the movement of *Manna* while we're flying out there."

"I know." I loaded the flight profile to main memory and as I did so the knot in my stomach seemed to loosen. "That's why I'll be piloting this ship, Will, rather than one of your buddies. We'll be accelerating away from the Sun at a hundred gee, agreed? Did you know that the Sun's acceleration on us here near Mars' orbit is only one three hundred thousandth of that? It has tiny effects on our motion."

"But what about *Manna's* movement in its orbit while we're on the way there? You've ignored that as well."

"For two reasons. First, *Manna* is so far out that it's not moving very fast in its orbit — only half a kilometer a second. More important, we don't know how far Lanhoff's team went in processing *Manna*. Is the body in its original orbit, or did they start it moving in toward the Sun?"

"I've no idea."

"Nor have I. The only thing we can do is fly out there and find out."

I looked at the clock. Time to get moving. "Better say your goodbyes," I went on. "There'll be plenty of chances for us to talk to each other in the next couple of weeks. Probably too many. Two hours from now we'll be on our way. Then we'll be deaf to outside signals until we're out in the Halo and turn off the drive."

"Is that so?" He looked intrigued. "But what about orders that come—"

"Bayes!" Anna Griss was calling softly from below.

Will was gone before I could swivel my chair.

I don't envy the life of the Downsiders, ten billion of them crawling over each other looking for a little breathing space. But there are certain experiences available on Earth and nowhere else in the Solar System.

For instance, I'm told that, during the great circular storms that sweep from the Earth tropics to the northern latitudes, there is an area at the very center — the "eye of the hurricane" as the Downsiders call it— where the wind drops to perfect stillness and the sky overhead turns to deep blue. That's something I'd like to see, just once.

The eye of the hurricane. That was the area of the living-capsule surrounding McAndrew during the *Hoatzin's* flight out to rendezvous with *Manna*.

With me, Anna Griss was in constant battle.

"What are you talking about, no messages?" she said. "I have to be in daily contact with Headquarters."

"Then I'll have to switch off the drive," I explained. "We can't get signals through the plasma shell."

"But that will slow us down! I told Headquarters that we'd only be away for one month — and it's a two-week trip each way even if we keep the drive on all the time."

We were standing by the robochef and I was programming the next meal. It took a few seconds for her last statement to penetrate.

"You told Headquarters *what*? That we'll only be away for a month?"

"That's right. Three days should be long enough to find out what's happening to *Star Harvester*. You said that yourself, and McAndrew agreed."

I turned to face her, noticing again the care she took to make her appearance as well-groomed and attractive as possible.

"Three days should be long enough, sure it should. But you'll be away for a lot more than a month. The trip is two weeks each way in shipboard time. It's twenty-five days each way in Earth time. There's no possible way you can get back home in a month."

Her face flushed red and her eyes glowed — she looked more attractive than ever. "How can that happen?"

"I don't know, but it's standard physics. Ask McAndrew." (I knew well enough, but I'd had more than I wanted of this conversation.)

It was like that all the time. We found it hard to agree on anything, and it became clear as soon as we were on the way that Anna Griss was used to delegating and not to doing. Poor old Will Bayes did triple duty. Luckily there was not too much that could be done without a communications link to Earth — except shout at Will and keep him on the run.

Yet McAndrew — I thought at first I was imagining it — McAndrew was the eye of the hurricane. When she was within two yards of him, Anna Griss became all sweetness and light. She humbly asked him questions about the drive and about time dilation; she deferred to his opinions on everything from diet to Dostoevsky; and she hung first on his word and then on his arm, blinking her eyelashes at him.

It was sickening.

And McAndrew — the great lout — he lapped it up.

"What's she doing?" I said to Bayes when the other two were out of earshot. "She's making a fool of herself."

He winked at me. "You think so, and I think so — but does he think so? Before we left she told me to get a full dossier about him and bring it on this trip. She's been reading it, too. You have to know Anna. What she wants, she gets. Wouldn't look bad for her personal records, would it, to have a five-year cohab contract with the most famous scientist in the System?"

"Don't be silly. She doesn't even like him."

"She does, you know." He stepped closer and lowered his voice. "I know Anna. She has appetites. She wants him, and I think she'd like a cohab contract."

I snorted. "With Mac? That's ridiculous! He belongs to — to science." And I fully believed it, until one morning I found myself applying a pheromonal amplifier behind my ears, and dressing in a new lime-green uniform that fitted a lot closer than my standard garb.

And McAndrew — the great lout — he never noticed or said one word.

While this was going on, we were hurtling outward away from the Sun. With our acceleration at a hundred gee, the living-capsule was snuggled in close to the mass-plate. The plate's gravitational attraction just about balanced the body force on us produced by the ship's acceleration, leaving us in a comfortable and relaxing half-gee environment. The tidal forces caused by the gravity gradient were noticeable only if you looked for them. McAndrew's vacuum drive worked flawlessly, as usual, tapping the zero point energy — "sucking the marrow out of spacetime," as one of Mac's colleagues put it.

"I don't understand," I'd once said to him. "It gets energy out of nothing."

McAndrew looked at me reproachfully. "That's what they used to say in 1910, when mad scientists thought you might get energy from the nucleus of an atom. Jeanie, I thought better of you."

All right, I was squelched — but I didn't understand the drive one bit better.

At the halfway mark we rotated the ship to begin

deceleration and I cut the drive while we did it. Anna Griss had an opportunity to send her backlog of messages, and finally gave Will Bayes a few hours of peace. I was amused to see that her communications gave the impression that she was running everything on the *Hoatzin*. Her increased absence from Headquarters she attributed to delays on the trip. If the level of scientific expertise in the Food Department matched her own she would probably get away with it.

For me, this should have been the best part of the mission, the reason that I would remain in space and never look for a Downside job. With the drive off we flew starward in perfect silence. I stayed by the port, watching the wheel of heaven as the ship turned.

The *Hoatzin* was within five percent of lightspeed. As we performed our end-over-end maneuver, the colors of the starscape Doppler-shifted slowly from red to blue. I caught a last glimpse of Sol and its attendants before the mass-plate shielded them from view. Jupiter was visible through the optical telescope, a tiny point of light a fifth of a degree away from the Sun's dazzling disk. Earth was gone. Its reflected photons had been lost on their hundred-and-fifty-billion-mile outward journey.

I turned the telescope ahead, in a hopeless search for *Manna*. It was a speck in the star-sea, as far ahead of us as the Sun was behind. We would not detect its presence for another two weeks. I looked for it anyway. Then the shield came on to protect us from the sleet of hard radiation and particles caused by our light-chasing velocity. The stars blinked out. I could pay attention again to events inside the *Hoatzin*.

With little else to occupy her attention, Anna delegated her chores to Will Bayes and concentrated everything on charming McAndrew. Will and I received the disdain and the dog work. I sat on my anger and bided my time.

As for Mac, he had disappeared again inside his head. We had loaded a library of references on Lanhoff and the organic materials of the Halo into the computer before we left the Institute. He spent many hours absorbing that information and processing it in the curiously structured personal computer he carries inside his skull. I knew better than to interrupt him. After just a couple of futile attempts to divert him, Anna learned the same lesson. No doubt about it: she was quick. No scientist, but when it came to handling people she did instinctively what I had taken years to learn. Instead of social chit-chat, she studied the same data that McAndrew had been analyzing and asked him questions about it.

"I can see why there ought to be a lot of pre-biotic organic stuff out in the Halo," she said during one of our planned exercise sessions. She was dressed in a tight blue leotard and pedaling hard at the stationary cycle. "But I never did follow Lanhoff's argument that there may be primitive life there, too. Surely the temperature's far too cold."

It was still the "Griss-Lanhoff" Theory for official records, but with us Anna had dropped her pretense of detailed knowledge of Lanhoff's ideas. She had been the driving force to carry his ideas to practical evaluation. We all knew it; for the moment that was enough for her. I had no doubt that we would see another change when we arrived back in the Inner System.

McAndrew was idly lifting and lowering a weighted bar. He hated exercise, but he grudgingly went along with general U.S.F. orders for spaceborne personnel.

"It is cold in the Halo," he said. "Just a few degrees above absolute zero, in most of the bodies. But it may not be *too* cold."

"It's much too cold for us."

"Certainly. That's Lanhoff's point. We know only about the enzymes found on Earth. They allow chemical reactions to proceed in a certain temperature regime. Why shouldn't there be other life-supporting enzymes that can operate at far lower temperatures?"

Anna stopped pedaling, and I paused in my toe-touching.

"Even at the temperatures here in the Halo?" she said.

"I think so." McAndrew paused in his leisurely bar-lifting. "Lanhoff argues that with plenty of complex organic molecules and with a hundred billion separate bodies available, a lot of things might develop in four billion years. He expected to find life somewhere out here — primitive life, probably, but recognizable to us. He was prepared to find it, and the *Star Harvester* was equipped to bring back samples."

We dropped the subject there, but it went running on in my mind while Anna took McAndrew off to program an elaborate meal. I could hear her giggling from the next room, while visions of a Halo civilization ran wild through my brain. Life had appeared there, evolved to intelligence. The Halo society had been disturbed by the arrival of our exploring ship. Lanhoff was a prisoner. His ship had been destroyed. The Inner System and the Halo would go to war...

All complete rubbish. I knew that even as I fantasized, and McAndrew pointed out why when we discussed it later.

"We got the way we are, Jeanie, because life on Earth is one long fight for limited resources. Our bloody-mindedness all started out as food battles, three billion years ago. The Halo isn't like that — *everything* will be part of the food supply. How much evolving would we have done if it rained soup every day and the mountains of Earth had been made of cheese? We'd still be single-celled organisms, happy as clams."

It sounded plausible. McAndrew was so bright that you tended not to question him after a while. But an hour or so later I was worrying again. It occurred to me that Mac was a physicist — when it came to biology he was way outside his field. And *something* had happened to Lanhoff and his ship. What could it have been?

I didn't mention it again, but I worried and fretted, while McAndrew and Anna Griss talked and laughed in the sleeping area and Will Bayes sat next to me in the control area, miserable with his own thoughts. He was so dominated by Anna that I often lost sight of him as an independent person when she was around. Now I found out what made him tick — security.

Poor Will. Looking for security he had joined the safest, most stable organization in Earth's government: the Food Department. That was the place for a solid, Earthbound, risk-free job. He had no desire for adventure, no wish to travel more than a mile from his little apartment. He had been in space only once before, as part of a meeting between the Council and the United Space Federation. Now he was embarked on a mission so far from home that he might survive even if the Sun went nova.

How had it happened? He didn't know. It didn't occur to him to blame Anna. He sat about, uncertain and unhappy. I kept him company, my own worry bump throbbing randomly until at last it was time to throttle the drive and begin final search and rendezvous. *Manna* should be less than ten million kilometers ahead of us.

"QUERY DISTANCE FOR *STAR HARVESTER* APPROACH? DEFAULT VALUE: ZERO."

Our computer began talking to us while we were still scanning ahead for first visual contact. No matter what had happened to the vessel's crew, *Star Harvester's* guidance and control system was still working. Automatic communication for identification and position-matching had begun between the two ships as soon as drive interference was low enough to permit signal transfer.

"Fifty thousand kilometers." I didn't want an immediate rendezvous. "Manual control."

"FIFTY THOUSAND KILOMETERS. CONTROL TRANSFERRED."

"We'll see nothing from that distance." Anna was impatiently watching the hi-mag viewing screen. "We're wasting time. Take us in closer."

We could now see the rough-cut oblong of *Manna* on the imaging radar. A bright cluster of point reflections at one end had to be the *Star Harvester's* assembly of sections. I suddenly had a new feel for the size of the body we were approaching. Lanhoff's ship was of the largest class in the U.S.F. fleet. Next to *Manna* it looked like specks of dust.

"Didn't you hear me?" Anna spoke more loudly. "I don't want a view from a million miles away — take us in closer. That's an order."

I turned to face her. "I think we should be cautious until we know what's going on. We can do a lot of overall checking from this distance. It's safer."

"And it wastes time." Her voice was impatient. "I'm the senior officer on this ship. Now, do as I say, and let's get in closer."

"Sorry." I couldn't delay this moment any longer. "You're the senior officer while we're in free flight, I agree. But when we're in a rendezvous mode with another ship, the pilot immediately has senior decision authority. Check the manuals. I have final say on our movements until we're on the way back to Earth."

There was a long pause while we sat eyeball to

eyeball. Anna's face took on a touch of higher color on the cheeks. McAndrew and Will Bayes held an uncomfortable silence.

"You've had this in mind all along, haven't you?" Anna said softly. Her voice was as cold as Charon. "Damn you, you counted on this. You're going to waste everybody's time while you play at being the boss."

She went through to the other communications department, and I heard the rapid tapping of keys. I didn't know if she was making an entry into the log, or merely calling out the section of the Manual that defines the transfer of authority to the pilot during approach and rendezvous. I didn't care. Super-caution has always paid off for me in the past. Why change a winning hand, even for Anna Griss? I concentrated my attention on the incoming data streams.

Half an hour later Anna came back and sat down without speaking. I was uncomfortably aware of her critical attention over my shoulder. I gestured to the central display screen, where the second series of remotely sensed observations from *Manna* was now appearing. The computer automatically checked everything for anomalies. One new set was displayed in flashing red for our attention.

"That's why I didn't want to rush. I don't think we've been wasting time at all. Mac, look at those radioactivity readings. What do you think of them?"

The computer had done its preliminary analysis, taking the ratio of radioactivity measurements from *Manna* to typical Halo bodies and to the general local background. McAndrew frowned at the smoothed values for a few seconds, then nodded.

"Uh-uh. They're high. About six hundred times as big as I would expect."

I took a deep breath. "So I think we know what happened to Lanhoff. One of the fusion units must have run wild when they were installing it. See now why I'm cautious, folks?"

Anna Griss looked stunned. "Then the crew all got a fatal overdose of radiation?"

"Looks like it." I had proved my point, but not in a way that gave me any satisfaction. I felt sick inside. When a fusion plant blows, there's no hope for the crew.

"No, Jeanie." McAndrew was frowning and rubbing at his sandy hairline. "You're jumping to conclusions. I said the radioactivity was six hundred times as big as it should be, and it is. But it's still low — you could live in it for years, and it wouldn't do you much harm. If a fusion plant had gone, the reading from *Manna* would be a hundred thousand times what we're measuring."

"But what else could give us abnormally high values?"

"I've no idea." He looked at me apologetically. "And we'll never know from this distance. Seems to me that Anna's right. We may have to get in a lot closer for a good look if we really want to find out."

Perhaps the idea that Lanhoff and his crew were almost certainly dead was hitting Anna hard for the first time. At any rate, there was no triumph in her expression as she watched me ease us gingerly forward until we were only ten thousand kilometers from the planetoid. We went slowly, all our sensor input channels wide open. I set the control system to hold us at a constant distance from the surface of *Manna*.

"That's as far as I'm willing to take us," I said. "We're a long way from home, and I won't risk our only way of getting back. Any closer look will have to be done with the transfer pod. Mac, I've not had time to watch the inputs. Is there anything about the ship or about *Manna* that's looking out of line?"

He had been muttering to himself over by a display screen. Now he frowned and pressed a sequence of control keys.

"Maybe. While you were busy I did a complete data transfer from *Star Harvester's* computer to ours. Lanhoff and his crew stopped feeding in new inputs a hundred and fifteen days ago — that's when the signals to Triton Station cut off — but the automatic sensors kept right on recording. See, here's the very first radioactivity reading from *Manna* when they arrived, and there's one taken just a few minutes ago. Look at 'em. Identical. And now look at this. This is the thermal profile of a cross-section through *Manna's* center."

A multi-colored blob filled the screen. It was a set of concentric ellipses, color coded to run from a dark red in its center portion to a violet on the outer boundary.

"Different colors represent different temperatures." McAndrew touched a button, and a dark ellipse appeared around the red and orange portions at the center of the image. "I've just put in the contour for zero degrees Celsius. See? Significant, eh?"

"See what?" said Anna. She was sitting close to McAndrew, their shoulders touching.

"The inside — inside the curve. It's warmer than the melting-point of ice. If *Manna* has a water-ice core, it must be liquid. There's a couple of kilometers of frozen surface, then that liquid interior."

"But we're out in the Halo," I protested. "We're billions of miles from a source of heat. Unless — did Lanhoff already put one of his fusion plants in there?"

"No." McAndrew shook his head. His eyes were sparkling. "The temperature distribution inside was like this before Lanhoff arrived. You're right, Jeanie, it looks impossible — but there it is. *Manna* is three hundred degrees warmer than it has any right to be."

There was a long silence. Finally Will Bayes cleared his throat.

"All right, I'll be the dummy. How can that happen?"

McAndrew gave a little bark of excitement. "Man, if I had a definite answer to that I wouldn't hold out on you. But I can make a good guess. There has to be a natural internal source of heat, something like uranium or thorium deep inside. That's consistent with the high radioactivity value, too." He turned to me. "Jeanie, you have to get us over there, so we can take a good look at the inside."

I hesitated. "Will it be safe?" I said at last. "If it's uranium and water — you can make a nuclear reactor from them."

"Yes — if you try really hard. But it wouldn't happen in nature. Be reasonable, Jeanie."

He was looking at me expectantly, while Anna sat silent. She liked to see him putting the pressure on me for a change.

I shook my head. "If you want to go over there and explore, I won't try to stop you. But my job is the safety of this ship. I'm staying right here."

Logic was all on my side. But even as I spoke I felt that I was giving the coward's answer.

From a distance of fifty kilometers, *Manna* already filled the sky ahead, a black bulk against the star field. *Star Harvester* hung as a cluster of glittering spheres near one end of the planetoid. It steadily grew in size on the screen as the pod moved in, one of its television cameras sending a crisp image back to my observation post on the *Hoatzin*. I could see the dozen Sections and the narrow connectors between them, hollow tubes that were flexible now but electromagnetically stiffened when the drive went on.

"Approaching outermost cargo sphere," said McAndrew. I could see him on the screen that showed the inside of the pod, and a third image showed and recorded for me the pod control settings exactly as he saw them himself.

"Everything still appears perfectly normal," he went on. "We'll make our entry of *Star Harvester* through the Control Section. What is it, Anna?"

He turned to where she was monitoring another sensor, one for which I was not receiving coverage.

"Cut in Unit Four," I said quickly.

At my command the computers sent the image Anna and Will were watching to fill the center screen. I saw a long shaft that extended from a cargo hold of *Star Harvester* and drove down to penetrate the rough surface of *Manna.* The camera tracked its length, switching to deep radar frequencies to generate an image where the shaft plunged below the planetoid's surface.

"Is that a drilling shaft?" I asked. "It looks as though they were getting ready to put a fusion plant in the middle of *Manna.*"

"Wouldn't make sense." McAndrew spoke in an abstracted grunt, and I saw him rubbing at the balding spot on the back of his head. "Lanhoff knew quite well that *Manna* has a liquid core — he had the same computer base to look at as we do. With that core he didn't need a fusion plant at all. The interior would be warm enough already for his enzymes to thrive."

"Was he looking for radioactive material?" I asked; but I could answer that question myself. "It wouldn't make sense. He could locate them the same way we did, from remote measurement. So why would he drill into the core?"

"I'll tell you why," said Anna suddenly. "That's the way Arne always was. Anytime he saw something that he didn't understand he wanted to investigate — he couldn't resist it. I'll bet he drilled to the core to take a closer look at something he'd detected in there — something he couldn't examine closely enough from outside."

The pod had been creeping in nearer and nearer to the hatches on the Control Section. I suddenly realized that once the three of them went inside I would be blind.

"Mac! As soon as you get in there, turn on all the monitors and tell the computer to send the signals back to me here on the *Hoatzin*." I raised my voice. "And one of you has to stay in the Control Section if you go down to the surface. *D'you hear me?*"

He nodded vaguely, but he was already moving towards the hatch. Anna followed him. The last thing I saw before the camera could no longer keep them in view was Will Bayes' face as he turned to take a last worried look around the pod.

Deserted, but in perfect working order; that was the conclusion after a thorough examination of the Control Section of *Star Harvester*.

I had followed on the remote monitors as the other three made their inspection, step by step, and I could not fault them for lack of caution.

"We'll not find Lanhoff and his crew here," said McAndrew finally, when they were back in the main control room. "They must have gone down into the interior of *Manna*. Look at this."

A computer-generated profile of the shaft leading down from the ship to the surface appeared on the screen in front of me. It penetrated the frozen outer crust and terminated in an airlock leading to the liquid core. In the graphics display the broad shaft looked like a hair-thin needle piercing an egg. I was astonished again by the size of the planetoid. Its liquid core held half a million cubic kilometers of liquid. Maybe we would never find Lanhoff and the other crew members.

"We know they went down there," went on McAndrew, as though he was reading my thoughts. He held up a big clear container full of a cloudy yellow fluid. "See? They brought back samples. I'll send you the analysis, but I can tell you now that the results are just what Lanhoff predicted."

"It's high-level organic materials," added Anna. She was looking at me in triumph. "I told you we had to come here to find anything useful. This is just as we expected, but even more concentrated than I hoped. We've found a mother lode. The whole inside of *Manna* is like a rich soup — one of us could probably drink it for dinner and feel well-fed."

Will Bayes was staring at it dubiously, as though he expected Anna to tell him to go ahead and take a swig. "There's things living in it," he said.

My old fears came running back. "Mac, be careful how you handle that. If there are organisms there..."

"Just single-celled ones." McAndrew was excited. "Lanhoff thought he might find primitive life here, and he was quite right about that."

"And it's DNA-based," added Anna. "The same as we are."

I looked more closely at the yellow broth. "So the old theories must be right? Life came to Earth from outside."

"That's the real significance of what they found on *Manna*," said McAndrew. "Life didn't originate on Earth. It began out here in the Halo, or somewhere even farther out, and drifted in to Earth — maybe in the head of a comet, or as smaller meteorites. But see the difference; down on Earth we've had pressures to make us evolve away from a single cell form. Here, there's heat from the radioactive materials in the middle of the planetoid, and there's food galore. There's no reason for evolution as we know it. That's why I don't share your worries, Jeanie, about going down to the interior. There's no evolutionary reason for predators on *Manna*. We won't find sharks and tigers here. It's the Garden of Eden."

Anna nodded her agreement and squeezed his arm. They were both so excited, I wondered if I were the irrational one. The more enthusiastic they became, the more uneasy I felt. No sharks and tigers, maybe — but wouldn't there still be natural selection, even if it went on very slowly?

Shades of Malthusian Doctrine: the number of organisms would follow an increasing geometric progression, and the food resources were finite. Eventually there would have to be a balance, a steady state where dying organisms were just replaced by new ones; and then natural selection ought to take over, with competition between different forms. I didn't have that logic explicitly in mind, all I knew was that something seemed wrong. And I knew that Mac was no biologist. I stared at the screen and shook my head.

"So what happened to Lanhoff and his crew?" I said.

There was a long, uneasy silence.

"Quite right, Jeanie," said McAndrew at last. "We still have no answer to that. But we're going to find one. Will can stay here, and Anna and I will go down there now."

"No." My pulse began to race. "I won't allow it. It's too dangerous."

"We don't agree," said Anna softly. "You heard McAndrew, he says we should look down there — and we'll go in our suits, so we'll be well protected."

Fools rush in where angels fear to tread. Anna Griss knew how to survive in an Earthbound bureaucratic free-for-all, but she was a long way from her home ground. And if she was relying on Mac's instincts to save their skins...

"No." My voice cracked. "Didn't you hear me? I absolutely forbid it. That's an order."

"Is it?" Anna didn't raise her voice. "But you see, we're not in the spacecraft rendezvous mode now, Captain Roker. The *Star Harvester* is tethered to the planetoid. That means I command here, not you." She turned to McAndrew. "Come on, let's make sure we're fully prepared. We don't want to take any risks."

Before I could speak again she reached forward to the monitor. I suddenly found that I was looking into a blank screen.

It took me five long minutes to patch in a substitute communications link between the computers of the *Hoatzin* and the *Star Harvester*.

When the auxiliary screen came alive I saw Will Bayes fiddling with the control bank.

"Where are they, Will?"

He turned quickly. "They're on the way down to the surface. Jeanie, I couldn't stop them. I said they shouldn't go, but Anna wouldn't take any notice of me. And she has Mac convinced, too."

I knew McAndrew — he hadn't taken any convincing at all. Show him an interesting intellectual problem, and preservation of life and limb came a poor second to curiosity.

"Don't worry about that, Will. Link me to the computer on board the transfer pod."

"What are you going to do?"

"Go after them. Maybe Mac is right, and they'll be fine, and in no danger. But I want to be the rearguard and trail along behind them, just in case."

Will could have probably flown the pod to pick me up in an emergency, and I knew that the computer could have done it with a single rendezvous command from me. But Will and the computer would have followed the book on permissible rates of acceleration and docking distances. I took remote control of the pod myself, overrode the computer, broke every rule in the Manual, and had the pod docked at the *Hoatzin* in less than fifteen minutes. Going back to the *Star Harvester* we beat that time by a hundred seconds.

Will was waiting at the main lock with his suit on. "Something has gone wrong," he said. "They told me they would send a signal every ten minutes, but it's been over twenty since the last one. I was going to go down and see what's happening."

"Did you see any weapons on board when you were looking over the ship earlier?" I asked.

"Weapons?" Will frowned. "No. Lanhoff had no reason to carry anything like that. Wait a minute, though, what about a construction laser? That can be pretty dangerous, and there are plenty of those in Section Six."

"Get one." I was preparing the transfer pod for a rapid departure from *Star Harvester* if we needed it. One time in a thousand, a precaution like that pays off.

"I'll get two."

Will was off along the tube between the Sections before I could argue with him. I didn't want him with me in the middle of *Manna* — I wanted him available to help me out if I ran into trouble myself.

What was I expecting? I had no idea, but I felt a lot better when I had my suit firmly closed and a portable construction laser tucked under one arm. Will and I went together to the entrance of the long tunnel that led down to the interior of *Manna*.

"Right. No farther for you." I looked at the peculiar way he was holding the laser, and wondered what would happen if he had to use it. "You stay here, at the head of the shaft. I'll send you a signal every ten minutes."

"That's what Anna said." His words echoed after me as I dropped away down the broad shaft.

The illumination came only from the light on my suit. Seen from the inside, the shaft out of the cargo hold dropped away in front of me like a dark, endless tunnel. *Manna's* gravity was negligible, so there were none of the Earth dangers of an accelerated fall. But I had to take care to remain clear of the side of the tunnel — it narrowed as we went deeper into the planetoid's crust. I drifted out to the center of the shaft, turned on the coupling between the suit's conducting circuits and the pulsed field in the tunnel wall, and made a swift, noiseless descent.

The three kilometer downward swoop took less than a minute. All the way to the airlock at the bottom I watched carefully for any sign that McAndrew and Anna had met trouble there. Everything was normal.

The drilling mechanism at the end of the shaft was still in position. Normally the shaft could extend itself through hard, frozen ice at a hundred feet an hour. When they came to the liquid interior, however, Lanhoff had arrested the progress of the drill and installed the airlock. It was a cylindrical double chamber about six meters across, with a movable metal wall separating the two halves.

I cycled through the first part of the lock, closed the wall, and went forward to the second barrier. I hesitated in front of it. The wall was damp with a viscous fluid. The airlock had been used recently. Anna and McAndrew had passed through here to the liquid core of the planetoid. If I wished to find them I must do the same.

Was there a port? I wanted to take a good look at the interior of *Manna* before I was willing even to consider going through into it.

The only transparent area was a tiny section a few inches across, where a small panel had been removed and replaced by a thin sheet of clear plastic. Lanhoff must have arranged it this way, to make an observation point before he would risk a venture beyond the lock. Despite his curiosity referred to by Anna, it suggested that he was a cautious man — and it seemed to increase the odds against me. I was diving blind, and in a hurry.

I drifted across and put the faceplate of my suit flat against the transparent plate. The only illumination in the interior was coming from my suit, and because it had to shine through the port I was confused by back-scattered light. I held my hand to shield my eyes, and peered in.

My first impression was of a snowstorm. Great drifting white flakes swam lazily across the field of view. As I adjusted to the odd lighting, the objects resolved themselves to white, feathery snowballs, ranging in size from a grape to a closed fist. The outer parts were in constant vibration, providing a soft-edged, uncertain shimmer as they moved through the pale yellow fluid of *Manna's* interior.

Even as I watched, the number and density of the white objects was increasing. The snowfall became a blizzard. And floating far away from me, almost at the limit of vision, I saw two great white shapes. They were travesties of the human form, bloated and blurred outlines like giant snowmen. Every second they grew bigger, as more and more snowballs approached and adhered to their surfaces. They were swelling steadily, rounding to become perfect spheres.

I shivered in my suit. Alien. The figures looked totally alien, but I knew what I had found. At their centers, unable to see, move, or send messages, were McAndrew and Anna. As I watched I thought of the guardian white corpuscles in my own blood-stream. The feathery balls were like them, busy leukocytes crowding around to engulf and destroy the foreign organisms that dared to invade the body of *Manna*.

How could I rescue them? They were in no danger for the first few minutes, but the snowballs would muffle the escape of heat from the suits. Unless the clinging balls were cleared away, Anna and McAndrew would soon die a blind and stifling death.

My first instinct was to open the lock and plunge through to the interior. Another look at the feathery snowballs changed my mind about that. They were thicker than ever, drifting up from the deep interior of the planetoid. If I went out there they would have me covered in less than a minute. The laser that I had brought with me was useless. If I used it in water, it would waste its energy turning a small volume close to me to steam. And I had no other weapon with me.

Return to the *Star Harvester*, and look for inspiration there? It might be too late for McAndrew and Anna.

I went across to the side of the lock. There was a dual set of controls for the drilling shaft there, installed so that drilling progress could be monitored and modified on the spot. If I started the drill, the fluid ahead would offer little resistance. The tunnel would extend further into the liquid, far enough to enclose the area where the two misshapen spheres were floating. So if I opened the lock first, then activated the drill...

The timing would be crucial. Once the lock was open, liquid would be drawn into the evacuated area around me. Then I would have to operate the drill unit so that the open lock moved to enclose the two swollen masses of snowballs, close the lock again, and pump the liquid out. But if I was too slow, the blizzard of snow would close in on me, too, and I would be as helpless as McAndrew and Anna.

Delay wouldn't help. I pressed the lever that opened the lock, moved to the side of the chamber, and started the drill extender.

Liquid rushed in through the opening aperture. I struggled to move forward against its pressure, fighting my way back to the lock control.

There was a swirling tide of white all around me. Feathered balls hit my suit and stuck to it, coating the faceplate in an opaque layer. Within thirty seconds I could not see anything, and my arms and legs were sluggish in their movements as I clung to the lock lever.

I had not anticipated that I would become blind so quickly. Were McAndrew and Anna already swept into the chamber by the advancing drill and the opened lock? I had no way of knowing. I waited as long as I dared, then heaved at the lever. My arm moved slowly, hampered by the mass of snow-spheres clinging to it. I felt the control close, and sensed the muffled roar of the pump. I tried to thrash my arms, to shake off the layers that clogged their movement. It was useless. Soon I was unable to move at all. I was in darkness. If the snowballs could tolerate vacuum, McAndrew and Anna and I would go the same way as Lanhoff; we'd be trapped inside our suits, our communication units useless, until the heat built up to kill us.

It was a long, long wait (only ten minutes, according to the communications link on board the ship — it felt like days). Suddenly there was a lightening of the darkness in front of my faceplate. I could move my arms again. The feather balls were falling off me and being pumped out through the airlock.

I turned around, peering through the one clear spot on my faceplate. There were two spherical blobs with me in the chamber, and they were gradually taking on human shapes. After another five minutes I could see parts of their suits.

"Anna! Mac! Turn around."

They clumsily rotated to face me. I saw them staring out of the faceplates, white-faced but undeniably alive.

"Come on. Let's get out of here."

"Wait." McAndrew was taking a bag from the side of his suit, opening it, and scooping up samples of liquid and snowballs. I decided that he was terminally crazy.

"Don't fool with that, Mac — let's get out of here."

What was the danger now? I didn't know, and I wasn't going to wait to find out. I reached out, grabbed his arm, and began to haul him back through to the other chamber. We were still sloshing in a chaos of fluid and floating feather balls.

Anna grabbed at my arm, so I was towing both of them. I could hear her teeth chattering.

"God," she said. "I thought we were dead. I knew it, it was just like being dead, no sound, nothing to see, not able to move."

"I know the feeling," I grunted — they were a weighty pair. "How did you get caught? I mean, why didn't you get back into the airlock as soon as the snowballs arrived?"

We were scooting back up the tunnel as fast as we could, McAndrew still clinging to his bucket of specimens.

"We didn't see any danger." Anna was gradually getting control of herself, and her grip on my arm had loosened. "When we first came through the lock there were maybe half a dozen of those fuzzballs in sight. McAndrew said we ought to get a specimen before we left, because they were a more complex lifeform than any that Lanhoff had reported. And then they started to arrive in millions, from all directions. Our suits were covered before we could get away — we didn't have a chance."

"But what are they — and what were they doing?" I said.

We had reached the top of the tunnel and entered the cargo sphere. There was no sign of Will Bayes — it occurred to me that I hadn't sent him a single signal of any kind since I left. He must be frantic. I hit the switch that would fill the chamber with air. For some reason I was keener to get out of that suit than I had ever been.

McAndrew placed his container on the floor and we all began to work our way free, starting with the helmets.

"What were they doing? Now that's a good question," he said. "While we were stuck in the middle of them down there, I had time to give it some thought."

Well, that sounded right. When McAndrew stops thinking, he'll be dead.

"Lanhoff and I made a big goof," he went on. "And for him it was a fatal one. We both argued that the food supply here was so plentiful that there'd be no pressure to evolve. But we forgot a basic fact. An organism needs more than food to survive."

"What else? You mean moisture?" I had my suit off, and air had never tasted so good.

"Moisture, sure. But as well as that it needs warmth. Here on Manna, the evolutionary pressure is to get near a heat source. If you're out too far from the center, you become part of the frozen outer layer. Those snowballs normally live down near the middle, getting as close as they can to the radioactive fragments that provide the warmth."

Anna was out of her suit. Now that we were safe, she was making a tremendous effort to gain her self-possession. Her shivering had stopped and she was even patting at her damp and tangled hair. She peered curiously down at the container of feathered snowballs. They were still moving slowly around in the yellow liquid.

"The radioactivity must speed up their rate of evolution, too," she said. "And I was thinking they wanted to *eat* us."

"I doubt that we're very appetizing, compared with their free soup," said McAndrew. "No, if there hadn't been so many of them they'd have been harmless enough. But when we came along, they sensed the heat given off by our suits, and they tried to cuddle up to us. They didn't want to eat us, all they were after was a place by the fireside."

Anna nodded. "This is going to create a sensation when we get to Earth. We'll have to take a lot of specimens back with us."

She was reaching down towards the open container. One of the snowballs had fully opened and was a delicate white mass of feathery cilia. She put out her forefinger as though she intended to touch it.

"*Don't do that!*" I shouted.

Maybe she was not even considering any such thing, but my loud command made her stiffen. She looked up at me angrily.

"You saved us, Captain Roker, and I appreciate that. But don't forget who is in charge of this expedition. And don't try to order me around — ever."

"Don't be a fool," I said. "I wasn't ordering you around — I was speaking for your own good. Don't you have any idea what might be dangerous?"

My own tone must have betrayed my impatience and anger. Anna stiffened, and her color went from white to red.

"McAndrew has pointed out that these lifeforms

would have been quite harmless if there had not been so many of them," she said. And then she reached forward into the container and deliberately touched the expanded snowball with her forefinger. She looked up at me. "Satisfied? They're perfectly harmless."

Then she screamed. The ball was clinging to her finger as she withdrew it, and the cilia had enveloped it as far as the second joint.

"It won't come off!" She began shaking her hand desperately. "It hurts."

I swung my helmet hard at her finger, and the edge caught the ball near its middle. It was jarred loose and flew across the chamber. Anna stood and looked ruefully at her hand. The finger was reddened and swollen.

"Damnation. It stings like hell." She turned accusingly to McAndrew and held forward her injured hand. "You fool. You told me they're harmless, and now look at my finger. This is your fault."

We all stared at her hand. The swelling on her forefinger seemed to be getting bigger and redder.

McAndrew had been standing there with a startled and perplexed expression on his face. Before I could stop him he picked up the laser that I had placed on the floor, aimed it at Anna, and pressed the switch. There was a crackle from the wall behind Anna, and the smoke of burned tissue. Her arm had been neatly severed above the elbow, and the wound cauterized with a single sweep of the instrument.

Anna looked at the stump with bulging eyes, groaned, and started to fall sideways to the floor.

"Mac!" I grabbed for the laser. "What the hell are you doing?"

His face was pale. "Come on," he said. "Let's get her to the robodoc. This isn't too serious — she'll have to wait to regenerate it until we get home and find a biofeedback machine, but we can't help that."

"But why did you do it?"

"I made one bad mistake, back there outside the air lock." We were hurrying back through the ship, supporting Anna between us.

"I don't want to make another one," he went on. "Lanhoff's notes on the single-celled organisms inside *Manna* pointed out that they didn't have a sexual method of reproduction, but they have something that resembles the plasmids down on Earth — they swap sections of DNA with each other, to get the mixing of offspring characteristics. I wondered about that when I read it, because it suggests a mechanism for speeding up an evolutionary process. But I skipped on past it, because I was so sure there would be no evolutionary pressures at work inside *Manna*."

We were almost at the Control Section of *Star Harvester*. Unless Will had gone mad and flown off in the transfer pod, we were only twenty minutes away from the *Hoatzin's* robodoc. Anna was coming out of her faint, and groaning a little.

"Mac, I still don't see it. Why does the evolution method of the creatures inside *Manna* mean you had to burn off Anna's arm?"

"If they do swap tissue regularly, their immune reaction systems have to recognize and tolerate the exchange. But we're not made like that — Anna's immune reaction system might mop up the materials that the snowball transferred to her bloodstream, but more likely the stuff would have killed her. I daren't take the chance."

We had come to the hatch that led to the transfer pod. Will Bayes stood there. For a fraction of a second he looked relieved, then he took in the whole scene. We were all pale and panting. I was dragging Anna along while she lay in a near-faint with only a stump of a right arm; and McAndrew, wild-eyed and lunatic, was bounding along behind us, still brandishing the laser.

Will backed away in horror, his hands held in front of him.

"Come on, man, don't just stand there," said McAndrew. "Get out of the way. We've got to get Anna over to our ship and let the doc have a go at her. The sooner the better."

Will took a hesitant step to one side. "She's not dead, then?"

"Of course she's not dead — she'll be as good as new once she's been through a regeneration treatment. We'll have to keep her sedated for the trip back, but she'll be all right."

I went to the controls of the pod, ready to take us back to the *Hoatzin*. It hadn't occurred to me that Anna would be quieted down for the return trip, but I wouldn't be the one to complain.

"You mean we're actually going home?" asked Will. His tone suggested that he had never expected to see Earth again.

"Just for a while." McAndrew had settled Anna as comfortably as he could, and now he was looking disconsolately around him for the bucket of lifeform samples that we had left behind in the Control Section of *Star Harvester*.

"We'll be back, Will, don't you worry," he said. "Anna was quite right: when Lanhoff found *Manna* he stumbled across a real treasure trove. We've hardly scratched the surface. As soon as we can get organized, there'll be another party from the Food Department. And I'm sure we'll all be here with it."

My attention was mainly on the controls, so I'm not sure that I heard Will's low mumble correctly. But I think he was saying something about a transfer to the Energy Department.

FIFTH CHRONICLE: ROGUEWORLD

The laws of probability not only permit coincidences; they absolutely insist on them.

I was sitting in the pilot's chair with McAndrew at my shoulder. Neither of us had spoken for a long time. We were in low polar orbit, sweeping rapidly across the surface of Vandell with all pod sensors wide open. I don't know what McAndrew was thinking, but my mind wasn't fully on the displays. Part of me was far away — one and a quarter light years away, back on Earth.

Why not? Our attention here was not necessary. The surveillance sensors were linked to the shipboard main computer, and the work was done automatically. If anything new turned up, we would hear of it at once. But nothing new could happen — nothing that mattered.

For the moment, I needed time to myself. Time to think about Jan; to remember her seventeen years, as a baby, as a slender child, as a fierce new intelligence, as a young woman; time to resent the chain of circumstance that had brought her and Sven Wicklund here, to die. Somewhere below these opalescent clouds, down on the cold surface of the planet, our sensor systems were seeking two corpses. Nothing else mattered.

I knew that McAndrew shared my sorrow, but he handled it in a different way. His attention was focussed on the data displays, in a concentration so intense that my presence didn't matter at all. His eyes lacked all expression. Every couple of minutes he shook his head and muttered to himself: "This makes no sense — no sense at all."

I stared at the screen in front of me, where the dark vortex had again appeared. It came and went, clearly visible on some passes, vanished on others. Now it looked like a funnel, a sooty conical channel down through the glowing atmosphere, the only break in the planet's swirling cloud cover. We had passed right over it twice before, the first time with rising hopes; but the sensors had remained quiet. It was not a signal. It had to be a natural feature, something like Jupiter's Red Spot, some random coincidence of twisting gas streams.

Coincidence. Again, coincidence.

"The laws of probability not only permit coincidences; they absolutely insist on them."

I couldn't get McAndrew's words out of my head.

He had spoken them months ago, on a day that I would never forget. It was Jan's seventeenth birthday, the first time of choice. I was down on Earth, choking on the dirty air, meeting with the new head of External Affairs. McAndrew was at his office at the Penrose

Institute. We were both trying to work, but I for one wasn't succeeding too well. I wondered what was going through Jan's head, waiting for graduation from the Luna system.

"Naturally, there will have to be some changes," Tallboy was saying. "That's to be expected, I'm sure you'll agree. We are reviewing all programs, and though I am sure that my predecessor and I" — for the third time he had avoided using Woolford's name — "agree on overall objectives, we may have slightly different priorities."

Dr. Tallboy was a tall man, with a lofty brow and a keen, intellectual eye. Although we had shaken hands and muttered the conventional greetings a couple of times before, this was our first working meeting.

I pulled my wandering attention back to him. "When will the program review be finished?"

He shook his head and smiled broadly (but there were no laugh lines around his eyes). "As I'm sure you know very well, Captain Roker, these things take time. There has been a change of Administration. We have many new staff to train. There have been new Budget cuts, too, and the Office of External Affairs has suffered more than most. We will continue all the essential programs, be assured of that. But it is also my mandate to expend public funds wisely, and that cannot be done in haste."

"What about the Penrose Institute's experimental programs?" I said — a bit abruptly, but so far Tallboy had offered nothing more than general answers. I knew I couldn't afford to seem impatient, but my meeting wouldn't last much longer.

He hesitated, then sneaked a quick look at the crib sheets of notes in front of him on the desk. It didn't seem to help, because when he looked up the fine and noble brow was wrinkled in perplexity.

"I'm thinking particularly of the Alpha Centauri expedition," I prompted him. "Dr. Tallboy, a quick go-ahead on that means a great deal to us."

"Of course." He was nodding at me seriously. "A great deal. Er, I'm not completely familiar with that *particular* activity, you understand. But I assure you, as soon as my staff review is completed..."

Our meeting lasted fifteen more minutes, but long before that I felt I had failed. I had come here to push for a decision, to persuade Tallboy that the program should go ahead as planned and approved by Woolford; but bureaucratic changes had changed everything. Forget the fact that McAndrew and I had been planning the Alpha Centauri expedition for a year; forget the fact that the *Hoatzin* had been provisioned, fuelled, and inspected, and the flight plans filed long since with the USF. Forget the masses of new observational equipment that we had loaded onto the ship with such loving care. That had been under the old Administration. When the new one came in everything had to start again from scratch. And not one damned thing I could do about it.

I did manage to extract one promise from Tallboy before he ushered me out with polite assurances of his interest and commitment to the Institute's work. He would visit the Institute personally, as soon as his schedule permitted. It wasn't anything to celebrate, but it was all I could squeeze out of him.

"He'll visit here *in person*?" said McAndrew — I had run for the phone as soon as I cleared the Office of External Affairs. "Do you think he'll do it?"

I nodded. "I didn't leave it up to him. I saw his secretary on the way out, and made sure that we're in the book. He'll do it."

"When?" McAndrew had been in Limperis' office when I called him, and it was the older man who leaned forward to ask the question.

"Eight days from now. That was the first gap in his schedule. He'll spend most of the day at the Institute."

"Then we're home free," said McAndrew. He was cracking his finger joints — a sure sign of high excitement. "Jeanie, we can put on an all-day show here that'll just blow him away. Wenig has a new E-M field stabilizer, Macedo says she can build a cheap detector for small Halo collapsars, and I've got an idea for a better kernel shield. And if we can ever get him to talk about it, Wicklund's cooking up something new and big out on Triton Station. Man, I'm telling you, the Institute hasn't been this productive in years. Get Tallboy here, and he'll go out of his mind."

Limperis shot a quick sideways glance at McAndrew, then looked back at the screen. He raised his eyebrows. I could read the expression on that smooth, innocent-looking face, and I agreed with him completely. If you wanted a man to quantize a nonlinear field, diagonalize a messy Hamiltonian, or dream up a delicate new observational test for theories of kernel creation, you couldn't possibly do better than McAndrew. But that would be his downfall now. He could never accept that the rest of the world might be less interested in physics than he was.

Limperis started that way, but years of budget battles as head of the Institute had taught him to play in a different league. "So what do you think, Jeanie?" he said to me, when Mac had finished babbling.

"I don't know." I shrugged. "I couldn't read Tallboy. He's an unknown quantity. We'd better look up his background, see if that gives us some clue to what makes him tick. As it is, you'll have to try it. Show him everything you've got at the Institute, and hope for the best."

"What about the Expedition?"

"Same for that. Tallboy acted as though he'd never

heard of Alpha Centauri. The *Hoatzin's* just about ready to go, but we need Tallboy's blessing. External Affairs controls all the—"

"*Call from Luna,*" cut in a disembodied voice. "*Central Records for Professor McAndrew. Level Two priority. Will you accept interrupt, or prefer re-schedule?*"

"Accept," said McAndrew and I together — even though it wasn't my call. It had to be from Jan.

"*Voice, tonal, display or hard copy output?*"

"Voice," replied McAndrew firmly. I was less sure of that. He had done it so that I could receive the message, too, but we would have to witness each other's disappointment if it was bad news.

"*Message for Arthur Morton McAndrew,*" went on the neutral voice. "*Message begins. January Pelham, ID 128-129-00476, being of legal age of choice, will file for parental assignment as follows:- Father: Arthur Morton McAndrew, ID 226-788-44577. Mother: Jean Pelham Roker, ID 547-314-78281. Name change filed for January Pelham Roker McAndrew. Parental response and acceptance is required. Reply via Luna free circuit 33, link 442. Message ends.*"

I had never seen McAndrew look so pleased. It was doubly satisfying to him to have me on the line when the word came through — I was sure that the Communications Group were trying to track me now through Tallboy's office, not knowing I was tapped into Mac's line.

"What's the formal date for parental assignment?" I asked.

There was a two second pause while the computer made confirmation of identity from my voiceprint, sent that information over the link from L-4 to Luna, decided how to handle the situation, and connected us all into one circuit. "*Message for Jean Pelham Roker. Message begins: January Pelham, ID 128—*"

"No need to repeat," I said. "Message received. Repeat, what is the formal date for parental assignment?"

"Two hundred hours U.T., subject to satisfactory parental responses."

"That's too soon," said McAndrew. "We won't have enough time for chromosomal confirmation."

"Chromosomal confirmation waived."

On the screen in front of me McAndrew blushed bright with surprise and pleasure. Not only had Jan filed for us as official parents as soon as legally permitted, she had done so without knowing or caring what the genetic records showed. The waiver was a definite statement: whether or not McAndrew was her biological father would make no difference to her; she had made her decision.

For what it was worth, I could have given my own assurance. Some evidence is just as persuasive to me as chromosomal mapping. No one who had seen that blind, inward look on Jan's face when she was tackling an abstract problem would ever doubt that she was McAndrew's flesh and blood. I had cursed that expression a hundred times, as McAndrew left me to worry alone while he disappeared on a voyage of exploration and discovery inside his own head.

Never mind; McAndrew had his good points.

"Parental acceptance by Jean Pelham Roker," I said.

"Parental acceptance by Arthur Morton McAndrew," said Mac.

Another brief pause, then: *"Acceptance received and recorded. Formal assignment confirmed for two hundred hours U.T. Arrange location through Luna link 33-442. Hard copy output follows. Is there additional transfer?"*

"No."

"Link terminated."

While the computer initiated hard copy output to the terminal at the Institute, I did a little calculation.

"Mac, we have a problem — Jan's acceptance ceremony is set for the same time as Tallboy's visit."

"Of course," He looked surprised that I hadn't seen it immediately. "We can handle it. She'll come out here. She'll want to visit — she hasn't been to the Institute since Wicklund went out to Triton Station."

"But you'll be too tied up with Tallboy to spend much time with her. What rotten luck."

McAndrew shrugged, and it was enough to start him talking. "Whenever a set of independent events occurs randomly in time or space, you'll notice event-clusters. They're inevitable. That's all there is to coincidences. If you assume that event arrival times follow a Poisson distribution, and just go ahead and calculate the probability that a given number will occur in some small interval of time, you'll find—"

"Take him away," I said to Limperis.

He slapped McAndrew lightly on the shoulder. "Come on. Coincidence or not, this is a day for celebration. You're a father now, and thanks to Jeanie we've got Tallboy coming out here to see the show." He winked at me. "Though maybe Jan will change her mind when she hears Mac talk for a few hours, eh, Jeanie? Poor girl, she's not used to it, the way you are."

McAndrew just grinned. He was riding too high for a little gentle joshing to have any effect. "If you pity the poor lass at all," he said, "it should be for the Philistine space-jock of a mother she'll be getting. If I wanted to talk to Jan about probability distributions, she'd listen to me."

She probably would, too. I'd seen her math profiles.

Limperis was reaching out to cut the connection, but Mac hadn't quite finished. "You know, the laws of probability not only permit coincidences," he said. "They—"

He was still talking when the screen went blank.

I had no more official business down on Earth, but I didn't head out at once. Limperis was quite right, it was a time for celebration — you didn't become a parent every day. I went over to the Asgard restaurant, up at the very top of Mile High, and ordered the full panoramic dinner. In some ways I wasted my money, because no matter what the sensories threw at me I hardly noticed them. I was thinking back through seventeen years, to the time when Jan was born, so small that she could put her whole fist in the old silver thimble McAndrew's friends gave her as a birthgift.

It was a few years later that I realized we had something exceptional on our hands — Jan had breezed through every test they could give her. I felt as though I had a window to McAndrew's own past, because I was sure he had been the same way thirty years earlier. The mandatory separation years hadn't been bad at all, because McAndrew and I had spent most of them on long trips out, where the Earth-years sped by in months of shipboard time. But I was very glad they were over now. In a few more days, McAndrew, Jan and I would be officially and permanently related.

By the time I finished my meal I probably wore the same foolish smile as I had seen on Mac's face before Limperis cut the video. Neither of us could see beyond the coming ceremony to a grimmer future.

The next few days were too busy for much introspection. The Penrose Institute had been in free orbit, half a million miles out, but to make it more convenient for Tallboy's visit Limperis moved us back to the old L-4 position. In a general planning meeting we decided what we would show off, and how much time could be spared for each research activity. I'd never heard such squabbling. The concentration of brain power found at the Institute meant that a dozen or more important advances were competing for Tallboy's time. Limperis was as impartial and diplomatic as ever, but there was no way he could smooth Macedo's feelings when she learned that she would have less than ten minutes to show off three years of effort on electromagnetic coupling systems. And Wenig was even worse — he wanted to be in on all the presentations, and still have time to promote his own work on ultra-dense matter.

At the same time McAndrew was having problems of quite a different kind with Sven Wicklund. That young physicist was still out on Triton Station, where he had gone complaining that the Inner System was all far too crowded and cluttered and he needed some peace and quiet.

"What the devil's he up to out there?" grumbled McAndrew. "I need to know for the Tallboy briefing, but a one-way radio signal out to Neptune takes four hours — even if he wanted to talk, and he doesn't. And I'm sure he's on to something new and important. Blast him, what am I supposed to report?"

I wasn't too sympathetic. To me it seemed no more than poetic justice. McAndrew had annoyed me and others often enough in the past, when he refused to talk about his own ideas while they were in development — "half-cooked", to use his phrase. Apparently Sven Wicklund was just the same, and it served Mac right.

But the Institute needed all the impressive material they could find, so Mac continued to send long and futile messages needling Wicklund to tell him something — anything — about his latest work. He got nowhere.

"And he's the brightest of the lot of us," said McAndrew. Coming from him that was a real compliment. His colleagues were less convinced.

"No, I don't think so," said Wenig when I asked him. "Anyway, it's a meaningless question. The two of them are quite different. Imagine that Newton and Einstein had lived at the same time. McAndrew's like Newton, as much at home with experiment as theory. And Wicklund's *all* theory, he needs help to change his pants. But it's still a fool question. Which is better, food or drink? — that makes as much sense. The main thing is that they're contemporaries, and they can talk to each other about what they're doing."

Except that Wicklund refused to do so, at least at this stage of his work. McAndrew finally gave up the effort to draw him out and concentrated on matters closer to home.

My own part in planning the show for Tallboy was a minor one. It had to be. My degrees in Gravitational Engineering and Electrical Engineering wouldn't get me in as janitor at the Institute. My job was to concentrate on the *Hoatzin*. Until we started work (budget permitting) on a more advanced model, this ship carried the best available version of the McAndrew Drive. It could manage a hundred gee acceleration for months, and a hundred and ten gee for as long as the crew was willing to forego kitchen and toilet facilities.

The Office of External Affairs officially owned *Hoatzin* and the Institute operated her, but I secretly thought of the ship as mine. No one else had ever flown her.

I had faint hopes that Tallboy might like a demonstration flight, maybe a short run out to Saturn. We could be there and back in a couple of days. The ship was all ready, for that and more — if he approved it, we were all set for the Alpha Centauri probe (forty-four days of shipboard time; not bad, when you remember that the first manned trip to Mars had taken more than nine months). We could be on our interstellar journey in a week or two.

All right, I wasn't being realistic; but I think everyone at the Institute nourished the secret dream that their project would be the one that caught Tallboy's imagination, occupied his time, and won his approval. Certainly the amount of work that went into preparation supported my idea.

The timing was tight but manageable. Jan would arrive at the Institute at 09:00, with the official parental assignment to take place at 09:50. Tallboy's grand show-and-tell began at 10:75 and went on for as long as he was willing to look and listen. Jan was scheduled to leave again at 19:90, so I had mixed feelings about Tallboy's tour. The longer he stayed, the more impressed he was likely to be, and we wanted that. But we also wanted to spend time with Jan before she had to dash back to Luna for graduation and sign-out.

In the final analysis everything went off as well — and as badly — as it could have. At 09:00 exactly Jan's ship docked at the Institute. I was pleased to see that it was one of the new 5-gee mini-versions of the McAndrew Drive, coming into use at last in the Inner System. My bet was that Jan had picked it just to please him. You don't need the drive at all for pond-hopping from Luna to L-4.

The parental assignment ceremony is traditionally conducted with a lot of formality. It was against custom to step out of the docking area as soon as the doors were opened, march up to the father-to-be, and grab him in a huge and affectionate hug. McAndrew looked startled for a moment, then swelled red as a turkeycock with pleasure. I got the same shock treatment a few moments later. Then instead of letting go, Jan and I held each other at arm's length and took stock.

She was going to be taller than me — already we were eye to eye. In three years she had changed from a super-smart child to an attractive woman, whose bright grey eyes told me something else: if I didn't take a hand, Jan would twist McAndrew round her little finger. And she knew I knew it. We stood smiling at each other, while a dozen messages passed between us; affection, pride, anticipation, sheer happiness — and challenge. Mac and I were getting a handful.

We gave each other a final hug, then she took my hand and Mac's and we went on through to meet with Limperis and the others. The official ceremony would not begin for another half hour, but we three knew that the important part was already completed.

"So what about your graduation present?" asked McAndrew, as we were waiting to begin. I had wondered about it myself. It was the first thing that most new children wanted to talk about.

"Nothing expensive," said Jan. "I think it would be nice just to make a trip — I've seen too much of Luna." Her tone was casual, but the quick sideways look at me told another story.

"Is that all?" said Mac. "Och, that doesn't sound like much of a present. We thought you'd be wanting a cruise pod, at the very least."

"What sort of trip?" I asked.

"I'd like to visit Triton Station. I've heard about it all my life, but apart from you, Jeanie, I don't know of anyone who's ever been there. And you never talk about it."

"I don't think that's a good idea at all," I said. The words popped out before I could stop them.

"Why not?"

"It's too far out — too isolated. And there'll be nothing at all for you to do there. It's a long way away." I had reacted before I had rational arguments, and now I was waffling.

Jan knew it. "A long way away! When the two of you have been light years out. You've been on trips thousands of times as far as Triton Station."

I hesitated and she bore in again. "You're the one who told me that most people stick around like moles in their own backyards, when the Halo's waiting for them and there's a whole Universe to be explored."

What could I say? That there was one rule for most people, and another for my daughter? Triton Station is in the backyard, in terms of interstellar space; but it's also out near the edge of the old Solar System, too far away for Inner System comforts. An excellent place for a message relay between the Halo and the Inner System, that's why it was put there in the first place. But it's small and spartan. And the station isn't down on Neptune's satellite, the way that most people think. It's in orbit around Triton, with just a small manned outpost on the surface of the satellite itself for supplies, raw materials, and cryogenics research. There are a few unmanned stations bobbing about in the icy atmosphere of Neptune itself, 350,000 kilometers away, but nobody in their right mind ever goes to visit them.

The sixty Station personnel are a strange mixture of dedicated researchers and psychological loners who find the Inner System and even the Titan Colony much too crowded for them. Some of them love it there, but as soon as the 100-gee balanced drive is in general use, Triton Station will be only a day and a half flight away and well within reach of a weekend vacation. Then I suppose the disgusted staff will curse the crowds, and move farther out into the Halo itself seeking their old peace and quiet.

"You'll be bored," I said, trying another argument. "They're more antisocial than you can imagine, and you won't know anybody there."

"Yes, I will. I know Sven Wicklund, and we always got along famously. He's still there, isn't he?"

"He is, blast him," said McAndrew. "But as to what he's been up to out there for the past six months..."

His voice tailed away and the old slack-jawed, half-witted look crept over his face. He was rubbing his fingers gently along his sandy, receding hairline, and I realized where his thoughts were taking him.

"Don't be silly, Mac. I hope you're not even considering it. If Wicklund won't tell you what he's doing, you don't imagine he'll talk to Jan about it, do you, if she's just at Triton Station for a short visit?"

"Well, I don't know," began McAndrew. "It seems to me there's a *chance*—"

"I feel sure he'll tell me," said Jan calmly.

Unfortunately, so was I. Wicklund had been bowled over by Jan when she was only fourteen and didn't have a tenth of her present firepower. If she could lead him around then with a ring through his nose, today with her added wiles it would be no contest.

"Let's not try to decide this now," I said. "The ceremony's already starting late, and then we have to get ready to meet Tallboy. Let's talk about it afterwards."

"Oh, I think we can decide it easily enough now," said McAndrew.

"No, that's all right," said Jan. "It can wait. No hurry."

Sorry, Jeanie, said her smile at me. *Game, set and match.*

After that I found it hard to keep my mind on Tallboy's visit. Luckily I wasn't on center stage most of the time, though I did tag along with the tour, watching that high forehead nodding politely, and his long index finger pointing at the different pieces of equipment on display. I also had a chance to talk to everyone when they completed their individual briefings.

"Impressive," said Gowers when she came out. She had been first one up, describing her theories and experiments on the focusing of light using arrays of kernels. A tough area of work. To set up a stable array of Kerr-Newman black holes called for solutions to the many-body problem in general relativity. Luckily there was no one in the System better able to tackle that — Emma Gowers had made a permanent niche for herself in scientific history years before, when she provided the exact solution to the general relativistic two-body problem. Now to test her approximations she had built a tiny array of shielded kernels, small enough that all her work was done through a microscope. I had seen Tallboy peering in through the eyepiece, joking with Emma as he did so.

"So he seems sympathetic?" I said.

"More than that." She took a deep breath and sat down. She was still hyper after her presentation. "I think it went very well. He listened hard and he asked questions. I was only scheduled for ten minutes, and we took nearly twenty. Keep your fingers crossed."

I did, as one by one the others went in. When they came out most of them echoed her optimism. Siclaro was the only questioning voice. He had described his system for kernel energy extraction, and Tallboy had given him the same attentive audience and nodded understandingly.

"But he asked me what I meant by 'spin-up'," Siclaro said to me as we stood together outside the main auditorium.

"That's fair enough — you can't expect him to be a specialist on this stuff."

"I know that." He shook his head in a worried fashion. "But that came at the end of the presentation. And all the time I was talking, he was nodding his head at me as though he understood everything — ideas a lot more advanced than simple spin-up and spin-down of a Kerr black hole. But if he didn't know what I meant at the end, how could he have understood any of the rest of it?"

Before I had time to answer, my own turn had arrived. I came last of all, and though I had prepared as hard as anyone I was not a central part of the show. If Tallboy had to leave early I would be cut. If he had time, I was to show him over the *Hoatzin*, and make it clear to him that we were all ready for a long trip, as soon as his office gave us permission.

His energy level was amazing. He was still cordial and enthusiastic after eight and a half hours of briefing, with only one short food break. We took a pod, just the two of us, and zipped over to the *Hoatzin*. I gave him a ten-minute tour, showing how the living area was moved closer to the mass disk as the acceleration of the ship was increased, to provide a net one-gee environment for the crew. He asked numerous polite general questions: how many people could be accommodated in the ship, how old was it, why was it called the inertia-less drive? I boggled a little at the last one, because McAndrew had spent large parts of his life explaining impatiently to anyone who would listen that, damn it, it *wasn't* inertia-less, that all it did was to balance off gravitational and inertial accelerations. But I went over it one more time, for Tallboy's benefit.

He listened closely, nodded that deep-browed head, and watched attentively as I moved us a little closer to the mass disk, so that we could feel the net acceleration on us increase from one to one-and-a-half gees.

"One more question," he said at last. "And then we must return to the Institute. You keep talking about *accelerations*, and making accelerations balance out. What does that have to do with us, with how heavy we *feel*?"

I stared at him. Was he joking? No, that fine-boned face was as serious as ever. He stood there politely waiting for my answer, and I felt that sinking feeling. I'm not sure what I told him, or what we talked about on the way back to the Institute. I handed him on to

McAndrew for a quick look at the Control Center, while
I hurried off to find Limperis. He was in his office, staring at a blank wall.

"I know, Jeanie," he said. "Don't tell me. I had to
sit in on every briefing except yours."

"The man's an *idiot,*" I said. "I think he means well,
but he's a complete, boneheaded moron. He has no
more idea than Wenig's pet monkey what goes on here
in the Institute."

"I know. I know." Limperis suddenly showed his age,
and for the first time it occurred to me that he was approaching retirement. "I hoped at first that it was just
my paranoia," he said. "I wondered if I was seeing
something that wasn't there — some of the others were
so impressed."

"How could they be? Tallboy had no idea what was
going on!"

"It's his appearance. That sharp profile. He *looks*
intelligent, so we assume he must be. But take the
people here at the Institute. Wenig looks like a mortician, Gowers could pass as a dumb-blonde hooker, and
Siclaro reminds me of a gorilla. And each of them a
mind in a million. We accept it that way round easily
enough, but not in reverse."

He stood up slowly. "We're like babies out here,
Jeanie; each of us with our own playthings. If anybody
seems to be interested in what we're doing, and nods
their head now and again, we *assume* they understand.
At the Institute, you interrupt if you don't follow an
argument. But that's not the way Earthside government
runs. Nod, and smile, and don't rock the boat — that's
the name of the game, and it will take you a long way.
You've seen how well it works for Dr. Tallboy."

"But if he doesn't understand a thing, what will his
report say? The whole future of the Institute depends
on it."

"It does. And God knows what will happen. I thought his background was physics or engineering, the way he kept nodding his head. Did you know his degree is in *sociology* and he has no hard scientific training at all? No calculus, no statistics, no complex variable, no dynamics. I bet the real quality of our work won't make one scrap of difference to his decision. We've all wasted a week." He sighed. "Horse shit. Well, come on. Tallboy will be leaving in a few minutes. We must play it to the end and hope he leaves with a positive impression."

He was heading for the door with me right behind when McAndrew hurried in.

"I've been wondering where you two had gone," he said. "Tallboy's at the departure dock. What a show, eh? I told you we'd do it, we knocked him dead. Even without Wicklund's work, we showed more new results today than he'll have seen in the past ten years. Come on — he wants to thank us all for our efforts before he goes."

He went bounding away along the corridor, full of enthusiasm, oblivious to the atmosphere in Limperis' office. We followed slowly after him. For some reason we were both smiling.

"Don't knock it," said Limperis. "If Mac were a political animal he'd be that much less a scientist. He's not the man to present your budget request, but do you know what Einstein wrote to Born just before he died? 'Earning a living should have nothing to do with the search for knowledge'."

"You should tell that to Mac."

"He was the one who told it to me."

There didn't seem much point in hurrying as we made our way to the departure dock. Tallboy had seen the best that we could offer. And who could tell? — perhaps McAndrew's enthusiasm would be more persuasive than a thousand hours of unintelligible briefings.

The mills of bureaucracy may or may not grind fine, but they certainly grind exceedingly slow. Long before we had an official report from Tallboy's office, the argument over Jan's visit to Triton Station was over. I had lost. She was on her way to Neptune. She had finagled a ride on a medium acceleration supply ship, and anytime now we should have word of her arrival. And McAndrew couldn't wait — Wicklund was still frustratingly coy about his new work.

By a second one of those coincidences that McAndrew insisted were inevitable, Tallboy's *pronunciamento* on the future of the Penrose Institute zipped in to the Message Center at the same time as Jan's first message from Triton Station. I didn't know about her space-gram until later, but Limperis directed the Tallboy message for general Institute broadcast. I was outside at the time, working near *Hoatzin*, and the news came as voice-only on my suit radio.

The summary: Siclaro's work on kernel energy extraction would proceed, and at a higher level (no surprise there, with the pressure from the Food and Energy Department for more compact power sources); Gowers would have her budget reduced by forty percent, as would Macedo. They could continue, but with no new experimental work. McAndrew had his support chopped in half. And poor Wenig, it seemed, had fared worst of all. The budget for compressed matter research was down by eighty percent.

I wasn't worried about McAndrew. If they cut his research budget to zero, he would switch to straight theory and manage very well with just a pencil and paper. But everyone else would suffer.

And me? Tallboy wiped me out at the very end of

the report, almost as an afterthought: experimental use of the *Hoatzin* was to be terminated completely, and the ship de-commissioned. There would be no expedition to Alpha Centauri or anywhere else beyond the Halo. Worst of all, the report referred to "previous unauthorized use of the balanced drive, and high-risk treatment of official property" — a direct knock at me and McAndrew. We had enjoyed free use of the ship under the previous Administration, but apparently Woolford had never thought to put it in writing.

I switched my suit to internal propulsion and headed back for the Institute at top speed. McAndrew knew I was outside, and he met me at the lock waving a long printout sheet. His mop of sandy hair was straggling into his eyes, and a long streak of orange stickiness ran down the front of his shirt. I guessed he had been at dinner when the report came in.

"Did you see it?" he said.

"Heard it. I was on voice-only."

"Well? What do you think?"

"Horrible. But I'm not surprised. I knew he hadn't understood a thing."

"Eh?" He stood goggling at me. "Are you trying to be funny? It's the most exciting news in years. I knew she'd find out. What a lass!"

I may not be as smart as McAndrew but I'm no fool. I can recognize a breakdown in communications when I see one. When Mac concentrates the world isn't there any more. It seemed to me odds-on that he had been thinking of something else and hadn't registered the Tallboy decision.

"Mac, stand still for a minute"—he was jiggling up and down with excitement—"and listen to me. The report from External Affairs is here, on the future of your programs."

He grunted impatiently. "Aye, I know about it — I

heard it come in." He dismissed the subject with a wave of his hand. "Never mind that now, it's not so important. *This* is what counts."

He shook the printout, stared at part of it, and went off into a trance. I finally reached out, removed it from his hand, and scanned the first few lines.

"It's from Jan!"

"Of course it is. She's on Triton Station. Do you realize what Wicklund's done out there?"

With Mac in this kind of mood, I'd never get his mind on to Tallboy. "No. What has he done?"

"He's solved it." He grabbed the spacegram back from me. "See, it's right here, can't you read? Jan didn't get the details, but she makes it clear enough. Wicklund has solved Vandell's Fifth Problem."

"Has he really?" I gently took the paper back from him. If it was news from Jan, I wanted to read it in full. "That's wonderful. It only leaves one question."

He frowned at me. "Many questions — we'll have to wait for more details. But which one are you thinking of?"

"Nothing you can't answer. But what in Heaven is Vandell's Fifth Problem?"

He stared at me in disgust.

I got an answer — eventually. But before I had all of it, we had been on a rambling tour of three hundred years of mathematics and physics.

"In the year 1900," he began.

"Mac!"

"No, listen to me. It's the right place to begin."

In the year 1900, at the second International Congress of Mathematicians in Paris, David Hilbert proposed a series of twenty-three problems to challenge the coming century. He was the greatest mathematician of his day, and his problems drew from a wide range of topics — topology, number theory, transfinite sets, and the foundations of mathematics itself. Each problem was important, and each was tough. Some were solved early in the century, others were shown to be undecidable, a few hung on for many decades; but by the year 2000 most of them had been wrapped up to everyone's reasonable satisfaction.

In the year 2000, the South African astronomer and physicist Dirk Vandell had followed Hilbert's precedent, and posed a series of twenty-one problems in astronomy and cosmology. Like Hilbert's problems they covered a wide range of topics, theoretical and observational, and every one was a skull-cruncher.

McAndrew had solved Vandell's Eleventh Problem when he was a very young man. From that work had emerged the whole theory for the existence and location of the kernel ring, the torus of Kerr-Newman black holes that circles the sun ten times as far out as Pluto. Nine years later, Wenig's partial solution of the Fourteenth Problem had given McAndrew the clue that led him to the vacuum-energy drive. Now, assuming that Jan's report were correct, the Fifth Problem had fallen to Wicklund's analysis.

"But why is it so important?" I asked McAndrew. "The way you describe it, I don't see practical uses. It's just a way of amplifying an observed signal without amplifying background noise — and it only applies when the original signal is minute."

He shook his head in vigorous disagreement. "It has a thousand applications. Vandell already proposed one when he first set the problem, and I'm sure Wicklund will tackle it as soon as his experimental equipment is working. He'll use the technique to look for solitaries — the rogue planets."

Rogue planets.

With those last two words, McAndrew brought the

explanation along to the point where it made sense to me. I could draw on my own formal training in classical celestial mechanics.

The possible existence of rogues went back a long way, farther than 1900. Probably all the way to Lagrange, who in his analysis of the three-body problem set up a mathematical framework to look at the motion of a planet moving in the gravitational fields of a binary star system. By 1880, that case was known to be "stable against ejection". In other words, the planet could have close approaches to each of the stars, and might suffer extremes of temperature, but it would never be completely expelled from the stellar system.

But suppose you have a system with three or more stars in it? That's not at all uncommon. Then the situation changes completely. A planet can pick up enough energy through a set of gravitational swing-bys past the stellar components to hurl it right out of the system. Once this happened it would become a sunless world, travelling alone through the void. Even if it later encountered another star, the chance of capture was minute. The planet would be a solitary, a rogue world. Astronomers had speculated for centuries about the existence and possible numbers of such planets, but without a scrap of observational evidence.

Vandell had defined the problem: *An Earth-sized planet shines only by reflected light. If it gives off radiation in the thermal infrared or microwave regions, the signal is swamped by the stellar background. Devise a technique that will permit the detection of a rogue planet as small as the Earth.*

Now it seemed that Wicklund had done it, and McAndrew was happy as a pig, while everybody else at the Institute gloomed about in reaction to Tallboy's effects on their work.

I sympathized with them. Rogue planets are fine, but

I could see no way in which they could make any practical difference to me. Mac and Sven Wicklund could have my share of them. I spent a lot of time over on the *Hoatzin,* wondering what to do next. I didn't belong at the Penrose Institute, the only thing I offered there was the ability to pilot the long trips out. Once that was over, I might as well go back to the Titan run.

Jan's next message back gave me mixed feelings, but at least it cheered me up.

"Not much to do out here," she wrote — she was the only person I have ever met who habitually *chats* via spacegram. "You were right, Jeanie. Wicklund's as bad as McAndrew, totally wrapped up in the work he's doing and won't take much notice of me. And the rest of them hate company so much they run and hide when we meet in the corridors. I've been spending a lot of time over on *Merganser.* I got the impression from you that she's an old hulk, but she's not. She may be an antique, but everything's still in good working shape. I've even been spinning-up the drive. If I can talk Wicklund into it maybe we can go off on a little bit of a trip together. He needs a rest (from physics!)."

That brought back some exciting memories. *Merganser* was one of the two original prototypes of the balanced drive, and McAndrew and I had ironed the bugs out of her personally. She was limited to a 50-gee acceleration, but still in good working order. I'd fly her anywhere. Mac seemed much less happy when he read the letter.

"I hope she knows what she's doing," he said. "That ship's not a toy. Do you think it's safe?"

"Safe as anything in the System. Jan won't have any trouble. We used *Merganser* for training before they mothballed her, don't you remember?"

He didn't, of course. He carries physics and mathematics in his head at an astonishing level of detail, but useful everyday information is another matter. He nodded at me vaguely, and wandered off to send more messages to Wicklund (who had to date provided no replies).

We heard from Jan again, just as the explicit order was coming in from Tallboy's office to de-commission *Hoatzin* and remove the supplies for the Alpha Centauri mission. I screwed up Tallboy's order into a tight ball and threw it across the room. Then I sat down to read what Jan had to say.

No preamble this time: "Wicklund says it works! He's already found three rogues, and expects a lot more. They must be a lot more common than anybody thought. Now sit back for the big news: *there's one only a light year away!* Isn't it exciting?"

Well, maybe — less so to me than to Mac, I was sure of that. I assumed that solitary planets would be rather rare, so one closer than the nearest star was a bit surprising. But it was her next words that shot me bolt upright and sent a tingle through my spine.

"*Merganser* is working perfectly now, all ready for a trip. I've persuaded Wicklund to take her out for a look at *Vandell* — that's what he wants to name the planet. I'm sure you don't approve, so I won't ask. Lots of love — see you when we get back."

Even as I screamed inside, I wasn't completely surprised. She was McAndrew's daughter all right — it was exactly the harebrained sort of thing he would have done.

Mac and I both played it very cool. That boneheaded pair, we said to each other. We might have guessed it, the follies of youth. They'll be in trouble when they get back, even though *Merganser* is an old ship that Triton Station can do what they like with.

But deep inside we both had other feelings. Wicklund

had sent the coordinates of Vandell to us before they left, and as Jan said it was close, less than a light year and a quarter away. Easily in *Merganser's* range, and a lure that any scientist worth his salt would find hard to resist, even without Jan's coaxing. Where had it come from, what was it made of, how long since it had been ejected from its parent star? — there were a hundred questions that could never be answered by remote observations, not even with the super-sensitive methods that Wicklund had developed.

But it was those same questions that made me so uneasy. If I've learned one thing wandering around inside and outside the Solar System, it's this: Nature has more ways of killing you than you can imagine. When you think you've learned them all, another one pops up to teach you humility — if you're lucky. If not, someone else will have to decide what did you in.

For a week after Jan's message I monitored the messages closely that came in from the outer relay stations. And every day I would ride over to *Hoatzin* and potter about there, sometimes with Mac, sometimes alone. I was supposed to be working on the decommissioning, but instead I would sit in the pilot's chair, check all the status flags, and think my own thoughts. Until finally, ten days after Jan and Wicklund had left, I went over to visit *Hoatzin* late one sleep period.

And found that the lock had been cycled since I left.

McAndrew was sitting in the pilot's chair, staring at the controls. I came quietly up behind him, patted him on the shoulder, and slipped into the copilot's seat. He turned towards me, straggly eyebrows raised.

"It's now or never," he said at last. "But what about Tallboy? What will he do to the Institute?"

I shrugged. "Nothing. Not if we make it clear that it's our fault."

I reached out and called for a destination reading. When I left, the coordinates had all been set to zero. Now they carried precise values.

"Do you think that anyone else suspects?" I said. "I checked the experimental logs in your lab today, and they were all current up to this afternoon — and you're always months behind. If I noticed that, maybe one of the others will."

He looked surprised. "Why should they? We've been careful not to talk about this when anyone else could hear."

There was no point in telling Mac that he was probably the world's worst person you'd want to keep a secret. I tapped him on the shoulder. "No point in worrying about it once we're on our way. Come on, Mac, move over — you're sitting in my chair. And think positively. We'll have a nice, long trip, just the two of us."

He stood up, rubbing at the back of his head the way he always did when he was embarrassed. "Och, Jeanie," he said. But he was smiling to himself as we changed seats.

The calculations were elementary, and I could do them as well as he could. *Merganser* would reach the rogue planet in about sixty days of shipboard time if they kept close to maximum acceleration all the way. We could be there in only 35 days of shipboard time, but that would pick up only ten days of inertial time. We would reach Vandell a couple of days after them. For me, that was two days too late.

Our drive wake left an ionization track across the whole width of the Solar System. Mac checked that there were no ships directly behind for us to burn a hole through, and while he was doing it I had a new idea and sent a message back to External Affairs. I said that we were about to perform a brief high-gee test of *Hoatzin's* drive before we took her in and decommissioned her. With luck, Tallboy's group would assume we had been the unhappy victims of a nasty accident, shooting out of the Solar System on a one-way journey when some control element of the drive unit had failed. Limperis and friends at the Institute wouldn't believe that, not as soon as they checked out our destination coordinates — but they would never tell their suspicions to Tallboy. Maybe they could even get some mileage from our disappearance, pointing out the need for more funds for reliability and system maintenance. Limperis could play that game with his eyes closed.

Perhaps everything would work out fine — until McAndrew and I came back. Then the truth would come out, and we'd be roasted for sure.

Neither of us could get too worried about that possibility. We had other things on our minds. As we raced out along the invisible scintillation of *Merganser's* drive, Mac dumped the data bank for information about Vandell's rogueworld. He didn't get much. We had coordinates relative to the Sun, and velocity components, but all they did was make sure we could find our way to the planet. Wicklund had been able to put an upper limit on its diameter using long base line interferometry, and estimated that we were dealing with a body no bigger than Earth. But we were missing the physical variables — no mass, internal structure, temperature, magnetic field, or physical composition, not even an estimate of rotation rate. Mac fumed, but at least I'd have a lot more information for him as soon as we got close. In the week before we left the Institute, I had put on board the *Hoatzin* every instrument that wasn't nailed down, anything that might

tell us something useful about Vandell without having
to go down there and set foot on its surface.

At a hundred gee acceleration you head out of the
Solar System on a trajectory that's very close to a
straight line. The gravitational accelerations produced by the Sun and planets are negligible by comparison,
even in the Inner System. We were bee-lining for a
point in the constellation Lupus, the Wolf, where
Vandell lay close in apparent position to an ancient
supernova fragment. Its explosion had lit up the skies
of Earth more than a thousand years ago, back in 1,006
A.D.; an interesting object, but we wouldn't be going
even a thousandth of the way out to it. Wicklund was
right, in interstellar terms Vandell's rogueworld sat in
Sol's backyard.

Without a complicated trajectory to worry about, I
went round and round with a different problem. When
the drives were on, both *Merganser* and *Hoatzin* were
blind to incoming messages, and drowned out any of
their own transmissions. Thus we had a chance to get
a message to Sven Wicklund and Jan only when their
drive was turned off, while they were coasting free to
rubberneck or study the starscape scenery from a
slightly different point of view. Even though they might
not be listening for an incoming signal when the drive
was off, their computer certainly would be, and it
would notify them of anything important.

But now see my problem: to send a message, we had
to switch our drive off, and that would delay our arrival a little bit every time we did it. Our signal would
then take days or weeks to reach *Merganser* — and
to receive it, their ship had to have its drive off at just
the right time. DON'T LAND was all I wanted to say.
But how would I know when to switch off our drive and
send an urgent message, so it would get to them just

when *their* drive was not operating?

I wrestled with that until my brains began to boil, then handed it over to McAndrew. He pointed out that we had knowledge of the occasions when their drive had been switched off, from the gaps in their drive wake. So making a best prediction was a straightforward problem in stochastic optimization. He solved it, too, before we had been on our way for a week. But the solution predicted such a low probability of successful contact that I didn't even try it — better to leave our drive on full blast, and try to make up some of their lead.

With the shields on to protect us from the sleet of particles and hard radiation induced by our light-chasing velocity, we had no sense of motion at all. But we were really moving. At turn-over point we were within one part in ten thousand of light speed.

If I haven't said it already, I'll say it now: the 100-gee balanced drive is nice to have, but it's a son of a bitch — you travel a lightyear in just over a month of shipboard time. Two months, and you've gone fifty lightyears. Four shipboard months, and you're outside the Galaxy and well on your way to Andromeda.

I calculated that two hundred days would put you at the edge of the Universe, 18 billion lightyears out. Of course, by the time you got there, the Universe would have had 18 billion more years to expand, so you wouldn't be at the *new* edge. In fact, since the "edge" is defined as the place where the velocity of recession of the Galaxies is light-speed, you'd still be 18 billion lightyears away from it — and that would remain true, no matter how long you journeyed. Worse still, if you arranged a trajectory that brought you to rest relative to the Earth, when you switched off the drive the Galaxies near you would be rushing away almost at light speed...

An hour or two of those thoughts, and I felt a new sympathy for Achilles in Zeno's old paradox, trying to catch the tortoise and never quite getting there.

Travel for a year, according to McAndrew, and you'd begin to have effects on the large-scale structure of space-time. The vacuum zero point energy tapped by the drive isn't inexhaustible; and as to what would happen if you kept on going...

An academic question, of course, as Mac pointed out. Long before that the mass plate would be inadequate to protect the drive, and the whole structure would disintegrate through ablative collision with intergalactic gas and dust. Very reassuring; but Mac's intrigued and speculative tone when he discussed the possibility was enough to send shivers up my spine.

The position fixes we needed to refine Wicklund's original position and velocity for Vandell rendezvous were made by our computer during the final three days of flight. Those observations and calibrations were performed in microsecond flashes while the drive was turned off, and at the same time we sent out burst mode messages, prepared and compressed in advance, to Merganser's projected position. We told them to send a return signal to us, but no counter message came in. There was nothing but the automatic "Signal received" from their shipboard computer.

One day before rendezvous we were close enough to throttle back the drive. We couldn't see Vandell or Merganser yet, but the ships' computers could begin talking to each other. It took them only a few seconds to collect the information I was interested in, and spit out a display summary.

No human presence now on board. Transfer pod in use for planetary descent trajectory. No incoming signals from pod.

I keyed in the only query that mattered: When descent?

Seven hours shipboard time.

That was it. We had arrived just too late. By now Jan and Sven Wicklund would be down on the surface of Vandell. Then another part of the first message hit me. *No incoming signals from pod.*

"Mac!" I said. "No pod signal."

He nodded grimly. He had caught it too. Even when they were down on the surface, there should be an automatic beacon signal to fix the pod's position and allow compensation for Doppler shift of communication frequency.

"No pod signal," I said again. "That means they're—"

"Aye." His voice was husky, as though there was no air in his lungs. "Let's not jump to conclusions, Jeanie. For all we know..."

But he didn't finish the sentence. The pod antenna was robust. Only something major (such as impact with a solid surface at a few hundred meters a second) would put it out of action. I had never known a case where the pod's comlink died and the persons within it lived.

We sat side by side in a frozen, empty silence as *Hoatzin* brought us closer to the rogue planet. Soon it was visible to our highest resolution telescopes. Without making a decision at any conscious level, I automatically set up a command sequence that would free our own landing pod as soon as the drive went off completely. Then I simply sat there, staring ahead at Vandell.

For much of our trip out I had tried to visualize what a planet would be like that had known no warming sun for millions or billions of years. It had floated free— for how long? We didn't know. Perhaps since our kind had descended from the trees, perhaps as long as any life had existed on Earth. For all that time, the planet had moved on through the quiet void, responsive only to the gentle, persistent tug of galactic gravitational and magnetic fields, drifting along where the stars were no more than distant pinpricks against the black sky. With no sunlight to breathe life onto its surface, Vandell would be cold, airless, the frozen innermost circle of hell. It chilled me to think of it.

The planet grew steadily in the forward screens. As the definition of the display improved, I suddenly realized why I couldn't relate the picture in front of me to my mental images. Vandell was *visible*, at optical wavelengths. It sat there at the center of the screen, a small sphere that glowed a soft, living pink against the stellar backdrop. As I watched the surface seemed to shimmer, with an evanescent pattern of fine lines running across it.

McAndrew had seen it too. He gave a grunt of surprise, cupped his chin in his hands, and leaned forward. After two minutes of silence he reached across to the terminal and keyed in a brief query.

"What are you doing?" I asked, when after another two minutes he showed no sign of speaking.

"Want to see what's in *Merganser's* memory. Should be some images from their time of first approach." He grunted and shook his head. "Look at that screen. There's no way Vandell can look like that."

"I was amazed to *see* it at visible wavelengths. But I'm not sure why."

"Available energy." He shrugged, but his gaze never left the display. "See, Jeanie, the only thing that can provide energy to that planet's surface is an internal source. But nothing I've ever heard of could give this much radiation at those frequencies, and sustain it over a long period. And look at the edge of the planet's disk. See, it's less bright. That's an atmospheric limb darkening, if ever I've seen one — an atmosphere, now, on a planet that should be as cold as space. Doesn't make any sense at all. No sense at all."

We watched together as *Merganser's* data bank fed across to our ship's computer and through the displays. The screen to our left flickered through a wild pattern of colors, then went totally dark. McAndrew looked at it and swore to himself.

"Explain that to me, Jeanie. There's the way that Vandell looked in the visible part of the spectrum when Jan and Sven were on their final approach — black as hell, totally invisible. We get here, a couple of days later, and we find *that*." He waved his arm at the central display, where Vandell was steadily increasing in size as we moved closer. "Look at the readings that Wicklund made as they came into parking orbit — no visible emissions, no thermal emissions, no sign of an atmosphere. Now see our readings: the planet is visible, above freezing point, and covered in clouds. It's as though they were describing one world, and we've arrived at a completely different one."

Mac often tells me that I have no imagination. But as he spoke wild ideas went running through my mind that I didn't care to mention. A planet that changed its appearance when humans approached it; a world that waited patiently for millions of years, then draped a cloak of atmosphere around itself as soon as it had lured a group of people to its surface. Could the changes on Vandell be interpreted as the result of *intention*, a deliberate and intelligent act on the part of something on the planet?

While I was still full of my furious fancies, a high-pitched whistle from the navigation console announced that the balanced drive had turned off completely. We had reached our rendezvous position, two hundred thousand kilometers from Vandell. I was moving away from the control panel, heading towards our own transfer pod, before the sound had ended. At the entrance I stopped and turned, expecting that McAndrew would be close on my heels. But he hadn't left the displays. He had called back the list of Vandell's physical parameters, showing mass, temperature, mean diameter, and rotation rate, and was staring at it blindly. As I watched he requested a new display of Vandell's rotation rate, which was small enough to be shown as zero in the standard output format.

"Mac!"

He turned, shook his head from side to side as though to banish his own version of the insane ideas that had crowded my mind when I saw the change in Vandell, and slowly followed me to the pod. At the entrance he turned for a last look at the screens.

There was no discussion of our move into the pod. We didn't know when, or even quite how, but we both knew that we had to make a descent to the surface of Vandell. Somehow we had to recover the bodies that lay beneath the flickering, pearly cloud shrouding the rogue world.

In another time and place, the view from the pod would have been beautiful. We were close enough now to explain the rosy shimmer. It was lightning storms, running back and forth across the clouded skies of Vandell. Lightning storms that shouldn't be there, on a world that ought to be dead. We had drained *Merganser's* data banks as we went round and round in low orbit. Not much new had come to light, but we had found the last set of instrument readings returned to the main computer when the other landing pod had made its approach to Vandell's surface: *Atmospheric pressure, zero. Magnetic field: negligible. Temperature, four degrees absolute. Surface gravity, four-tenths gee.*

Planetary rotation rate, too small to measure.

Then their pod had touched down, with final relative velocity of only half a meter a second — and all transmissions had ceased, instantly. Whatever had killed Jan and Sven Wicklund, direct impact with the surface couldn't be the culprit. They had landed gently. And if they hadn't been killed by collision when they landed...

I tried to ignore the tiny bud of hope that wanted to open in my mind. I had never heard of a pod being destroyed without also killing anyone inside it.

Our instruments had added a few new (and odd) facts to that earlier picture. The "atmosphere" we were seeing now was mainly dust, a great swirling storm across the whole of Vandell, littered by lightning flashes through the upper part. It was hot, a furnace breath that had no right to exist. Vandell was supposed to be *cold.* Goddammit, it should be drained of every last calorie of heat. McAndrew had told me so, there was no way the planet could be warm.

Round and round, orbit after orbit; we went on until I felt that we were a fixed center and the whole universe was gyrating around us, while I stared at that black vortex (it came and went from one orbit to the next, now you see it, now you don't) and McAndrew sat glued to the data displays. I don't think he looked at Vandell itself for more than ten seconds in five hours. He was thinking.

And me? The pressure inside was growing — tearing me apart. According to Limperis and Wenig, I'm cautious to a fault. Where angels fear to tread, I not only won't rush in, I don't want to go near the place. That's one reason they like to have me around, to exercise my high cowardice quotient. But now I wanted to fire our retro-rockets and get down there, down on-to Vandell. Twice I had seated myself at the controls, and fingered the preliminary descent sequence (second nature, I could have done that in my sleep). And twice McAndrew had emerged from his reverie, shook his head, and spoken: "No, Jeanie."

But the third time he didn't stop me.

"D'ye know where you're going to put her down, Jeanie?" was all he said.

"Roughly." I didn't like the sound of my voice at all. Too scratchy and husky. "I've got the approximate landing position from *Merganser's* readings."

"Not there." He was shaking his head. "Not quite there. See it, the black tube? Put us down the middle of that funnel — can you do it?"

"I can. But if it's what it looks like, we'll get heavy turbulence."

"Aye, I'll agree with that." He shrugged. "That's where they are, though, for a bet. Can you do it?"

That wasn't his real question. As he was speaking, I began to slide us in along a smooth descent trajectory. There was nothing to the calculation of our motion, we both recognized that. Given our desired touchdown location, the pod's computer would have a minimum fuel descent figured in fractions of a second.

I know McAndrew very well. What he was saying — not in words, that wasn't his style — was simple: *It's going to be dangerous, and I'm not sure how dangerous. Do you want to do it?*

I began to see why as soon as we were inside the atmosphere. Visibility went down to zero. We were descending through thick smoke-like dust and flickering lightning. I switched to radar vision, and found I was looking down to a murky, surrealistic world, with a shattered, twisted surface. Heavy winds (without an atmosphere? — what were winds?) moved us violently from side to side, up and down, with sickening free-fall drops arrested by the drive as soon as they were started.

Thirty seconds to contact, and below us the ground heaved and rolled like a sick giant. Down and down, along the exact center of the black funnel. The pod shook and shivered around us. The automatic controls seemed to be doing poorly, but I knew I'd be worse — my reaction times were a thousandfold too slow to compete. All we could do was hold tight and wait for the collision.

Which never came. We didn't make a featherbed landing, but the final jolt was just a few centimeters a second. Or was it more? I couldn't say. It was lost in the continuing shuddering movements of the ground that the pod rested on. The planet beneath us was alive. I stood up, then had to hold on to the edge of the control desk to keep my feet. I smiled at McAndrew (quite an effort) as he began an unsteady movement towards the equipment locker.

He nodded at me. *Earthquake country.*

I nodded back. *Where is their ship?*

We had landed on a planet almost as big as Earth, in the middle of a howling dust storm that reduced visibility to less than a hundred yards. Now we were proposing to search an area of a couple of hundred million square miles — for an object a few meters across. The needle in a haystack had nothing on this. Mac didn't seem worried. He was putting on an external support pack — we had donned suits during the first phase of descent.

"Mac!"

He paused with the pack held against his chest and the connectors held in one hand. "Don't be daft, Jeanie. Only one of us should be out there."

And that made me mad. He was being logical (my specialty). But to come more than a lightyear, and then *one* of us go the last few miles ... Jan was *my* daughter too — my only daughter. I moved forward and picked up another of the packs. After one look at my face, Mac didn't argue.

At least we had enough sense not to venture outside at once. Suited up, we completed the systematic scan of our surroundings. The visual wavelengths were useless — we couldn't see a thing through the ports — but the microwave sensors let us look to the horizon. And a wild horizon it was. Spikes of sharp rock sat next to crumbling mesas, impenetrable crevasses, and tilted blocks of dark stone, randomly strewn across the landscape.

I could see no pattern at all, no rule of formation. But over to one side, less than a mile from our pod, our instruments were picking up a bright radar echo, a reflection peak stronger than anything that came from the rocky surface. It must be metal — could only be metal — could only be Jan's ship. But was it intact? Lightning-fused? A scoured hulk? A shattered remnant, open to dust and vacuum?

My thoughts came too fast to follow. Before they had reached any conclusion we had moved to the lock, opened it, and were standing on the broken surface of Vandell. McAndrew automatically fell behind to let me take the lead. Neither of us had any experience with this type of terrain, but he knew my antennae for trouble were better than his. I tuned my suit to the reflected radar signal from our pod and we began to pick our way carefully forward.

It was a grim, tortuous progress. There was no direct path that could be taken across the rocks. Every tenth step seemed to bring me to a dead end, a place where we had to retrace our steps halfway back to our own pod. Beneath our feet, the surface of the planet shivered and groaned, as though it was ready to open up and swallow us. The landscape as our suits

presented it to us was a scintillating nightmare of
blacks and greys. (Vision in non-visible wavelengths is
always disconcerting — microwave more than most.)

Around us, the swirling dust came in shivering waves
that whispered along the outside of our helmets. I could
detect a definite cycle, with a peak every seven minutes
or so. Radio static followed the same period, rising and
falling in volume to match the disturbance outside.

I had tuned my set to maximum gain and was
transmitting a continuous call signal. Nothing came
back from the bright radar blip of the other pod. It was
now only a couple of hundred yards ahead but we were
approaching agonizingly slowly.

At fifty yards I noticed a lull in the rustle around us.
I switched to visible wavelengths, and waited impatiently while the suit's processor searched for the best
combination of frequencies to penetrate the murk.
After half a second the internal suit display announced that there would be a short delay; the sensors were
covered with ionized dust particles that would have to
be repelled. That took another ten seconds, then I had
an image. Peering ahead on visible wavelengths I
thought I could see a new shape in front of us, a flat
oval hugging the dark ground.

"Visible signal, Mac," I said over the radio. "Tell
your suit."

That was all I could say. I know the profile of a pod,
I've seen them from every angle. And the silhouette
ahead of us looked *wrong*. It had a twisted, sideways
cant, bulging towards the left. I increased pace, stum-
bling dangerously along smooth slabs and around
jagged pinnacles, striding recklessly across a quiver-
ing deep abyss. Mac was following if I got in trouble
— unless he was taking worse risks himself. I could
hear his breath, loud on the suit radio.

It was their pod. No doubt at all. And as I came

closer I could see the long, gaping hole in one side. It takes a lot to smash a transfer pod beyond repair, but that one would never fly again. Inside it would be airless, lifeless, filled with the choking dust that was Vandell's only claim to an atmosphere.

And the people inside? Would Jan or Sven have thought to wear suits before descent? It would make a difference only to the appearance of the corpses. Even with suits, anything that could kill their signal beacon would kill them too.

I took my final step to the pod, stooped to peer in through the split in the side, and stopped breathing. Somewhere deep inside me, contrary to all logic, there still lived a faint ghost of hope. It died as I looked. Two figures lay side by side on the floor of the pod, neither of them moving.

I groaned, saw Mac coming to stand beside me, and switched on my helmet light for a better view of the interior. Then I straightened up so fast that my head banged hard on the pod's tough metal.

They were both wearing suits, their helmets were touching — and as the light from outside penetrated the interior of the pod, they swung around in unison to face me. They were both rubbing at their suit faceplates with gloved hands, clearing a space in a thick layer of white dust there.

"Jan!" My shout must have blasted Mac rigid. "Sven! Mac, they're alive!"

"Christ, Jeanie, I see that. Steady on, you'll burst my eardrums." He sounded as though he was going to burst himself, from sheer pleasure and relief.

We scrambled around to the main hatch of the pod and I tried to yank it open. It wouldn't move. Mac lent a hand, and still nothing would budge — everything was too bent and battered. Back we went to the hole

in the ship's side, and found them trying to enlarge it
enough to get out.

"Stand back," I said. "Mac and I can cut that in a
minute."

Then I realized they couldn't hear me or see me.
Their faceplates were covered again with dust, and
they kept leaning together to touch helmets.

"Mac! There's something wrong with their suits."

"Of course there is." He sounded disgusted with my
stupidity. "Radios not working — we already knew
that. They're communicating with each other by direct
speech through the helmet contact. Vision units are
done for, too — see, all they have are the faceplates,
and the dust sticks and covers them unless they keep
on clearing it. The whole atmosphere of this damned
planet is nothing more than charged dust particles. Our
suits are repelling them, or we'd see nothing at visible
wavelengths. Here, let me in there."

He stuck his head through the opening, grabbed the
arm of Jan's suit, and pulled us so that we were all four
touching helmets. We could talk to each other.

And for that first ten minutes that's what we did;
talk, in a language that defies all logical analysis. I
would call it the language of love, but that phrase has
been used too often for another (and less powerful)
emotional experience.

Then we enlarged the hole so they could climb out.
At that point I thought that we had won, that our
troubles and difficulties were all over. In fact, they
were just starting.

Their pod was in even worse shape than it looked.
The battering from flying boulders that had ruined the
hull should have left intact the internal electronics,
computers, and communications links, components with
no moving parts that ought to withstand any amount
of shaking and violent motion. But they were all dead.

The pod was nothing but a lifeless chunk of metal and plastics. Worse still, all the computer systems in Jan and Sven's suits had failed too. They had no radios, no external vision systems — not even temperature controls. Only the purely mechanical components, like air supply and suit pressure, were still working.

I couldn't imagine anything that could destroy the equipment so completely and leave Jan and Sven alive, but those questions would have to come later. For the moment our first priority was the return to the other pod. If I had thought it dangerous work coming, going back would be much worse. Jan and Sven were almost blind, they couldn't step across chasms or walk along a thin slab of rock. Without radios, I couldn't even tell them to back up if I decided we had to retrace part of our path.

We all four linked hands, to make a chain with Mac on the left-hand end and me on the right, and began a strange crab-like movement back in the direction of the other pod. I daren't hurry, and it took hours. Four times I had to stop completely, while the ground beneath us went through exceptionally violent paroxysms of shaking and shuddering. We stood motionless, tightly gripping each other's gloved hands. If it was scary for me, it must have been hell for Jan and Sven. Mac and I were their lifeline, if we lost contact they wouldn't make twenty meters safely across the broken surface. While the shaking went on, I was picking up faint sounds in my radio. McAndrew and Wicklund had their helmets together, and Wicklund seemed to be doing all the talking. For five minutes I heard only occasional grunts from Mac through his throat mike.

"Right," he said at last. "Were you able to pick up any of that, Jeanie? We have to get a move on. Go faster."

"Faster? In these conditions? You're crazy. I know

it's slow going, but we all have plenty of air. Let's do it right, and get there in one piece."

"It's not air I'm worried about." He was crowding up behind us, so that we were all bumping into each other. "We have to be in the pod and off the surface in less than an hour. Sven's been tracking the surges of seismic activity and dust speed, ever since they landed and everything went to hell. There's a bad one coming an hour and a half from now — and I mean *bad.* Worse than anything we've felt so far. A lot of the minor cycles we've been feeling since we came out on the surface will all be in phase. They'll all add together."

Worse than anything we had felt so far. What would it be like? It wasn't easy to imagine. Nor was the cause — but *something* had taken Vandell's smooth and quiet surface and crumpled it to a wild ruin in the few hours since the other pod had landed.

Against my instincts I began to take more risks, to climb over more jagged rocks and to walk along shelves that might tilt and slide under our weight. I think that at this point it was worse for McAndrew and me than for Sven and Jan. They could walk blind and trust us to keep them safe; but we had to keep our eyes wide open, and study all the dangers around us. I wanted to ask Mac a hundred questions, but I didn't dare to focus his attention or mine on anything except the immediate task.

At our faster pace we were within a hundred meters of the pod in twenty minutes, with what looked like a clear path the rest of the way. That was when I heard a grunt and curse over the suit radio, and turned to see McAndrew sliding away to one side down a long scree of loose gravel. Last across, he had pushed Sven Wicklund to safety as the surface began to break. He fell, scrabbled at the ground, but couldn't get hold of anything firm. He rolled once, then within seconds was lost from view behind a black jumble of boulders.

"Mac!" I was glad that Jan couldn't hear my voice crack with panic.

"I'm here, Jeanie. I'm all right." He sounded as though he was out on a picnic. "My own fault, I could see it was breaking away when Sven was on it. I should have looked for another path instead of following him like a sheep."

"Can you get back?"

There was a silence, probably thirty seconds. In my nerved-up state it seemed like an hour. I could hear Mac's breath, faster and louder over the radio.

"I'm not sure," he said at last. "It's a mess down here, and the slope's too steep to climb straight up. Damned gravel, I slide right back down with it. It may take me a little while. You three had better keep going and I'll catch up later. Time's too short for you to hang around waiting."

"Forget it. Hold right there, I'm coming back after you." I leaned to set my helmet next to Jan's. "Jan, can you hear me?"

"Yes. But speak louder." Her voice was faint, as though she was many meters away.

"I want you and Sven to stand right here and don't move — not for anything. Mac's stuck, and I have to help him. I'll be just a few minutes."

That was meant to be reassuring, but then I wondered what would happen if I was too optimistic about how long it would take me. "Give me twenty minutes, and if we're not back then, you'll have to get to the pod on your own. It's straight in front as you're facing now, about a hundred meters away. If you go in a straight line for fifty paces, then clear your faceplates, you should be able to see it."

I knew she must have questions, but there was no

time to answer them. Mac's tone suggested it would be completely fatal to be on Vandell's surface, unprotected, when the next big wave of seismic activity hit us.

I knew exactly where Mac had gone, but I had a hard time seeing him. The rock slide had carried with it a mixture of small and large fragments, from gravel to pebbles to substantial boulders. His struggles to climb the slope had only managed to embed him deeper in loose materials. Now his suit was three quarters hidden. His efforts also seemed to have carried him backwards, so with a thirty degree gradient facing him I didn't think he'd ever be able to get out alone. And farther down the slope lay a broad fissure in the surface, of indeterminate depth.

He was facing my way, and he had seen me too. "Jeanie, don't come any closer. You'll slither right down here, the same as I did. There's nothing firm past the ledge you're standing on."

"Don't worry. This is as far as I'm coming." I backed up a step, nearer to a huge rock that must have weighed many tons, and turned my head so the chest of Mac's suit sat on the crosshairs at the exact center of my display. "Don't move a muscle now. I'm going to use the Walton, and we don't have time for second tries."

I lifted the crosshairs just a little to allow for the effects of gravity, then intoned the Walton release sequence. The ejection solenoid fired, and the thin filament with its terminal electromagnet shot out from the chest panel on my suit and flashed down toward McAndrew. The laser at the tip measured the distance of the target, and the magnet went on a fraction of a second before contact. Mac and I were joined by a hair-thin bond. I braced myself behind the big rock. "Ready? I'm going to haul you in."

"Aye, I'm ready. But why didn't I think of using the Walton? Damnation, I didn't need to get you back here, I could have done it for myself."

I began to reel in the line, slowly so that Mac could help by freeing himself from the stones and gravel. The Izaak Walton has been used for many years, ever since the first big space construction jobs pointed out the need for a way to move around in vacuum without wasting a suit's reaction mass. If all you want is a little linear momentum, the argument went, why not take it from the massive structures around you? That's all that the Waltons do. I'd used them hundreds of times in free fall, shooting the line out to a girder where I wanted to be, connecting, then reeling myself over there. So had Mac, and that's why he was disgusted with himself. But it occurred to me that this was the first time I'd ever heard of a Walton being used on a planetary surface.

"I don't think you could have done it, Mac," I said. "This big rock's the only solid one you could see from down there, and it doesn't look as though it has a high metal content. You'd have nothing for the magnet to grab hold of up here."

"Maybe." He snorted. "But I should have had the sense to try. I'm a witless oaf."

What that made me, I dreaded to think. I went on steadily hauling in the line until he had scrabbled his way up to stand by my side, then switched off the field. The line and magnet automatically ran into their storage reel in my suit, and we carefully turned and headed back to the other two.

They were just where I had left them. They stood, helmets touching, like a frozen and forlorn tableau in Vandell's broken wilderness. It was more than fifteen minutes since I had gone back to Mac, and I could imagine their uneasy thoughts. I leaned my helmet to touch both theirs.

"All present and safe. Let's go."

Jan gave my arm a great squeeze. We formed our chain again, and crabbed the rest of the way to the pod. It wasn't quite as easy as it had looked, or as I suggested to Jan, but in less than fifteen minutes we were opening the outer hatch and bundling Sven and Jan into it.

The lock was only big enough for two at a time. They were out of their useless suits by the time that McAndrew and I could join them inside. Jan looked pale and shaky, ten years older than her seventeen years. Sven Wicklund was as blond and dreamy-looking as ever, still impossibly young in appearance. Like McAndrew, his own internal preoccupations partly shielded him from unpleasant realities — even now he was brandishing a piece of paper covered with squiggles at us. But Jan and Sven had both held together, keeping their composure well when death must have seemed certain. It occurred to me that if you wanted to find a rite of passage to adulthood, you wouldn't find a tougher one than Jan had been through.

"Just look at this," Sven said as soon as we were out of the hatch. "I've been plotting the cycles —"

"How long before it hits?" I interrupted.

"Four minutes. But—"

"Get into working suits, both of you." I was already at the controls. "I'm taking us up as soon as I can, but if we're too late I can't guarantee that the pod hull will survive. You know what happened to yours."

The ascent presented no problem of navigation — I had plenty of fuel, and I intended to go straight up with maximum lift. There would be time to worry about rendezvous with *Merganser* and *Hoatzin* when we were safely away from Vandell.

I believe in being careful, even on the simplest takeoff, so all my concentration was on the control sequences. I could hear Jan, McAndrew and Wicklund babbling to each other in the background, until I told them to get off my suit frequency and let me think. Vandell was still a complete mystery world to me, but if the others had answers, those, like the problem of ship rendezvous, could wait until we were off the surface.

Wicklund's predictions for the timing of the next wave of violence proved to be unnecessary. I could see it coming directly, in the values provided by the pod's field instruments. Every gauge reading in front of me was creeping up in unison as we lifted off; ionization levels, surface vibrations, dust density, electric and magnetic fields — readouts flickered rapidly higher, and needles turned steadily across their dials like the hands of an old-fashioned clock.

Something big was on its way. We lifted into a sky ripped by great lightning flashes, burning their way through the clouds of charged dust particles. The ascent we made was rapid. Within a few seconds we had reached three kilometers. And then, as I was beginning to relax a little and think that we had been just in time, the readings in front of me went mad. External field strengths flickered up so fast in value that the figures were unreadable, then warning lights came on. I heard the screech of a fatal overload in my suit's radio, and saw the displays in front of me blank out one after another. The computer, after a brief mad flurry of a binary dump across the control screen, went totally dead. Suddenly I was flying blind and deaf. All the electronic tools that every pilot relied on were now totally disabled.

It was useless information, but suddenly I understood exactly what had killed the signal beacon from Jan and Sven's pod without also killing them. Before the displays in front of me died, the electric and magnetic field strengths had risen to an impossible level. Even with partial shielding from the pod's hull, their intensity was enough to wipe out magnetic storage — that took care of computers, communications equipment, displays, and suit controls. If the suits hadn't been designed with manual overrides for certain essentials so that Jan and Sven could control their air supply, that would have been the end.

Now our pod had the same problem as theirs. We hadn't been pelted with boulders, as they had when they were sitting on the surface of Vandell, but we had no computer control of our flight and we were being whipped around the sky by the changing magnetic fields.

It wasn't necessary for me to change to manual control. When the computer died, it dumped everything in my lap automatically. I gritted my teeth, tried to keep us heading straight up (not easy, the way we were being tilted and rocked) and refused to decrease thrust even though the pod shuddered as though it was getting ready to disintegrate.

I'm blessed with an iron stomach, one that doesn't get sick no matter how much lurching and spinning it takes. McAndrew isn't, and Jan takes after him. They couldn't communicate with me, but I could take their misery for granted.

It was worth the discomfort. We were getting there, rising steadily, while the pink glow around the pod's ports faded towards black. As our altitude increased I looked at the internal pressure gauge — thank God for a simple mechanical gadget. It was showing normal pressure, which meant that the hull hadn't been breached on our ascent. I allowed myself the luxury of a quick look around me.

McAndrew was slumped forward in his straps, head

down as low as he could get it. Sven and Jan were both leaning back, arms linked. All the faceplates were clear, so that I knew none of them had vomited in their suit — no joke, since the internal cleaning systems that would usually handle the mess were out of action.

The turbulence around the pod grew less. Stars were coming into view outside the ports as I turned us into an orbit that spiralled outwards away from Vandell. I was looking for *Hoatzin*. Our orbit was clumsy and wasteful of fuel compared with what the navigation computer would have provided. But give me some credit, I was receiving no reference signals from the ship. All I had was instinct and experience.

Scooting along over the clouds I could now see a pattern to the lightning. It moved in great waves over the surface, reaching peaks in places, fading elsewhere. We had lifted from a point where all the peaks had converged, but now it was fading to look no different from the rest. Or almost so; the faint shadow of the black funnel still dipped down into the murk.

I felt a tap on my shoulder. Mac was gesturing at me, then at the helmet of his suit. I nodded and broke the seal on my own helmet. We were outside the danger zone, and it was important to re-establish contact among the group. The search for *Hoatzin* and *Merganser* might take hours, with no assistance from automated scan instruments or radio receipt of homing signals. Meanwhile, I wanted some explanations. It was clear that McAndrew and Wicklund between them had more idea than I did what had been happening to us.

Three miserable, greenish-yellow faces emerged from the helmets. No one had thrown up, but from the look of them it had been a close thing.

"I thought it was bad when the storm hit us on the surface," said Jan. "But that was even worse. What did you do to us, Jeanie? I thought the pod was coming apart."

"So did I." Suit helmet off, I reached back to massage the aching muscles in my neck and shoulders. "It almost did. We lost the computers, the communications, the displays — everything. What *is* this crazy planet, anyway? I thought the laws of nature were supposed to be the same all over the Universe, but Vandell seems to have a special exemption. What in hell did you two *do* to the place, Jan? It was quiet as a grave until you got at it."

"It damn near was one," said McAndrew. "If you hadn't...."

He paused and swallowed. "We know what happened. That's what we were talking about before you shook us to pieces. If we'd been a bit smarter, we could have inferred it ahead of time and none of this would have happened. How much did you hear on the way up?"

I shook my head. "I tuned you out — remember? I had other things on my mind. Are you telling me you *understand* that mess down there? I thought you said it made no sense at all."

While we spoke I had taken us up to the correct height above Vandell for rendezvous with *Hoatzin*. Now it would need a steady and simple sweep to find our ship.

McAndrew wiped his hand across his pale, sweating forehead. He was looking awful, but less like a dying pickle as the minutes passed. "It didn't make sense," he said huskily. "Nothing ever does before you understand it, and then it seems obvious. I noticed something odd just before we left *Hoatzin* to go into the pod — Sven had wondered about the same thing, but neither of us gave it enough significance. Remember the list of physical variables that they recorded for Vandell when they first arrived here? No electric and magnetic fields, negligible rotation rate, no atmosphere, and cold as the pit. Does any one of those observations suggest anything to you?''

I leaned against the padded seat back. My physical exertions over the past half hour had been negligible, but tension had exhausted me totally. I looked across at him.

"Mac, I'm in no condition for guessing games. I'm too tired. For God's sake, get on with it."

He peered at me sympathetically. "Aye, you're right. Let me begin at the beginning, and keep it simple. We know that Vandell was quiet until *Merganser's* pod landed on its surface. Within minutes of that, there was massive seismic activity and terrific electric and magnetic disturbances. We watched it, there were waves of activity over the whole planet — but they all had one focus, and one point of origin: where the pod landed." As McAndrew spoke his voice became firmer, strengthening now that he was back on the familiar ground of scientific explanation. "Remember the dark cone that we followed in to the surface? It was the only anomaly visible over the whole surface of the planet. So it was obvious. The impact of the pod caused the trouble, it was the trigger that set off Vandell's eruption."

I looked around at the others. They all seemed happy with the explanation, but to me it said absolutely nothing. I shook my head. "Mac, I've landed on fifty planets and asteroids through the System and the Halo. Never once has one shaken apart when I tried to set foot on it. So *why*? Why did it happen to Vandell?"

"Because—"

"*Because Vandell is a rogue world*," interrupted Sven Wicklund. We all stared at him in amazement. Sven usually never said a word about anything (except of course physics) unless he was asked a direct question. He was too shy. Now his blond hair was wet with perspiration, and there was still that distant, mystic look on his face, the look that vanished only when he laughed. But his voice was forceful. Vandell had done something to him, too.

"A rogue world," he went on. "And one that does not rotate on its axis. That is the crux of this whole affair. Vandell rotates too slowly for us to measure it. McAndrew and I noticed, but we thought it was no more than a point of academic interest. As Eddington pointed out centuries ago, almost everything in the Universe seems to rotate — atoms, molecules, planets, stars, galaxies. But there is no law of nature that *obliges* a body to rotate relative to the stars. Vandell did not, but we thought it only a curious accident."

He leaned towards me. "Think back to the time — how many million years ago? — when Vandell was first ejected from its stellar system. It had been close to the system's suns, exposed to great forces. It was hot, and maybe geologically active, and then suddenly it was thrown out, out into the void between the stars. What happened then?"

He paused, but I knew he was not expecting an answer. I waited.

He shrugged. "Nothing happened," he said. "For millions or billions of years, Vandell was alone. It slowly lost heat, cooled, contracted — just as the planets of the Solar System cooled and contracted after they were first formed. But there is one critical difference: the planets circle the Sun, and each other. As tensions inside build up, tidal forces work to release them. Earth and the planets release accumulating internal stresses through sequences of small disturbances — earthquakes, Marsquakes, Jupiterquakes. They can never build up a large store of pent-up energy. They are nudged continuously to internal stability by the other bodies of the system. But not Vandell. It wanders alone. With no tidal forces to work on it — not even the forces caused by its rotation in the galactic gravitational and magnetic fields — Vandell became super-critical. It was a house of cards, unstable against small disturbances. Apply one shock, and all the stored energy would be released in a chain reaction."

He paused and looked around. Then he blushed and seemed surprised at his own sudden eloquence. We all waited. Nothing else was forthcoming.

I had followed what he said without difficulty, but accepting it was another matter. "You're telling me that everything on Vandell came from the pod's landing," I said. "But what about the dust clouds? And why the intense fields? And how could they arise from an internal adjustment — even a violent one? And why were there peaks in the disturbance, like the one when we lifted off?"

Sven Wicklund didn't answer. He had apparently done his speaking for the day. He looked beseechingly for support to McAndrew, who coughed and rubbed at his head.

"Now, Jeanie," he said. "You could answer those questions for yourself if you wanted to give it a minute's thought. You know about positions of unstable equilibrium as well as I do. Make an infinitesimal displacement, and produce an unbounded change, that's the heart of it. Compared with the disturbances on Vandell for the past few million years, the landing of a pod was a super-powerful shock — more than an infinitesimal nudge. And you expect a set of spherical harmonics — with a pole at the source of energy — when you distribute energy over a sphere. As for the fields, I'll bet that you're not enough of a student of science to know what a Wimshurst machine is; but I've seen one. It was an old way of generating tremendous electromagnetic fields and artificial lightning — using simple friction of plates against each other. Vandell's crustal motion could generate fields of billions of volts, though of course they'd only last a few hours. We were there right at the worst time."

We looked back at the planet. To my eye, it was maybe a little less visible, the lightning flashes less intense across the dusty clouds.

"Poor old Vandell," said Jan. "Peaceful for all these years, then we come and ruin it. And we wanted to study a rogue planet, a place of absolute quiet. It'll never be the way it was before we got here. Well, never mind, there should be others. When we get back we'll tell people to be more careful."

When we *get back.*

At those words, the world snapped into a different focus. For twelve hours I had been completely absorbed by the events of the moment. Earth, the Office of External Affairs, the Institute, they had not existed for me two minutes ago. Now they were present again, still far away — I looked out of the port, seeking the bright distant star of the Sun — but *real.*

"Are you all right, Jeanie?" asked Jan. She had observed my sudden change of expression.

"I'm not sure."

It was time we told her everything. About Tallboy's decision on the future of the Institute, about the cancellation of the Alpha Centauri expedition, the proposed de-commissioning of the *Hoatzin*, and the way we had disobeyed official orders to follow them to Vandell. It all came rolling out like a long-stored fury.

"But you saved our lives," protested Jan. "If you hadn't taken the ship we'd be dead. Once they know that, they won't care if you ignored some stupid regulation."

McAndrew and I stared at her, then at each other.

"Child, you've got a lot to learn about bureaucracy,"
I said. "I know it all sounds ridiculous and trivial out
here — damn it, it is ridiculous and trivial. But once
we get back we'll waste weeks of our time, defending
what we did, documenting everything, and writing
endless reports on it. The fact that you would have died
won't make one scrap of difference to Tallboy. He'll
follow the rule book."

There was a moment of silence, while Mac and I
pondered the prospect of a month of memoranda.

"What happened to the old Administrator?" asked
Jan at last. "You know, the one you always talked about
before. I thought he was your friend and understood
what you were doing."

"You mean Woolford? There was a change of Administration, and he went. The top brass change with
the party, every seven years. Woolford left, and Tallboy
replaced him."

"Damn that man," said McAndrew suddenly. "Everything ready for the Alpha Centauri expedition, heaps
of supplies and equipment all in place; and that buf-
foon signs a piece of paper and kills it in two seconds."

Ahead of us, I saw a faint blink against the starry
background. It had to be *Hoatzin's* pulsed beacon, sending a brief flash of light outwards every two seconds.
I made a first adjustment to our orbit to take us to
rendezvous, and pointed out the distant ship to the
others. Mac and Sven moved closer to the port, but Jan
surprised me by remaining in her seat.

"Seven years?" she said to me thoughtfully. "The Administration will change again in seven years. Jeanie,
what was the shipboard travel time you planned to
Alpha Centauri?"

I frowned. "From Earth? One way, standing start to
standing finish, would take *Hoatzin* about forty-four
days."

"So from here it would be even less." She had a strange gleam in her eyes. "I noticed something before we set out. Vandell sits in Lupus, and that's a neighboring constellation to Centaurus. I remember thinking to myself before we started, it's an odd coincidence, but we'll be heading in almost the same direction as Mac and Jeanie. So Alpha Centauri would take less time from here, right? Less than forty-four days."

I nodded. "That's just in shipboard time, of course. In Earth time we would have been away —" I stopped abruptly. I had finally reached the point where Jan had started her thinking.

"At least eight and a half years," she said. "Alpha Centauri is 4.3 lightyears from earth, right? So by the time we get back home, we'll find a new Administration and Tallboy will be gone."

I stared at her thoughtfully. "Jan, do you know what you're saying? We can't do that. And as for that 'we' you were using, I hope you don't think that Mac and I would let you and Sven take the risk of a trip like that. It's out of the question."

"Can't we at least talk about it?" She smiled. "I'd like to hear what Mac and Sven have to say."

I hesitated. "Oh, all right," I said at last. "But not now. Let's at least wait until we're back on board *Hoatzin*. And don't think I'll let you twist those two around, the way you usually do."

I frowned, she smiled.

And then I couldn't help smiling back at her.

That's the trouble with the younger generation. They don't understand why a thing can't be done, so they go ahead and do it. I hope that when the history of the first Alpha Centauri expedition is written, they'll tell how it all *really* started.

APPENDIX: The science in the science fiction

1. Kernels, black holes, and singularities.

Kernels feature most prominently in the first Chronicle, but they are assumed and used in all the others, too. A kernel is actually a Ker-N-le, which is shorthand for Kerr-Newman black hole.

To explain Kerr-Newman black holes, it is best to follow McAndrew's technique, and go back a long way in time. We begin in 1915. In that year, Albert Einstein published the field equations of general relativity in their present form. He had been trying different possible formulations since about 1908, but he was not satisfied with any of them before the 1915 set. His final statement consisted of ten coupled, nonlinear, partial differential equations, relating the curvature of space-time to the presence of matter.

The equations are very elegant and can be written down in tensor form as a single short line of algebra. But written out in full they are horrendously long and complex — so much so that Einstein himself did not expect to see any exact solutions, and thus perhaps didn't look very hard. When Karl Schwarzschild, just the next year, produced an exact solution to the "one-body problem" (he found the gravitational field produced by an isolated mass particle), Einstein was reportedly quite surprised.

This "Schwarzschild solution" was for many years considered mathematically interesting, but of no real physical importance. People were much more interested in looking at approximate solutions of Einstein's field equations that could provide possible tests of the theory. Everyone wanted to compare Einstein's ideas on gravity with those introduced two hundred and fifty years earlier by Isaac Newton, to see where there might be detectible differences. The "strong field" case covered by the Schwarzschild solution seemed less relevant to the real world.

For the next twenty years, little was discovered to lead us towards kernels. Soon after Schwarzschild published his solution, Reissner and Nordstrom solved the general relativity equations for a spherical mass particle that also carried an electric charge. This included the Schwarzschild solution as a special case, but it was considered to have no physical significance and it too remained a mathematical curiosity.

The situation finally changed in 1939. In that year, Oppenheimer and Snyder were studying the collapse of a star under gravitational forces — a situation which certainly *did* have physical significance, since it is a common stellar occurrence.

Two remarks made in their summary are worth quoting directly: *"Unless fission due to rotation, the radiation of mass, or the blowing off of mass by radiation, reduce the star's mass to the order of the sun, this contraction will continue indefinitely."* In other words, not only can a star collapse, but if it is heavy enough there is no way that the collapse and contraction can be stopped. And "the radius of the star approaches asymptomatically its gravitational radius; light from the surface of the star is progressively reddened, and can escape over a progressively narrower range of angles." This is the first modern picture of a black hole, a body with a gravitational field so strong that light cannot escape from it. (We have to say "modern picture" because Laplace in 1795 noted as a curiosity that a sufficiently massive body could have an escape velocity from its surface that exceeded the speed of light; in a sense, he predicted the black hole before the end of the eighteenth century.)

Notice that the collapsing body does not have to contract indefinitely if it is the size of the sun or smaller, so we do not have to worry that the Earth, say, or the Moon, will shrink indefinitely to become a black hole. Notice also that there is a reference to the "gravitational radius" of the black hole. This was something that came straight out of the Schwarzschild solution, the distance where the reddening of light became infinite, so that any light coming from inside that radius could never be seen by an outside observer. Since the gravitational radius for the Sun is only about three kilometers, if the Sun were squeezed down to this size conditions inside the collapsed body defy the imagination. The density of matter must be about twenty billion tons per cubic centimeter.

You might think that Oppenheimer and Snyder's paper, with its apparently bizarre conclusions, would have produced a sensation. In fact, it aroused little notice for a long time. It too was looked at as a mathematical oddity, a result that physicists needn't take too seriously.

What was going on here? The Schwarzschild solution had been left on the shelf for a generation, and now the Oppenheimer results were in their turn regarded with no more than mild interest.

One could argue that in the 1920's the attention of leading physicists was elsewhere, as they tried to drink from the fire-hose flood of theory and experiment that established quantum theory. But what about the 1940's and 1950's? Why didn't whole groups of physicists explore the consequences for general relativity and astrophysics of an indefinitely collapsing stellar mass?

Various explanations could be offered, but I favor one that can be stated in a single word: Einstein. He was a gigantic figure, stretching out over everything in physics for the first half of this century. Even now, he casts an enormous shadow over the whole field. Until his death in 1955, researchers in general relativity and gravitation felt a constant awareness of his presence, of his genius peering over their shoulder. If Einstein had not been able to penetrate the mystery, went the unspoken argument, what chance do the rest of us have? Not until after his death was there a resurgence of interest and spectacular progress in general relativity. And it was one of the leaders of that resurgence, John Wheeler, who in 1958 provided the inspired name for the Schwarzschild solution needed to capture everyone's fancy: the *black hole*.

We still have not reached the kernel. The black hole that Wheeler named was still the Schwarzschild black hole, the object that McAndrew spoke of with such derision. It had a mass, and possibly an electric charge, but that was all. The next development came in 1963, and it was a big surprise to everyone working in the field.

Roy Kerr, at that time associated with the University of Texas at Austin, had been exploring a particular set of Einstein's field equations that assumed an unusually simple form for the metric (the metric is the thing that defines distances in a curved space-time). The analysis was highly mathematical and seemed wholly abstract, until Kerr found that he could produce a form of exact solution to the equations. The solution included the Schwarzschild solution as a special case, but there was more; it provided in addition another quantity that Kerr was able to associate with *spin*.

In the Physical Review Letters of September, 1963, Kerr published a one-page paper with the not-too-catchy title, "Gravitational field of a spinning mass as an example of algebraically special metrics." In this paper he described the Kerr solution for a *spinning black hole*. I think it is fair to say that everyone, probably including Kerr himself, was astonished.

The Kerr black hole has a number of fascinating properties, but before we get to them let us take the one final step needed to reach the kernel. In 1965 Ezra Newman and colleagues at the University of Pittsburgh published a short note in the Journal of Mathematical Physics, pointing out that the Kerr solution could be generated from the Schwarzschild solution by a curious mathematical trick, in which a real coordinate was replaced by a complex one. They also realized that the same trick could be applied to the *charged* black hole, and thus they were able to provide a solution for a rotating, charged black hole: the Kerr-Newman black hole, that I call the *kernel*.

The kernel has all the nice features admired by McAndrew. Because it is charged, you can move it about using electric and magnetic fields. Because you can add and withdraw rotational energy, you can use it as a power source and a power reservoir. A Schwarzschild black hole lacks these desirable qualities. As McAndrew says, it just sits there.

One might think that this is just the beginning. There could be black holes that have mass, charge, spin, axial asymmetry, dipole moments, quadrupole moments, and many other properties. It turns out that this is not the case. *The only properties that a black hole can possess are mass, charge, spin and magnetic moment*—and the last one is uniquely fixed by the other three.

This strange result, often stated as the theorem "A black hole has no hair" (i.e. no detailed structure), was established to most people's satisfaction in a powerful series of papers in 1967-1972 by Werner Israel, Brandon Carter, and Stephen Hawking. A black hole is fixed uniquely by its mass, spin, and electric charge. Kernels are the end of the line, and they represent the most general kind of black hole that physics permits.

After 1965, more people were working on general relativity and gravitation, and other properties of the Kerr-Newman black holes rapidly followed. Some of them were very strange. For example, the Schwarzschild black hole has a characteristic surface associated with it, a sphere where the reddening of light becomes infinite, and from within which no information can ever be sent to the outside world. This surface has various names: the surface of infinite red shift, the trapping surface, the one-way membrane, and the event horizon. But the Kerr-Newman black holes turn out to have *two* characteristic surfaces associated with them, and the surface of infinite red shift is in this case distinct from the event horizon.

To visualize these surfaces, take a hamburger bun and hollow out the inside enough to let you put a round hamburger patty entirely within it. For a Kerr-Newman black hole, the outer surface of the bread (which is a sort of ellipsoid in shape) is the surface of infinite red shift, the "static limit" within which no particle can remain at rest, no matter how hard its rocket engines work. Inside the bun, the surface of the meat patty is a sphere, the "event horizon", from which no light or particle can ever escape. We can never find out anything about what goes on within the meat patty's surface, so its composition must be a complete mystery (you may have eaten hamburgers that left the same impression). For a rotating black hole, these bun and patty surfaces touch only at the north and south poles of the axis of rotation (the top and bottom centers of the bun). The really interesting region, however, is that between these two surfaces — the remaining bread, usually called the *ergosphere*. It has a property which allows the kernel to become a power kernel.

Roger Penrose pointed out in 1969 that it is possible for a particle to dive in towards a Kerr black hole, split in two when it is inside the ergosphere, and then have part of it ejected in such a way that it has more *total* energy than the whole particle that went in. If this is done, we have extracted energy from the black hole.

Where has that energy come from? Black holes may be mysterious, but we still do not expect that energy can be created from nothing.

Note that we said a *Kerr* black hole — not a Schwarzschild black hole. The energy we extract comes from the rotational energy of the spinning black hole, and if a hole is not spinning, no energy can possibly be extracted from it. As McAndrew remarked, a Schwarzschild hole is dull, a dead object that cannot be used to provide power. A Kerr black hole, on the other hand, is one of the most efficient energy sources imaginable, better by far than most nuclear fission or fusion processes. (A Kerr-Newman black hole allows the same energy extraction process, but we have to be a little more careful, since only part of the ergosphere can be used.)

If a Kerr-Newman black hole starts out with only a little spin energy, the energy-extraction process can be worked in reverse, to provide more rotational energy— the process that McAndrew referred to as "spin-up" of the kernel. "Spin-down" is the opposite process, the one that extracts energy. A brief paper by Christodoulou in the Physical Review Letters of 1970 discussed the limits on this process, and pointed out that you could only spin-up a kernel to a certain limit, termed an "extreme" Kerr solution. Past that limit (which can never be achieved using the Penrose process) a solution can be written to the Einstein field equations. This was done by Tomimatsu and Sato, and presented in 1972 in another one-page paper in Physical Review Letters. It is a very odd solution indeed. It has no event horizon, which means that activities there are not shielded from the rest of the universe as they are for the usual kernels. And it has what is referred to as a "naked singularity" associated with it, where cause and effect relationships no longer apply. This bizarre object was discussed by Gibbons and Russell-Clark, in 1973, in yet another paper in Physical Review Letters.

That seems to leave us in pretty good shape. Everything so far has been completely consistent with current physics. We have kernels that can be spun up and spun down by well-defined procedures — and if we allow that McAndrew could somehow take a kernel past the extreme form, we would indeed have something with a naked singularity. It seems improbable that such a physical situation could exist, but if it did, space-time there would be highly peculiar. The existence of certain space-time symmetry directions — called Killing vectors — that we find for all usual Kerr-Newman black holes would not be guaranteed. Everything is fine.

Or is it?

Oppenheimer and Snyder pointed out that black holes are created when big masses, larger than the Sun, contract under gravitational collapse. The kernels that we want are much smaller than that. We need to be able to move them around the Solar System, and the gravitational field of an object the mass of the Sun would tear the system apart. Unfortunately, there was no prescription in Oppenheimer's work, or elsewhere, to allow us to make small black holes.

Stephen Hawking finally came to the rescue. Apart from being created by collapsing stars, he said, black holes could also be created in the extreme conditions of pressure that existed during the Big Bang that started our Universe. Small black holes, weighing no more than a hundredth of a milligram, could have been born then. Over billions of years, these could interact with each other to produce more massive black holes, of any size you care to mention. We seem to have the mechanism that will produce the kernels of the size we need.

Unfortunately, what Hawking gave he soon took away. In perhaps the biggest surprise of all in black hole history, he showed that *black holes are not black.*

General relativity and quantum theory were both developed in this century, but they have never been combined in a satisfactory way. Physicists have known this and been uneasy about it for a long time. In attempting to move towards what John Wheeler terms the "fiery marriage of general relativity with quantum theory", Hawking studied quantum mechanical effects in the vicinity of a black hole. He found that particles and radiation can (and must) be emitted from the hole. The smaller the hole, the faster the rate of radiation. He was able to relate the mass of the black hole to a *temperature*, and as one would expect, a "hotter" black hole pours out radiation and particles much faster than a "cold" one. For a black hole the mass of the Sun, the associated temperature is lower than the background temperature of the Universe. Such a black hole receives more than it emits, so it will steadily increase in mass. However, for a small black hole, with the few billion tons of mass that we want in a kernel, the temperature is so high (ten billion degrees) that the black hole will radiate itself away in a gigantic and rapid burst of radiation and particles. Furthermore, a rapidly spinning kernel will preferentially radiate particles that decrease its spin, and a highly charged one will prefer to radiate charged particles that reduce its overall charge.

These results are so strange that in 1972 and 1973 Hawking spent a lot of time trying to find the mistake in his own analysis. Only when he had performed every check that he could think of was he finally forced to accept the conclusion: black holes aren't black after all; and the smallest black holes are the least black.

That gives us a problem when we want to use power kernels in a story. First, the argument that they are readily available, as leftovers from the birth of the Universe, has been destroyed. Second, a Kerr-Newman black hole is a dangerous object to be near. It gives off high energy radiation and particles.

This is the point where the science of Kerr-Newman black holes stops and the science fiction begins. I assume in these stories that there is some as-yet-unknown natural process which creates sizeable black holes on a continuing basis. They can't be created too close to Earth, or we would see them. However, there is plenty of room outside the known Solar System — perhaps in the region occupied by the long-period comets, from beyond the orbit of Pluto out to perhaps a lightyear from the Sun.

Second, I assume that a kernel can be surrounded by a shield (not of matter, but of electromagnetic fields) which is able to reflect all the emitted particles and radiation back into the black hole. Humans can thus work close to the kernels without being fried in a storm of radiation and high-energy particles.

Even surrounded by such a shield, a rotating black hole would still be noticed by a nearby observer. Its gravitational field would still be felt, and it would also produce a curious effect known as "inertial dragging".

We have pointed out that the inside of a black hole is completely shielded from the rest of the Universe, so that we can never know what is going on there. It is as though the inside of a black hole is a separate Universe, possibly with its own different physical laws. Inertial dragging adds to that idea. We are used to the notion that when we spin something around, we do it relative to a well-defined and fixed reference frame. Newton pointed out in his *Principia Mathematica* that a rotating bucket of water, from the shape of the water's surface, provides evidence of an "absolute" rotation relative to the stars. This is true here on Earth, or over in the Andomeda Galaxy, or out in the Virgo Cluster. It is not true, however, near a rotating black hole. The closer that we get to one, the less that our usual absolute reference frame applies. The kernel defines its own absolute frame, one that rotates with it. Closer than a certain distance to the kernel (the "static limit" mentioned earlier) everything *must* revolve — dragged along and forced to adopt the rotating reference frame defined by the spinning black hole.

2. The McAndrew balanced drive.

This device makes a first appearance in the Second Chronicle, but it is used in all the subsequent stories.

Let us begin with well-established science. Again it starts at the beginning of the century, in the work of Einstein. In 1908, he wrote as follows:

"We...assume the complete physical equivalence of a gravitational field and of a corresponding acceleration of the reference system..."

And in 1913:

"An observer enclosed in an elevator has no way to decide whether the elevator is at rest in a static gravitational field or whether the elevator is located in gravitation-free space in an accelerated motion that is maintained by forces acting on the elevator (equivalence hypothesis)."

This equivalence hypothesis, or equivalence principle, is central to general relativity. If you could be accelerated in one direction at a thousand gees, and simultaneously pulled in the other direction by an intense gravitational force producing a thousand gees, you would feel *no force whatsoever.* It would be just the same as if you were in free fall.

As McAndrew said, once you realize that fact, the rest is mere mechanics. You take a large circular disk of condensed matter (more on that in a moment), sufficient to produce a gravitational acceleration of, say, 50 gee on a test object (such as a human being) sitting on the middle of the plate. You also provide a drive that can accelerate the plate away from the human at 50 gee. The net force on the person at the middle of the plate is then zero. If you increase the acceleration of the plate gradually, from zero to 50 gee, then to remain comfortable the person must also be moved in gradually, starting well away from the disk and finishing in contact with it. The life capsule must thus move in and out along the axis of the disk, depending on the ship's acceleration: high acceleration, close to disk; low acceleration, far from disk.

There is one other variable of importance, and that is the *tidal forces* on the human passenger. These are caused by the changes in gravitational force with distance — it would be no good having a person's head feeling a force of one gee, if his feet felt a force of thirty gee. Let us therefore insist that the rate of change of acceleration be no more than one gee per meter when the acceleration caused by the disk is 50 gee.

The gravitational acceleration produced along the axis of a thin circular disk of matter of total mass M and radius R is a textbook problem of classical potential theory. Taking the radius of the disk to be 50 meters, the gravitational acceleration acting on a test object at the center of the disk to be 50 gee, and the tidal force there to be one gee per meter, we can solve for the total mass M, together with the gravitational and tidal forces acting on a body at different distances Z along the axis of the disk.

Table 1 shows the design of the McAndrew balanced drive for such a case. The distance of the passengers from the center of the plate ranges from 246 meters, where the plate produces a gravitational acceleration on passengers of 1 gee, and if the drive is off there is a net force of 1 gee on them; to zero meters, where the plate produces a gravitational acceleration on passengers of 50 gee, the drive accelerates them at 50 gee, and they feel as though they are in free fall. Notice that the tidal force is a maximum, at one gee per meter, when the passengers are closest to the disk.

This device will actually work as described, with no science fiction involved at all, if you can provide the plate of condensed matter and the necessary drive. Unfortunately, this turns out to be non-trivial. All the distances are reasonable, and so are the tidal forces. What is much less reasonable is the mass of the disk that we have used. It is a little more than 9 trillion tons; such a disk 100 meters across and one meter thick would have an average density of 1,170 tons per cubic centimeter.

This density is modest compared with that found in a neutron star, and tiny compared with what we find in a black hole. Thus we know that such densities do exist in the Universe. However, no materials available to us on Earth today even come close to such high values — they have densities that fall short by a factor of more than a million. And the mass plate would not work as described, without the dense matter. We have a real problem.

It's science fiction time again: let us assume that in a couple of hundred years we will be able to compress matter to very high densities, and hold it there using powerful electromagnetic fields. If that is the case, the mass plate needed for McAndrew's Drive can be built. It's certainly massive, but that shouldn't be a limitation — the Solar System has plenty of spare matter available for construction materials. And although a 9 trillion ton mass may sound a lot, it's tiny by celestial standards, less than the mass of a modest asteroid.

With that one extrapolation of today's science it sounds as though we can have the McAndrew balanced drive. We can even suggest how that extrapolation might be performed, with plausible use of present physics.

Unfortunately, things are not as nice as they seem. There is a much bigger piece of science fiction that must be introduced before the McAndrew Drive can exist as a useful device. We look at that next, and note that it is a central concern of the Third Chronicle.

Suppose that the drive mechanism is the most efficient one consistent with today's physics. This would be a photon drive, in which any fuel is completely converted to radiation and used to propel the ship. There

TABLE I.
Acceleration and tidal effects along mass plate axis.

Distance from disk center (meters)	Acceleration produced by disk (gees)	Tidal effect (gees/meter)
0	50	1.0
2.0	48	1.0
5.0	45	0.99
10.2	40	0.94
15.7	35	0.87
21.9	30	0.77
28.9	25	0.65
37.5	20	0.51
49.0	15	0.36
66.5	10	0.22
103.1	5	0.08
246.2	1	0.01

is certainly nothing in present science that suggests such a drive is theoretically impossible, and some analysis of matter-antimatter reactions indicates that the photon drive could one day be built. Let us assume that we know how to construct it. Then, even with this "ultimate" drive, McAndrew's ship would have problems. It's not difficult to calculate that with a fifty gee drive, the conversion of matter to radiation needed to keep the drive going will quickly consume the ship's own mass. More than half the mass will be gone in a few days, and McAndrew's ship will disappear from under him.

Solution of this problem calls for a lot more fictional science than the simple task of producing stable condensed matter. We have to go back to present physics and read it as Richard Nixon must have read the American Constitution — looking for loopholes. We need to find inconsistencies in the overall picture of the Universe provided by present day physics, and exploit these as necessary.

The best place to seek inconsistencies is where we already know we will find them — in the meeting of general relativity and quantum theory. If we calculate the energy associated with an absence of matter in quantum theory — the "vacuum state" — we do not, as common sense would suggest, get zero. Instead we get a large, positive value, E_0, per unit volume. In classical thinking, one could argue that the zero point of energy is arbitrary, so that one can simply start measuring energies from the value E_0. But if we accept general relativity, this option is denied to us. Energy, of any form, produces space-time curvature. We are therefore not allowed to change the definition of the origin of the energy scale. Once this is accepted, the energy of the vacuum state cannot be talked out of existence. It is real, if elusive, and its presence provides the loophole that we need.

Again, we are at the point where the science fiction enters. If the vacuum state has an energy associated with it, I assume that this energy is capable of being tapped. Doesn't this then, according to relativity ($E = mc^2$), suggest that there is also *mass* associated with the vacuum, contrary to what we think of as vacuum? Yes, it does, and I'm sorry about that, but the paradox is not of my creation. It is implicit in the contradictions that arise as soon as you try to put general relativity and quantum theory together.

Richard Feynman, one of the founders of quantum electrodynamics, addressed the question of the vacuum energy, and computed an estimate for the equivalent mass per unit volume. The estimate came out to 2 billion tons per cubic centimeter. The energy in 2 billion tons of matter is more than enough to boil all Earth's oceans (powerful stuff, vacuum). Feynman, commenting on his vacuum energy estimate, remarks:

"Such a mass density would, at first sight at least, be expected to produce very large gravitational effects which are not observed. It is possible that we are calculating in a naive manner, and, if all of the consequences of the general theory of relativity (such as the gravitational effects produced by the large stresses implied here) were included, the effects might cancel out; but nobody has worked all this out yet. It is possible that some cutoff procedure that not only yields a finite energy for the vacuum state but also provides relativistic invariance may be found. The implications of such a result are at present completely unknown."

With that degree of uncertainty at the highest levels of present-day physics, I feel not at all uncomfortable in exploiting the troublesome vacuum energy to service McAndrew's Drive.

The Third Chronicle introduces two other ideas that

are definitely science fiction today, even if they become science fact a few years from now. If there are ways to isolate the human central nervous system and keep it alive independently of the body, we certainly don't know much about them. On the other hand, I see nothing that suggests this idea is impossible in principle — heart transplants were not feasible 30 years ago, and until this century blood transfusions were rare and highly dangerous. A century hence, today's medical impossibilities should be routine.

The Sturm Invocation for vacuum survival is also invented, but I believe that it, like the Izaak Walton introduced in the Fifth Chronicle, is a logical component of any space-oriented future. Neither calls for technology beyond what we have today. The hypnotic control implied in the Invocation, though advanced for most practitioners, could already be achieved. And any competent engineering shop could build a Walton for you in a few weeks — I am tempted to patent the idea, but fear that it would be rejected as too obvious or inevitable a development.

3. *Beyond the known Solar System: life from space, the kernel ring, the life ring, rogue planets, and Vandell's Fifth Problem.*

Only the First Chronicle takes place completely within the conventional, nine planet Solar System. The others occur at least partly in the Halo, or Outer System, which I define to extend from the distance of Pluto from the Sun, out to a little over a lightyear. Within this radius, the Sun is still the primary gravitational influence, and controls the orbits of objects moving out there.

To give an idea of the size of the Halo, we note that Pluto lies at an average distance of about 6 billion kilometers from the Sun. This is 40 astronomical units, where the astronomical unit, usually abbreviated to a.u., is defined as the mean distance of the Earth from the Sun. The a.u. provides a convenient yardstick for measurements within the Solar System. One lightyear is about 63,000 a.u. (inches in a mile, is how I remember it). So the volume of space in the Halo is 4 billion times as large as the sphere enclosing all nine known planets.

By Solar System standards, the Halo is thus a huge region. But beyond Pluto, we know remarkably little about it. For example, there are almost certainly additional planets out there. The search for Pluto was inspired early this century by differences between theory and observation in the orbits of Uranus and Neptune. When Pluto was found, it soon became clear that it was not nearly heavy enough to produce the observed irregularities. The obvious explanation is yet another planet, farther out than the ones we know.

Previous calculations of the orbit and size of this tenth planet to reconcile observation and theory for Uranus and Neptune suggest a rather improbable object, out of the orbital plane that all the other planets move in and about seventy times the mass of the Earth. I don't believe this particular object exists.

On the other hand, observational equipment and techniques for faint objects are improving rapidly. I am willing to place a substantial bet that some new planet beyond Pluto will be found by the early 1990's.

The one thing we know for sure about the Halo is that it is populated by comets. The Halo is often called the Oort Cloud, since the Dutch astronomer Oort suggested thirty years ago that the entire Solar System is enveloped by a cloud of cometary material, to a radius of perhaps a lightyear. He regarded this region as a "cometary reservoir", containing perhaps a hundred billion comets. Close encounters between comets out in the Halo would occasionally disturb the orbit of one of them enough to divert it to the Inner System, where it would appear as a long-period comet when it came close enough to the Sun. Further interactions with Jupiter and the other planets would then sometimes convert the long-period comet to a short-period comet, such as Halley's or Encke's comet, which we observe repeatedly each time they swing by close to the Sun.

Most comets, however, continue their lonely orbits out in the Cloud, never approaching the Inner System. They do not have to be small to be invisible to us. The amount of sunlight a body receives is inversely proportional to the square of its distance from the Sun; the apparent area it presents to our telescopes is also inversely proportional to the square of its distance from Earth. For bodies in the Halo, the reflected light that we receive from them thus varies as the inverse fourth power of their distance from the Sun. A planet with the size and composition of Uranus, but half a lightyear away, would be 7 trillion times as faint. And we should remember that Uranus itself is faint enough that it was not discovered until 1781, when high-quality telescopes were available. So far as present-day detection powers are concerned, there could be almost anything out there in the Halo.

One of the things that may be there is life. In a carefully argued but controversial theory developed over the past 20 years, Hoyle and Wickramasinghe have advanced the idea that space is the natural place for the creation of "pre-biotic" molecules in large quantities. Pre-biotic molecules are compounds such as carbohydrates, amino acids, and chlorophyll, which form the necessary building blocks for the development of life. Simpler organic molecules, such as methyl cyanide and ethanol, have already been observed in interstellar clouds.

Hoyle and Wickramasinghe go further. They state explicitly: *"We shall argue that primitive living organisms evolve in the mixture of organic molecules, ices and silicate smoke which make up a comet's head."*

The science fiction of the Fourth Chronicle consists of these two assumptions:

1. The complex organic molecules described by Hoyle and Wickramasinghe are located in a particular region of the Halo, a "life ring" that lies between 3,200 and 4,000 a.u. from the Sun;

2. The "primitive living organisms" have evolved quite a bit further than Hoyle and Wickramasinghe expected, on at least one body of the Oort Cloud.

The Halo offers so much scope for interesting celestial objects of every description that I assume we will find a few more there. In the Second Chronicle, I introduced the collapsed objects, high-density bodies that are neither stars nor conventional planets. The dividing line between stars and planets is usually decided by whether or not the center of the object supports a nuclear fusion process and contains a high density core of "degenerate" matter. Present theories place that dividing line at about a hundredth of the Sun's mass — smaller than that, you have a planet; bigger than that you must have a star. I assume that there are in-between bodies out in the Halo, made largely of degenerate matter but only a little more massive than Jupiter.

I also assume that there is a "kernel ring" of Kerr-Newman black holes, about 300 to 400 a.u. from the Sun, and that this same region contains many of the collapsed objects. Such bodies would be completely undetectable using any techniques of present-day astronomy.

As, of course, rogue planets would be; which brings us to Vandell's Fifth Problem.

David Hilbert did indeed pose a set of mathematical problems in 1900, and they served as much more than a summary of things that were "hard to solve". They were concise and exact statements of questions, which, if answered, would have profound implications for many other problems in mathematics. The Hilbert problems are both deep and difficult, and have attracted the attention of almost every mathematician of the twentieth century. Several problems of the set, for example, ask whether certain numbers are "transcendental" — which means they can never occur as solutions to the usual equations of algebra (more precisely, they cannot be roots of finite algebraic equations with algebraic coefficients). These questions were not disposed of until 1930, when Kusmin and Siegel proved a more general result than the one that Hilbert had posed. In 1934 Gelfond provided another generalization.

At the moment there is no such "super-problem" set defined for astronomy and cosmology. If there were, the one I invented as Vandell's Fifth Problem would certainly be a worthy candidate, and might take generations to solve. (Hilbert's Fifth Problem, concerning a conjecture in topological group theory, was finally solved in 1952 by Gleason, Montgomery, and Zippin.) We cannot even imagine a technique, observational instrument or procedure that would have a chance of detecting a rogue planet. The existence, frequency of occurrence, and mode of escape of rogue planets raise many questions concerning the stability of multiple-body systems moving under their mutual gravitational attractions — questions that cannot be answered yet by astronomers and mathematicians.

In general relativity, the exact solution of the "one-body problem" as given by Schwarzschild has been known for more than 60 years. The relativistic "two-body problem", of two objects orbiting each other under mutual gravitational influence, has not yet been solved. In *non-relativistic* or Newtonian mechanics, the two-body problem was disposed of three hundred years ago by Newton. But the non-relativistic solution for more than two bodies has not been found to this day, despite three centuries of hard work.

A good deal of progress has been made for a rather simpler situation that is termed the "restricted three-body problem". In this, a small mass (such as a planet or small moon) moves under the influence of two much larger ones (stars or large planets). The large bodies define the gravitational field, and the small body moves in this field without contributing significantly to it. The restricted three-body problem applies to the case of a planet moving in the gravitational field of a binary pair of stars, or an asteroid moving in the combined fields of the Sun and Jupiter. It also offers a good approximation for the motion of a small body moving in the combined field of the Earth and Moon. Thus the problem is of practical interest, and the list of workers who have studied it in the past 200 years includes several of history's most famous mathematicians: Euler, Lagrange, Jacobi, Poincaré, and Birkhoff. (Lagrange in particular provided certain exact solutions that include the L-4 and L-5 points, famous today as proposed sites for large space colonies.)

The number of papers written on the subject is huge — Victor Szebehely, in a 1967 book on the topic, lists over 500 references, and restricts himself to only the major source works.

Thanks to the efforts of all these workers, a good deal is known about the possible solutions of the restricted three-body problem. One established fact is that the small object cannot be thrown away to infinity by the gravitational interactions of its two large companions. Like much of modern astronomy, this result is not established by looking at the orbits themselves. It is proved by general arguments based on a particular constant of the motion, termed the Jacobian integral.

Unfortunately, those arguments cannot be applied in the general three-body problem, or in the N-body problem whenever N is bigger than two. It is presently *conjectured* by astronomers, but not proved, that ejection to infinity is possible whenever more than three bodies are involved. In such a situation, the lightest member of the system is most likely to be the one ejected. Thus, rogue planets can probably be produced when a stellar system has more than two stars in it. As it happens, this is rather common. Solitary stars, like the Sun, are in the minority. Once separated from its stellar parents, the chances that a rogue will ever again be captured to form part of a star system are remote. To this point, the Fifth Chronicle's discussion of solitary planets fits known theory, although it is an admittedly incomplete theory.

So how many rogue planets are there? There could conceivably be as many as there are stars, strewn thick across the Galaxy but completely undetectable to our instruments. Half a dozen may lie closer to us than the nearest star. Or they may be an endangered species, vanishingly rare among the varied bodies that comprise the celestial zoo.

In the Fifth Chronicle I suggest that they are rather common — and that's acceptable to me as science fiction, because there is absolutely no information available one way or the other.

This seems to be one case where we will probably not know the right answer for a long time. And it may be that we will never know it by simply sitting here close to the Sun and observing. We may find the truth only when we send our probes and exploration ships, manned or unmanned, out towards the stars.

They will almost certainly not be powered by Kerr-Newman black holes, nor tap resonance modes of the vacuum energy, nor use the McAndrew Drive, nor discover life-bearing planetoids and rogue planets out in the Halo. But I believe that the ships will be built; and when they are they will employ ideas, technology, and energy sources to make today's boldest science fiction appear timid, clumsy, small-scale, and unimaginative.

And, being what we are, we will take the new developments for granted and label them as dull technology. We will look back with nostalgia on the romantic old times, the simple bygone days of space shuttles, nuclear power plants, automobiles, television, grown food, and computers big enough to fill your whole hand.

Best-Selling Science Fiction from TOR

☐	48-549-2	**Paradise** Dan Henderson	$2.95
☐	48-531-X	**The Taking of Satcon Station** Barney Cohen and Jim Baen	$2.95
☐	48-555-7	**There Will Be War** J.E. Pournelle	$2.95
☐	48-566-2	**The McAndrew Chronicles** Charles Sheffield	$2.95
☐	48-567-0	**The Varkaus Conspiracy** John Dalmas	$2.95
☐	48-526-3	**The Swordswoman** Jessica Amanda Salmonson	$2.75
☐	48-584-0	**Cestus Dei** John Maddox Roberts	$2.75

DAVID DRAKE

●●●●●●●●●●●●●●●●●●●●●●●●●●●

☐	48-541-7	**Time Safari**	$2.75
☐	48-552-2	**The Dragon Lord**	$2.95
☐	48-544-1	**Skyripper**	$3.50

C.M. Kornbluth

☐	48-512-2	**Not This August** C.M. Kornbluth revised by Frederik Pohl	$2.75
☐	48-543-3	**The Syndic** C.M. Kornbluth revised by Frederik Pohl	$2.75
☐	48-570-0	**Gunner Cade/Takeoff** C.M. Kornbluth and Judith Merril	$2.95

Buy them at your local bookstore or use this handy coupon:
Clip and mail this page with your order

PINNACLE BOOKS, INC. – Reader Service Dept.
1430 Broadway, New York, NY 10018

Please send me the book(s) I have checked above. I am enclosing $＿＿＿＿＿ (please
add 75¢ to cover postage and handling). Send check or money order only—no cash
or C.O.D.'s.

Mr./Mrs./Miss＿＿＿＿＿＿＿＿＿＿＿＿＿＿＿＿＿＿＿＿＿＿＿＿＿＿＿＿＿

Address＿＿＿＿＿＿＿＿＿＿＿＿＿＿＿＿＿＿＿＿＿＿＿＿＿＿＿＿＿＿＿

City＿＿＿＿＿＿＿＿＿＿＿＿＿＿＿＿＿＿ State/Zip＿＿＿＿＿＿

Please allow six weeks for delivery. Prices subject to change without notice.
Canadian orders must be paid with U.S. Bank check or U.S. Postal money order only.

Best-Selling Science Fiction from TOR